"So are you going to give me that kiss now?" Rio asked.

"What kiss?"

"The one you almost landed on me when we were sharing a moment over the cake."

"What makes you think I wanted to kiss you then?" Yvonne parried.

"Because I loved your cake so much?"

She found herself smiling despite herself. "You don't let things go, do you?"

He pointed at his chest. "World Champion Bull Rider, remember? Focused, tenacious, and successful."

"And I'm your next challenge?"

He studied her for a long moment. "Yeah. I suppose you are." He sounded almost as surprised by his answer as she was.

"I'm not a prize to be won."

"I get that." He nodded.

"So even if I kiss you because you liked my cake it doesn't mean you've won anything."

"I understand."

"It's just a kiss." She was no longer sure which of them she was trying to convince.

"Okay."

He moved even closer, his broad shoulders blocking the waning evening sunlight as his mouth came down over hers in the gentlest of butterfly kisses. Even that was almost too much as she reached blindly for something to anchor herself to. Her hand came to rest on his shoulder, and then curved around his neck to keep him exactly where she wanted him . . .

Books by Kate Pearce

The House of Pleasure Series
SIMPLY SEXUAL
SIMPLY SINFUL
SIMPLY SHAMELESS
SIMPLY WICKED
SIMPLY INSATIABLE
SIMPLY FORBIDDEN
SIMPLY CARNAL
SIMPLY VORACIOUS
SIMPLY SCANDALOUS
SIMPLY PLEASURE (e-novella)
SIMPLY IRRESISTIBLE (e-novella)

The Sinners Club Series
THE SINNERS CLUB
TEMPTING A SINNER
MASTERING A SINNER
THE FIRST SINNERS (e-novella)

Single Titles
RAW DESIRE

The Morgan Brothers Ranch
THE RELUCTANT COWBOY
THE MAVERICK COWBOY
THE LAST GOOD COWBOY
THE BAD BOY COWBOY
THE BILLIONAIRE BULL RIDER

Anthologies
SOME LIKE IT ROUGH
LORDS OF PASSION
HAPPY IS THE BRIDE

Published by Kensington Publishing Corporation

THE
BILLIONAIRE
BULL RIDER

KATE PEARCE

ZEBRA BOOKS
KENSINGTON PUBLISHING CORP.
http://www.kensingtonbooks.com

ZEBRA BOOKS are published by

Kensington Publishing Corp.
119 West 40th Street
New York, NY 10018

All Kensington titles, imprints, and distributed lines are available at special quantity discounts for bulk purchases for sales promotion, premiums, fund-raising, educational, or institutional use.

Special book excerpts or customized printings can also be created to fit specific needs. For details, write or phone the office of the Kensington Sales Manager: Attn.: Sales Department. Kensington Publishing Corp., 119 West 40th Street, New York, NY 10018. Phone: 1-800-221-2647.

Zebra and the Z logo Reg. U.S. Pat. & TM Off.

First Printing: August 2018
ISBN-13: 978-1-4201-4473-4
ISBN-10: 1-4201-4473-1

eISBN-13: 978-1-4201-4474-1
eISBN-10: 1-4201-4474-X

10 9 8 7 6 5 4 3 2 1

Printed in the United States of America

ACKNOWLEDGMENTS

Many thanks to Genevieve Turner and Keri Ford for reading this book through for me. Big thanks to Angela Ollivett Smith for letting me sit in the kitchen at Sweet Eatz and watch her work her culinary wonders, *and* for the wonderful sin cake recipe.

I also owe a big debt of gratitude to my merry band of translators: Marianne Bell Calloway for the French, and Chris Almeida for the Brazilian Portuguese. Any mistakes are definitely my own.

If you enjoy the Morgan Ranch series, please check out my website at www.themorgansranch.com.

Chapter One

"Ah." Yvonne Payet kicked off her shoes, leaned back precariously in her chair and flung her arms wide. "*Sunday.*"

It was the only day of the week when she didn't have to get up at four in the morning to start baking for her coffee shop. Of course, she would have to go to bed early for the Monday morning start, but at least she'd had four glorious hours of extra sleep. She led such a glamorous, exciting life. . . .

A tap on the back door had her turning her head.

"Hey, Yvonne! Can I come in?"

"Be my guest, January. Door's open." Her apartment was actually above the shop, but she was currently sitting in the stark steel splendor of the industrial kitchen, where she did all her baking. She'd come down to get some croissants out of the pantry, and never made it back up the stairs.

"Hey, girlfriend!"

She smiled as January Morgan breezed in, and took a seat opposite her at the table. Her friend wore her usual jeans, and a yellow Morgan Ranch T-shirt topped with a cozy blue fleece.

"Hey yourself."

"You ready?" January looked expectantly at her.

Yvonne blinked. "For what?"

"You've forgotten, haven't you?" January sighed.

"No, I haven't forgotten. I'm just . . ." Yvonne waved a vague hand around her head. "Okay, I've forgotten. Just don't tell me I promised you five hundred choux buns for your guests at the ranch this morning?"

"Nope. You agreed to come up to the ranch and have lunch with me."

"Is that all?"

January widened her eyes. "What else would it be?"

"You and Avery have a terrible habit of introducing me to attractive men."

"That's terrible?" January did the wide-eyed innocent thing, but Yvonne wasn't fooled.

"Well, not exactly, *terrible,* but I'm not really in a position to date anyone at the moment. I work fourteen-hour days, I'm still getting over being dumped by you know who, and I'm picky as hell."

"Like that's supposed to stop us?"

Yvonne sighed. "Obviously not. Just because you and Avery are insufferably happy with your Morgan brothers doesn't mean that you have to try and match all your friends up as well."

"Yes, it does," January pointed out. "It's the rule. We love you, and we're determined to find a man worthy of you, unlike He Who Shall Not Be Named."

"Isn't that Voldemort?"

"You know who I mean," January said darkly, and made encouraging motions at Yvonne like she was herding chickens. "Go and get ready. It's almost eleven o'clock."

Grumbling, Yvonne rose and headed for the stairs. "I'm not going riding."

"I didn't say you had to," January called out. "By the way, do you have any éclairs left over?"

"Pink box on the second shelf in the large refrigerator. It has your name on it."

"Cool! Thanks!"

Yvonne had already showered, so all she had to do was pick something to wear that she didn't mind getting ruined at the ranch. It wasn't the sort of place where you sauntered around in designer heels without getting horseshit all over them.

She carefully applied her makeup, and brushed out her long, dark hair. No jeans because that might create the impression that she was willing to get back on a horse, so capri pants, old shoes, and a striped T-shirt in navy and white.

"Very French," she murmured to herself, grabbing a jacket and sliding her feet into her favorite pair of old wedges. "*Tres jolie.*"

When Yvonne got downstairs, January was sitting at the table texting. She looked up and nodded her approval.

"I don't know how you get ready so fast. You always look so chic."

"All those years in France at catering college rubbed off on me, I suppose." Yvonne grimaced at her striped shirt. "Maybe I should put on a beret, and bring one of my French sticks to look really authentic."

"Or a bicycle and a string of onions around your neck?" January asked helpfully. "I don't think you need *too* many accessories."

"Less is certainly more, especially on a cow farm," Yvonne muttered as she picked up her purse and put on her sunglasses. "Let's go."

She enjoyed the drive out to the ranch, which was just outside the boundary of Morgantown, where she lived and worked. The ranch had been there for over a hundred and fifty years and was still run by the Morgan family. The town—the second attempt to found a settlement in the area—was also named in their honor.

January had come to the ranch to complete her research for her doctorate and had ended up marrying the oldest son, Chase Morgan, who was a Silicon Valley entrepreneur on the side. Chase was also a good man who adored his wife, which made him okay with Yvonne.

"Is Avery going to be there?" Yvonne asked.

"Yup. I think everyone but Rachel is home for a change."

"Nice. Morgans everywhere."

January chuckled. "It does get a bit overwhelming sometimes."

"Yes, all that testosterone in one place." Yvonne mock scowled. "All those hot, unattainable men."

"Like you were ever interested in any of them." January snorted.

"True. I've never had a thing for cowboys. I like my men docile, subservient, and beta."

"Yeah, right. Good luck with finding that around here."

"Luck has nothing to do with it," Yvonne said. "I'm just too busy to give some man the attention he thinks he deserves. Running a business is hard."

January shot her a concerned sideways glance. "You certainly work too hard. Have you thought about getting an assistant?"

"Finding a good assistant out here is like finding a good man now that all the Morgans are taken," Yvonne said firmly.

"You should ask Avery. She has lots of contacts in the hotel industry."

"I *have* asked her." Yvonne sighed. "It's the fact that we're out in the sticks and I can't pay much that sucks."

"What about finding someone to train up?"

"I've been doing that, but it's very time consuming. Every time I get them to a decent level of competence, they leave for the big city and I'm back at square one." Yvonne fiddled with her seat belt. "Want me to get the gate?"

"No need. They're all automatic now." January punched in a code. "Chase set it up last week. We're expecting our first full guest list over spring break, so he wanted to make sure everyone would be secure."

"Are you excited?"

"Excited and terrified at the same time. I don't think we're going to fail, but you never know what's going to happen when you put horses and new riders in the mix together."

Yvonne patted her friend's arm. "You'll be fine. I bet Chase has a plan for every contingency."

"He does." January chuckled. "Including one for an alien invasion, or California experiencing a massive earthquake and us ending up in the sea or on the coast."

"If I didn't know your OCD, nerdy husband, I'd be laughing right now, but I suspect he really has got plans for that."

January drew the big truck up in the circular driveway in front of the old ranch house. It was a Victorian structure with a slate roof, a deep porch, and fancy spiral woodwork. The original barn now housed the new and improved horse stables, and the tastefully designed guest cabins were secreted behind the new welcome center on a downward slope.

Yvonne sucked in a great big lungful of fresh air, and sighed happily as she alighted from the truck. She loved the ranch and enjoyed spending time there. Opening the rear door, she gathered up the pink boxes containing extra lunchtime treats and balanced them carefully in her arms. There were already several trucks parked in the driveway, and one fancy car.

"Who does that car belong to?" She pointed at the Mercedes.

"One of Chase's partners is here," January said way too casually over her shoulder. "Didn't I mention that?"

"No, strangely enough, you did not." Yvonne followed her friend up the steps to the main house. "Traitor." She sniffed appreciatively as January opened the screen door. "Ruth's cooking a roast. My favorite thing to eat on a Sunday."

"Lamb, I believe," January said. "With all the trimmings." She hesitated at the bottom of the stairs. "Matt is a really nice guy. I think you'll like him a lot."

"Well, look who's here!" Ruth Morgan, the tiny woman who ruled over the whole Morgan clan, looked up from stirring something on the stove, and smiled at Yvonne. "I haven't seen you for ages."

"I've been really busy." Yvonne placed the boxes in the old green 1950s refrigerator. "Business has picked up."

"It's the same around here. I never thought I'd live to see the ranch thriving like this." Ruth lowered the temperature and peered into the pan. "I never thought I'd get all my grandchildren back either. God is very good."

"Amen." Yvonne crossed herself out of habit. "Can I help you with anything?"

"Not yet. Why don't you go into the parlor and keep Matt company while I finish up?"

Yvonne meekly did as she was told. It seemed the whole Morgan family was intent on finding her a new man. . . .

An hour later, she was sitting at a packed table, jostling elbows with various Morgans and their wives and girlfriends in a somewhat competitive match to get as much food on their plates as humanly possible. Boy, those men could eat. Matt was seated opposite her, and he occasionally smiled like they were united as outsiders in the noisy fray.

He *was* a nice guy. Good looking in that blond California nerd way and intelligent enough to immediately grasp what her business entailed, and how hard she worked. He'd asked some great questions and given her a couple of things to think about.

"The lamb is excellent, Mrs. Morgan." A new voice entered the conversation.

"Thank you, Rio," Ruth said. "And how are you settling in, dear?"

Yvonne looked down the table at the speaker, who was wedged between Ry and HW Morgan. He wore a black shirt with some kind of logo on it, and had the tanned, outdoor look of a cowboy. His accent held a hint of southern America, but she couldn't pin it down more than that. Having been to Sunday lunch at the Morgans' before, Yvonne figured he must be one of the new spring hires being welcomed onboard.

"I am settling in very well, thank you, Mrs. Morgan. I grew up on a ranch, so this feels very much like coming home."

His voice was soft and so melodious that Yvonne found herself smiling. He caught her staring and winked at her. Maybe not so young and sweet after all . . .

"Who's ready for dessert?" Ruth stood up. "I have cheesecake, and whatever Yvonne brought from the store."

There were several fake groans, but no one seemed willing to say no. Yvonne jumped up to help while the others cleared the table. The cowboy helped as well, stacking plates into the dishwasher with great speed and efficiency.

"Let me get that for you." Matt held the door of the refrigerator open as she took out the desserts.

"Thanks." She flashed him a smile. "Do you like éclairs, cream slices, or meringue?"

"I like all of them." He patted his stomach. "Unfortunately, my personal trainer would kill me if I *ate* any of them."

The new cowboy gave a hastily concealed snort. Yvonne offered him a sharp look and received a sunny smile in return.

"We won't tell him if you don't." Yvonne set the boxes on the countertop and looked around for some plates.

"Here you go." The cowboy slid a pile of plates in front of her. Up close, he had very brown eyes and long eyelashes that she immediately coveted. He wasn't that much taller than her in her two-inch wedges, which made him around five-foot-ten.

"Thank you."

"They look good. Where did you buy them?"

"Thank you. I got them at the coffee shop in town," Yvonne said as she expertly decanted the cream slices onto the plate without breaking the thin layers of pastry and custard.

"That fancy place with the pink and white awning, and the tables outside?"

"Yes." Yvonne offered him a brief smile. "I own it."

"Yeah? That's awesome." He took two of the plates and transferred them to the table.

Now his accent sounded typically American. . . .

She allowed him to help her liberate the rest of the pastries and then sat down, helping herself from the carafe of French vanilla coffee Ruth placed on the table.

"These are great, Yvonne." January made a moaning sound that drew the immediate attention of her husband. "If I could marry twice, I'd marry this éclair."

"Marrying the pastry chef would be the best idea," Matt chimed in. "Then you'd have a renewable resource." He beamed at Yvonne. "We should talk about that."

"Our wedding or the cakes?" she countered.

He laughed, and the conversation went off in another direction.

Despite everyone protesting, Yvonne somehow won the right to finish cleaning the kitchen with the cowboy and Matt. Ruth was watching TV in the parlor, and everyone else had dispersed. Yvonne had a thing about leaving her workspaces clean, and actually enjoyed the process of restoring order. Matt had no idea what to do, but was willing to be ordered around, and the other guy, Rio, just got on with it, seeming to know instinctively what to do and how to do it. He'd make an excellent kitchen assistant if he weren't already a ranch hand.

They kept the conversation to a minimum, giving Yvonne plenty of time to consider what she thought about Matt and his prospects as a boyfriend. The major issue was that he lived in San Francisco, which, although quite close, was still a plane or long drive away. January and Chase managed their relationship like that, but they were very committed to making it work.

Matt did have a lot of the qualities she liked in a man. He was intelligent, good looking, but not out of her league, and he really did listen when she talked. But there was no "'zing" there, nothing that made her want to kiss his socks off, no hint of sexual attraction. But she'd been there, had that, and had the broken marriage to prove it. Perhaps it was time to start with a friendship and hope it would grow into something more durable.

Matt would certainly understand her work schedule, seeing as he was pretty committed to the angel venture capital company he ran with Chase and Jake. And maybe not having him around all the time would work, too. They could both concentrate on their businesses and enjoy their relationship on the side.

Matt's cell buzzed, and he fished it out of his pocket and grimaced. "Sorry, I've got to take this. Back in a minute."

Yvonne carried on putting things away, finishing with the huge pile of silverware, which she carefully dried, and polished with the dishtowel.

"Do you know where this should go?"

She blinked into the gorgeous brown eyes of the cowboy, and then let her gaze fall to the glass bowl cupped in his large, capable hands.

"Up there." She pointed over her head. "Second cupboard on the right."

"Thanks." He reached up and put the bowl away. "I'm glad someone knows where everything goes. I'm working on it, but there are still a few things that elude me."

"Are you here for the season?" Yvonne asked.

"Kind of." He considered her, his keen gaze taking everything in. "I know Ry and HW from the rodeo. They asked me to come and help out." He barely paused to breathe. "Would you consider going on a date with me?"

She blinked at him. "*What*?"

He pointed at his chest. "Me." Then pointed at her. "Go out with you."

Great . . . her one day off, and someone was hitting on her. She put up with it at her café because pouring hot drinks over customers' laps was apparently bad for business, but she didn't have to smile and let it happen right now.

"I heard what you said, but . . . I think they're trying to set me up with Matt."

"Okay. Do you like Matt?"

Yvonne frowned. "I've only just met him."

"But you'd go out with him?"

"Maybe."

"Then seeing as you've only just met *me*, you *could* go out with me instead."

"Your logic is . . ." She shook her head. She really didn't want to deal with another cocky cowboy, but he was a guest of the Morgans. "So, so lame."

The door banged and Matt came back in. "Sorry about that." He looked around the kitchen. "Looks like you two have everything covered. Shall we go and join Ruth in the parlor?"

Rio watched Yvonne leave the kitchen with Matt, the exasperation at his expense still lingering in her eyes.

Jeez. Talk about messing things up from the get-go. He wanted to slap a hand over his *own* mouth. He was supposed to be a smooth-talking charmer, yet he'd come across like a two-bit bumbling teenager asking out his first girl. No wonder she'd looked at him with such bemusement. A woman as beautiful as Yvonne Payet was probably used to dealing with drooling fools, which was exactly what he'd turned into the moment he'd seen her.

And then he'd had to listen to the Morgans working out how they were going to fix her up with Matt, who was a really nice guy, but—

"Hey." HW put his head around the door. "What's up?"

"Just getting myself more coffee." Rio busied himself finding a mug. "What's the plan for the afternoon?"

"Some of us are 'napping.'" HW gave him a lascivious wink. "The rest are thinking about taking a walk around the ranch."

"Why walk when there are horses to spare?" Rio wondered.

"Yvonne doesn't like to ride, and neither does Avery. Matt's not very confident either. Did you think he hit it off with Yvonne? She seemed to like him."

"What's not to like?" Rio agreed.

"You can ride out if you want," HW said. "I'll make your excuses. It'll give you a chance to get used to the different horses so you can match them with the guests."

"I thought I was here to teach the newbies bull riding?" Rio asked.

"Sure, you are." HW gave his famous patented smile. "But we're hoping you'll pitch in with the other stuff as well."

"Only if you double my wages?"

HW punched Rio's shoulder. "Seeing as I'm not paying you a dime, sure, why not?"

* * *

Halfway along the gentle, winding path shielded by pine trees Chase had constructed beside Morgan Creek, Rio managed to catch up with Yvonne, who had outpaced both Avery and Matt. She glanced over as he reached her side, but didn't speak.

"I want to apologize," Rio said.

She shrugged. "I've heard some lousy chat-up lines in my time, but that was pretty dire."

"That's because it wasn't planned," Rio said ruefully. "It sort of just fell out of my mouth before I used my brain. I'm usually much better than that."

"At flirting? I should hope so or you've probably never gotten laid in your life."

"Ah. That probably explains it." He nodded. "I've always wondered what I was doing wrong." He fought back a grin. "I'll have to work on my technique."

She gave him that amused don't-mess-with-me stare again. "Not with me."

"I should imagine you're pretty good at shooting down lame bullshit from guys, aren't you? You could tell me where I'm going wrong."

They'd reached the end of the path, where a series of picnic tables was laid out overlooking one of the minor waterfalls on the creek. The roar of the water was loud with the rush of melting snow from the Sierra Mountains above. She turned to face him, her hands tucked in the pockets of her jeans.

"It's not my job to help amateurs work out their best lines."

"True." He met her gaze. "I'm really sorry."

She considered him for a long moment. "Okay. Apology accepted." She sighed. "I probably over-reacted. I deal with it six days a week at my café, and for once I didn't have to grit my teeth, smile, and pretend everything was fine. You just caught me on my day off."

"I'm sorry," Rio said again. "I really am."

He wanted to throw caution to the wind, and ask her out again, but the thought of her turning him down flat held him back. He was better than that, and she definitely deserved more. He took a seat on the corner of one of the tables, and looked out over the rushing waters of the creek. The ranch was a truly magical place steeped in history and tradition.

"I love it out here," Yvonne said.

Rio glanced over at her in surprise. He'd expected her to ignore him for quite a while. Maybe she really had forgiven him, and moved on.

"Me, too." Inwardly he grimaced as he dropped yet another inane reply. "The scenery is spectacular and the people even better."

"The Morgans are good people." She sat down on the top of the picnic table, her feet on the seat. "You met the twins on the rodeo circuit?"

"Yeah." He smiled. "I was twenty-three, I'd barely spoken English for years, and I had five hundred dollars to my name. The twins took me in, introduced me to the other guys from Brazil, and made sure nobody hazed me too much. How did you end up in Morgantown?"

"I came through here once by accident when we missed the turn-off for the highway. It kind of stuck in my memory because there was nowhere to buy a decent cup of coffee—only the stuff in the general store." She smiled, and it was like a shot of pure tequila. "When I was looking for a place to set up my business, I called a couple of my old friends, and ended up here."

"From what I hear, everyone is glad you got lost that day."

Her smile dimmed. "It's a good place to make friends, and put down roots."

"But not so good for business?"

She swung around to study him, her hands now tucked into the pockets of her jacket. "My, you are full of questions today, aren't you?"

He shrugged. "I've never seen myself as shy. If I want to know something, I always prefer to ask outright."

"Like when you asked me out even though I told you I was thinking about going out with Matt?"

"Exactly." He loved the way she sparred with him.

She regarded him for a long minute, and shook her head.

"What?" Rio protested. "I heard that the café was doing very well."

"From whom?"

"Everyone. So what's the problem?"

"Lack of trained staff."

"Ah. Beauty comes with a price, eh?" He let his gaze travel around the stark splendor of the isolated valley protected by the massive Sierra Mountains. "What are you going to do about that?"

"Why? Have you decided to give up on ranching, and apply for a job in my kitchen?"

"Maybe." He winked at her. "A man can't live on beef alone."

She rolled her eyes and redirected her gaze over the top of his head. "Avery and Matt are here. Did you know Avery used to be a barrel racer?"

"Yeah. Ry told me." Something told *him* that she was trying to get rid of him. It was quite a new experience. He wasn't sure whether to laugh or cry.

Yvonne hopped gracefully down off the table and headed toward the incoming pair.

"Hey." Matt greeted her with a smile. "I was just asking Avery about a good place to take you out to eat tonight. She suggested the hotel would be the easiest, or the Red Dragon Bar if you wanted it louder."

Yvonne didn't even look back in Rio's direction as she smiled and took Matt's hand. "The hotel will be great. Just remember I have to be home by nine."

Only then did she look at Rio and sent his wink right back to him.

Rio opened his mouth to say something, and then shut it again. Yvonne might have won the first round, but he was here all summer, and Matt was going back to San Francisco. . . .

Competition was his middle name, and he hated to lose. Soon, *he* would be the man taking the gorgeously smart Yvonne Payet out for dinner, and Matt would be consigned to history.

Chapter Two

Yvonne loved her kitchen. It was the only place where she was in complete control—well, as complete as the recipe and the demands of the cooking gods allowed her to be. The surfaces were clean; her supplies were labeled, dated, and kept in an easy-to-access system, which made pulling together the ingredients for anything super easy.

And then there was Tom, her latest apprentice from the community college. . . .

"I dunno, like, what happened, Yvonne. One minute, everything was, like, in the bowl. The next, my hand slipped, and the cake batter sort of, like, got everywhere."

"I can see that."

Yvonne took in the globs of pink that covered his apron, dripped from his covered hair, and decorated the plain white walls.

"I'll clean up," Tom offered.

"That would be good." Yvonne smiled into his anxious eyes. This was his third shot at a youth apprenticeship, and probably his last before he was kicked off the program. "It's okay. Nothing is on fire this time, and this is *totally* fixable. Clean the walls, the work surfaces, and most importantly, yourself, and then start again."

"Okay." Tom blew out his breath. "Thanks for not shouting at me, Yvonne."

She returned to her end of the kitchen, and started counting croissants again. The café was open, but it wasn't that busy yet so Lizzie, who worked out front, could manage without her.

Tom started whistling as he cleaned up. He was a good kid, and he definitely had potential, but, like all the college kids, he still needed a lot of supervision. . . . Yvonne wrote down the number of croissants and started on the chocolate-filled ones. She had four birthday cakes to make today, as well as the usual café fare, and time was tight.

Her young apprentice was supposed to be making the cake batters so that she could get the sponge bases cooled down before she attempted the filling and frosting. She loved making individual cakes. They were a creative challenge, and she always enjoyed that.

Next week, she was going to sit down with her accountant and go through the books again. She was making enough money to survive, which was great, and the new contracts with Morgan Ranch would ease her financial concerns even more, but she still worried. She never forgot that most small businesses failed, and she hated the thought of being financially insolvent.

She loved her café with its striped pink and black awning over the door, the small bistro tables and chairs set out on the raised wooden sidewalk. It reminded her of her last summer in Paris, when she'd been in love and everything had been wonderful.

So much for that. . . .

Lizzie popped her head around the door. "Do you

have another tray of chocolate chip muffins? They're going like crazy today."

"Sure. I'll bring some out to you."

Yvonne went into the large, cooled larder and brought out a batch of the muffins she'd baked at five that morning. The chocolaty smell wafted over her, and she inhaled appreciatively. Some pastry chefs lost their taste for sweet things when they worked with them all day, but not her. She'd bathe in chocolate if she had the time, and the money.

Using her shoulder to open the kitchen door, she backed into the shop, and almost bumped into a man standing at the counter. He wore the local uniform of jeans, T-shirt, and a cowboy hat.

"Hey."

Belatedly, she recognized the new hand from the ranch who had asked her out.

"Hey, Ross."

"It's Rio, but never mind." His smile was warm, and there was a twinkle in his eye that she bet slayed almost every female between the ages of two and one hundred and two. "I came in for some coffee, and got waylaid by the muffins." He chuckled. "I think I inhaled the last one, and asked if there were any more."

"Happens a lot around here."

He eased his arm around her back, and carefully closed the kitchen door. "Don't want you to get smacked in the back of the head."

"Are you sure you've never worked in a restaurant before?" She put the tray of muffins down on the back counter, and started shifting them across into the glass display cabinet.

"I worked as a waiter to make ends meet when I first joined the rodeo." His smile was wry. "Got into trouble going in the out door once, and caused a plate pile-up. Never did it again."

"I bet." She finished with the muffins, and spent a moment rearranging the display to make it look more appealing.

Lizzie came over with a large cup of to-go coffee, and handed it to Rio with a blush and a cute smile.

"Here you are. I'll just get your muffin."

"Thank you, Lizzie."

Lizzie went even redder as she found a paper bag and fiddled around with the tongs.

The cowboy took a sip of his coffee, and sighed. "Yeah. That hits the spot. How did your date with Matt go?"

Yvonne raised an eyebrow. She really should go back into her kitchen and stop playing with fire, but she couldn't seem to help herself. "What's it got to do with you?"

"After listening to the whole Morgan family setting you up for a week, I'm kind of invested."

"You're just hoping it was a disaster."

He widened his brown eyes. "Why ever would you think that?"

"Because then you could jump in and ask me out again."

He considered her for a long moment as a dimple slowly emerged on his right cheek. "True."

She liked the way he acknowledged a hit so easily, and decided to be gracious. "Actually, it went really well."

"Damn." He sighed. "So are you two a couple now?"

"I didn't say that." She hedged. "There are a lot of things we need to discuss before we get to that stage."

"Discuss? Sounds more like a board meeting than the start of a relationship."

"Like you'd know about either of those things."

He winced and pressed a hand to his heart. "Ouch."

"You're welcome." Yvonne gave him her best smile. Rio might be a pain, but it was fun having someone to spar with who didn't seem to take offense. "Have a great day."

He hesitated. "Actually, there *was* something I wanted to discuss with you."

"Didn't we just do that?"

"This is something else entirely." He gestured at the nearest table. "Can we sit down?"

Yvonne glanced back at the kitchen, where she hoped Tom was behaving himself. "Okay, but I only have a minute."

He held out her chair and waited until she was settled before he took the seat opposite, his brown gaze serious.

"I hear you make birthday cakes."

"Yes."

"Could you make a thank-you cake for Mrs. Morgan? She's been very kind to me, and although I know she loves to bake, I thought it would be nice if she didn't have to for a change."

"That's a lovely idea."

Okay, so he was funny *and* nice.

"I'm not sure what her favorite flavor is. Do you know?"

He looked directly into her eyes, and Yvonne felt that flicker of attraction she was trying to ignore spark between them again.

"She loves anything coffee flavored," Yvonne said. "And chocolate, so maybe some kind of flourless chocolate cake?"

"Sounds good to me. When do you think you'll be able to get it done?"

"Not until the end of the week." Yvonne paused.

She knew that the ranch hands didn't earn much above minimum wage. "My cakes aren't cheap, but seeing as it's for Ruth, I—"

He cut her off with a wave of his hand. "That's very kind of you, but I can afford to pay the full price."

"You were successful in the rodeo thing then?"

"Successful enough." His smile returned. "And I've made a few investments over the years that give me a decent income."

Was that his gentle way of getting back at her jibe about him not knowing his way around a boardroom?

"I'm sorry." Yvonne made a face. "I hate people judging me on my appearance, and I guess I did the same to you."

He shrugged one elegant shoulder. "I should have told you although I'm willing to help out when needed, I didn't just come to the ranch as a working hand. HW asked me to teach a class on bull riding."

"That's what you do?" Yvonne crinkled her nose.

"Yes."

"Is it a big thing in the rodeo?" Yvonne asked innocently. She sort of knew from the Morgans about bull riding, but she wasn't going to let *Rio* know that. He was way too confident and assured already.

"You could say that." He took another sip from his cup and glanced behind him as the door opened and about six people filed in looking desperate for coffee. "I won't keep you. Let me know how much I owe you for the cake, and when it will be ready."

"Will do." Yvonne rose to her feet and made sure he picked up his bagged muffin. "Thanks for coming in."

"Thanks for baking." He tipped his black cowboy hat to her and headed for the door. "I'll see you soon."

He was almost at the door before he turned back

and locked gazes with her. For some reason, her knees literally wobbled.

"Can I give you my cell number?"

"Sure!" Yvonne said brightly, aware that she'd been staring at his Wrangler-covered ass, and picked up one of the order pads. "Fire away."

Rio closed the door of the café behind him, and smiled. *What a woman.* She baked, she looked like a million dollars, and she was as sharp as a tack. Why some man hadn't gone all caveman on her and carted her off already was a mystery. Except she'd probably have something to say if anyone tried that on her. . . .

But she sounded like she was about to enter into a relationship with Matt, and he wouldn't interfere. It wasn't his style. Being a bull rider who risked his life for eight seconds of perfection, he had a deep appreciation for the gods of fate and destiny. If he and Yvonne were meant to be a couple, it would happen. To be fair, Matt really wasn't up for the challenge of a woman like Yvonne. It would be kinder if one of the Morgan brothers pointed that out to Matt. Blue was known for his honesty, so maybe Rio would have a quiet word with him just to help move things along a bit.

Morgantown was starting to wake up around him. Spring break traffic attempting to avoid the freeway for a gentler drive through the great state of California was already building up. The Morgans were talking about making downtown vehicle free, and he was totally behind the idea. Every time one of the massive big rigs thundered through Main Street, the small town was shaken to its foundations. They could do with some kind of bypass for the big stuff and a decent parking lot behind the town for the tourists.

His cell buzzed, and he took it out of his pocket to see a new number flashing on the screen, followed by a text from Yvonne. She was nothing if not efficient. He was just about to put his cell away when he noticed the buildup of voice mail and reluctantly accessed them.

Six of them were from the same admin. The seventh was different.

"Call me, immediately. I know you are in the country."

His father's voice boomed in his ear and he winced. *Yeah. Call the old man.* It wasn't like they hadn't spoken for five years or anything. His father was too used to getting his own way, and Rio wasn't having it. He was no longer a scared teenager begging to be understood, begging to be allowed to live his life as he wanted to. He was also no longer one of his father's management team. They'd parted on bad terms, and as far as he was concerned, nothing had changed.

He shoved his phone back in his pocket, and continued along the raised wooden sidewalk to the post office, which was just by Yvonne's café. He checked the ranch box, and found a letter from his mother, which made him smile. Unlike his father, his mother hated to use the phone, and preferred to write him long, chatty letters, which, due to the vagaries of the Brazilian post coupled with his crazy travel schedule, often took quite a while to reach him.

His half sister, Josie, kept him up to date by texting him, which meant that if there were ever a real emergency at home, he'd know soon enough. When his maternal grandmother had died, he'd gotten on a plane two hours later and been there for the funeral. Sometimes it was a very small world. He grimaced at the thought of his father.

Sometimes too small.

"Yo, Rio! You ready to go?"

He turned to see HW Morgan standing by his truck and waved in return.

"I'm coming."

He'd intended to go into the general store and buy himself a new straw cowboy hat to replace his black one, but that could wait until tomorrow. He'd had a much better time in the coffee shop chatting to Yvonne—the woman who made him blurt out stuff like a teenager with his first crush. For some reason, he didn't seem able to turn on his famous charm and flirt with her. He suspected she'd see straight through him anyway. . . .

He strode toward his parking spot, unlocking the doors so that HW could get in the passenger side. At least he and Yvonne had a cake to bond over. Today would be all about learning the layout of Morgan Ranch. Tomorrow, the first guests were arriving, and his time would no longer be his own.

Yvonne wrote a note to herself about the chocolate cake for Ruth Morgan and added it to her calendar. Tom had successfully made some new pink cake batter and had the ovens up to temperature, so all was good. She set him to making the next batch, reminding him to read through the whole recipe before he started, while she greased up the four pans she needed and dolloped the batter in, weighing each pan to make sure they were even.

After sliding the pans into the industrial-sized oven, she set a timer and consulted the day planner on her laptop. Something about the date resonated and she stopped to consider it. How could she have forgotten? Ten years ago, she'd gone to study in Paris and she'd met Paul. Six years ago, on this very day, she'd married him, and they'd moved back to the United States to start a business together.

Now he was back in France, and they were no longer a couple. . . .

Yvonne sighed. She couldn't believe she'd forgotten such an important moment in her life. Had she become used to the loneliness? Had she allowed her job to consume her so that she wouldn't care about the past anymore? Paul would probably agree with that. He'd always thought she took everything too seriously, and that work had become a priority over him.

But a business didn't run itself. . . .

She just about took in the details of the next cake and the regular list of breads and pastries for the café before she closed her calendar. Clicking back to her home page, she gave in to the temptation to Google her ex, and soon found pictures of his latest successful eatery in Paris.

She studied the photos, her head tipped to one side. He still looked good, but she no longer felt that pang of loss, that sense that she was incomplete without him that had dragged her down after the first two years of his departure. Her friends Avery and Nancy had been there for her, and her work had saved her. She looked around her immaculate kitchen and took a deep breath. She had her coffee shop. She was well liked in her community, and usually that was enough.

An email notification popped up on the top right of her screen, and she did a double take.

Je pense tres fort a toi aujourd'hui. Meilleurs voeux. Paul.

He was *thinking* about her today? Why now? Why hadn't he thought about breaking her heart when he'd walked out on her four years ago after barely two years of marriage?

Yvonne let out an exasperated breath. Men sucked. There was no other explanation for it. She closed her laptop, washed her hands, and dived into the business of the day. It was almost lunchtime, when the café would be filled with tourists, and Lizzie would need all the help she could get. They'd lost a waitress last week and were down to two again.

After giving Tom a new set of very specific instructions, Yvonne tidied her hair, put on a white apron over her severe black dress, and went to do battle out front. She paused to survey the filled tables and wished she had the money to expand into the shop next door. Having two separate counters, one for takeout, and one for sit-down guests, would probably be way more efficient.

But then she'd need more staff. . . .

Fixing a bright smile on her face, she hurried behind the counter, picked up a notepad and pen, and went to check the tables out front. Paul might have his fancy line of bistros in Paris, but she had Morgantown, and a steady flow of customers with a sweet tooth just like hers.

She took her first order from a businesswoman with a cell phone jammed to her ear, mainly by guesswork and lots of pointing, but she was used to that, and moved on to the next table. In her secret opinion, the French had a lot more respect for the value of a relaxing meal than Americans ever would.

There was a group clustered around one of the small tables with the wide-eyed stares of a family who'd been driving for days. Their two small kids were chattering like magpies, and the mother looked exhausted. Having spent several vacations trapped in the back of a car while her parents "saw America," Yvonne had all the sympathy in the world for her.

She handed out lunch menus that contained some great options for the kids. "Welcome to Yvonne's. Now what can I get you to drink?"

Chapter Three

"That's right. Just hunker down, find your natural center, and hold on to the rope," Rio repeated patiently to the teenager who was currently astride the artificial bucking bull in one of the Morgan Ranch barns. He had a group of about ten trying out his first bull-riding class, which was quite enough for him.

"What do you mean, my natural center?" Troy asked dubiously.

Rio patted the guy on his lower back just above his jeans. "Here, like if you were riding a Harley. Relax your hips and settle in."

"Oh, right!"

Rio stepped out of the way and headed for the controls. "I'll start you off slow. Remember, try and keep one hand locked in the rope while holding the other high."

"Got it."

In the way of most teens, Troy sounded way more confident than he should be. Rio shared an amused glance with Troy's parents, who were obviously torn between wanting their son to succeed and worrying he'd fall and hurt himself. Even if he did fall, there was a pit full of soft foam for him to land on. When Rio had first jumped on the back of a bull, he'd had nothing but his own deluded cloak of invincibility and an incredibly hard head.

"All right! Let's get this bull bucking!" Rio shouted as the bull began a slow rock and roll to the right.

Troy managed to stay on the whole eight seconds, and whooped with delight as Rio offered to speed things up. It didn't take long for the teen to end up in the pit, but as he was grinning when he emerged from the foam forms, Rio guessed he'd enjoyed himself.

"Hey, Dad! How about I forget about college and do this instead?" Troy yelled.

Rio hid a smile at the horrified expression on the father's face, and busied himself resetting the controls. His father had looked exactly the same when he'd finally found out what Rio had ended up doing.

It was heating up inside the barn. Rio wished he'd gotten around to buying a white straw cowboy hat, and decided to go back into town after he was done for the day. Maybe he'd get a chance to drop in on Yvonne as well.

"Can I have a try?"

Jolted out of his pleasant dream of Yvonne's beautiful face, Rio looked down at Elsa, who was Troy's grandmother, and something of a live wire.

"Sure, you can." He patted her shoulder. "Show that young grandson of yours how it's done, right?"

She elbowed him in the ribs. "I'd rather watch you. I've seen you on TV. I can't believe you're here right now doing this on a ranch!" Her voice became concerned. "Don't they pay you enough, dear?"

He patted her shoulder. "I'm just helping out my friend, Elsa. Don't worry about me."

He helped her climb up onto the back of the bull

and showed her how to wrap her rope and secure her gloved hand under the coils. She threw her left hand high over her head and let out a loud yell right in his ear, making him wince.

"Let it go, cowboy!" she shrieked as Rio hurried to do her bidding.

She hung on for the whole eight seconds, but declined his invitation to speed up the bull. He was just returning from helping her down when Troy spoke up.

"Will you show us how it's done, Rio, please? I want to get a picture."

Rio glanced around the group to find them all nodding encouragingly at him. "Okay, if that's what you all want. Tomorrow we're going to work on your technique, and get you anticipating what's going to happen rather than just reacting so that you can adjust your seat and balance accordingly."

"Awesome." Troy and his younger brother grinned and high-fived each other.

Rio turned to Elsa. "How about you handle the controls so I don't get too many surprises? Just start at level three, and move it up to the top from there. It's preprogrammed to throw in a few tricks at that point."

"Will do." Elsa took control, and nodded at him to proceed.

Riding a mechanical bull was nothing like riding a real one. Even the best, most up-to-date machines didn't have that belligerent streak that a living, breathing top-class fifteen-hundred-pound bucking bull had. Every single time a rider climbed on the back of one of those overbred beasts, he took his life in his hands and risked it all.

Rio rewound the rope and settled the coils in the palm of his hand, giving them one last tighten as he settled into place. With a nod at Elsa, he raised his right hand high over his head and the bull gathered speed, whirling and turning like a demented circus ride. But nothing could unseat him. Here, he was in his element, in his zone, and here, he truly believed he was unbeatable.

The buzzer went, and eight seconds flashed on the scoreboard. He undid his rope and performed a flashy dismount, much to the enjoyment of the Morgan Ranch guests, who hollered and applauded him. He raised his hat, and came back to the side of the pit, ready to answer questions.

It was only then that he noticed they'd been joined by January Morgan and a smiling Yvonne. He settled himself at one of the tables, and tried his best to reply to the torrent of questions. It wasn't the first time he'd done an exhibition ride, but it was still fun.

After a while, January announced that lunch was ready, and everyone headed for the welcome center. Rio took off his hat and wiped his brow.

"Phew. It's getting hot in here."

"You're really something to watch on the back of a bull," Yvonne said.

"Thanks." He glanced down at her, surprised that she'd remained behind, and shrugged. "It's my job."

"I've never thought about how hard a body has to work to stay in one place and in one piece on the back of a bull."

"It's just a dance." He sat down on the corner of the table, and took off his shirt to reveal his black T-shirt beneath.

"A deadly one."

"Sure, but that's why it's so challenging and so amazing when you get it right."

She angled her head to one side to look up at him. "What does it feel like?"

He grinned. "You're not going to like my answer."

"Try me."

"Okay, it's like having the best sex ever—when everything is moving perfectly in harmony, and you know you're going to have the biggest climax of your life."

"Wow." She let out a slow breath. "That's almost . . . poetic."

"It's the closest I've ever gotten to describing how it feels."

"I suppose when you're risking your life to stay on the back of something for eight seconds, sex and death probably do come to mind," Yvonne mused.

"And life. You appreciate every brilliant millisecond of that. When you're having a good ride, everything seems to slow down, and you experience every breath, every tiny shift in the bull's weight in a different, more visceral way."

Yvonne nodded. "So, just like sex."

"Yeah." It was his turn to grin at her. "Exactly. Not that I've ever had sex like that according to you."

"*Have* you?" Yvonne asked.

He met her intense gaze with his own. "Once or twice. How about you?"

"Maybe when I was younger, and believed in true love and all that stuff," she countered.

"You don't believe in love?" He raised his eyebrows.

"Not really."

This time, her smile was meant to put a distance between them, but he'd never been one to worry about jumping a few hard fences.

"Why not?"

"The usual reasons." She stood and handed him his shirt. "You should stop with all this macho black stuff, and buy some summer clothes. You must be cooking alive in there."

"And you would know about cooking." He rubbed an absent hand over his T-shirt, which clung to the outline of his abs. Her gaze dropped to the motion of his fingers, and a bolt of pure lust struck him right in the gut. Time to change the subject before he did something insane like take her in his arms and kiss her until she was plastered against him and begging him to—

He hastily cleared his throat. "I was planning on visiting Maureen's store tomorrow."

"Good idea." She started back toward the house, and he followed her like a lamb. She was moving fast, her long, slim legs in denim capris eating up the ground. Maybe she'd seen something in his eyes that had betrayed his sudden flare of interest. Maybe he'd imagined the reciprocal heat in hers. It wasn't like him to get so . . . *poetical* with a woman so fast, but the words had tumbled out of him because, when she turned that bright green gaze on him, she deserved that— deserved his honesty.

"How's my cake coming along?" He went for the most neutral subject he could think of.

"I haven't even started it yet."

"Oh, that's right. You said the end of the week."

She stopped walking and turned to face him. "I don't like this."

"This what?"

She poked him in the chest. "This *thing* between us."

"That we're attracted to each other? We don't have to do anything about it, do we?" He attempted a shrug even as he rejoiced that she was feeling it too. "We're both adults."

"I don't have time for any complications right now."

"I'm a complication?" Rio nodded. "But you have time for Matt? I totally don't get it."

Her eyes flashed. "*Matt* is . . . different."

"From me?" He knew he should stop talking, but somehow he couldn't stop. "He's a nice guy, yeah, but he sure is different."

Yvonne raised her chin. "Matt is all I can handle right now. You, on the other hand, strike me as extremely high-maintenance."

"*Me*?" Rio blinked at her. "Whatever gave you that idea?"

She folded her arms across her chest—never a good sign. "You're an athlete. A successful one."

"So?"

"You're used to women throwing themselves at you."

"I never suggested you throw yourself at me," Rio protested.

"No, because you *assume* that, with that killer smile and amazing body, any woman you meet will immediately fall into your arms, no shoving required."

He allowed himself a slow victorious smile. "You think I'm hot."

She made a dismissive gesture. "That's all you got out of everything I just said to you? Typical!"

"I think you are one of the most beautiful women I've ever met," he said quietly.

"Don't." She glared at him. "Don't do that, go all sincere on me, and what do my looks have to do with anything anyway?"

"Hey, you started it," Rio protested.

"*What*?"

He ran a hand down over his chest and stomach. "You said I was hot. I just reciprocated in kind."

"I did not say—" She stopped talking, and sighed. "Okay, I did say you were hot."

He batted his eyelashes at her. "And maybe you hurt

my feelings by treating me like an object rather than a person?"

"Oh, good Lord, I certainly didn't mean to do that." She reached for his hand. "I—"

"Just kidding." He took her fingers and brought them to his lips to kiss. "I'm totally fine with you thinking I'm hot."

"You are infuriating."

"I know." He pretended to look modest. "It's an integral part of my hotness."

She rolled her eyes and eased her hand out of his. "Look, can we just be friends?"

"We can certainly try." Rio nodded.

"Okay, then."

"Okay."

She started walking again, and this time Rio made no effort to keep up with her. She did have a point. He wasn't looking for a girlfriend at this point in his life. He had a career to maintain, and a lifestyle that looked glamorous from the outside but mainly consisted of endlessly moving from city to city and hotel to hotel between events. Not many women wanted to join their men on tour, and not many long-distance relationships survived without someone being unfaithful.

Yvonne was settled in Morgantown, she had a successful business, and she was happy with her life. He got that. He craved that settled normality like a drug sometimes. Coming from a separated family, he'd had to balance not only living in two countries but two parents who hated each other. He'd never had that kind of security. He'd always been the bridge between them, a bridge they'd both wanted to cleave in half so they could claim him for their own.

Rio shrugged off the memories and turned toward

the ranch house, where he was staying. He had nothing of value to offer Yvonne—nothing she would value anyway—so maybe it would be better if they could try and be friends. He let his gaze drift upward to the horse barn where she was talking to January, her expressive face wreathed in smiles as she gesticulated with her hands in a very French way.

Yeah, friends it would have to be because, right now, he didn't think he had the ability to turn his back and walk away from her completely.

"So how did it go with Matt?" January asked in her most casual voice, which didn't fool Yvonne one bit. "Are you two seeing each other now?"

Yvonne followed her friend into the kitchen of the ranch house, forcing herself not to look back and see where Rio had gone. She couldn't quite believe she'd sat there and had such a personal conversation with him when she barely even knew the guy. But there was something about his quiet, elegant confidence that appealed to her senses. And seeing him on the back of the bull, his body arched in the fluid motion of an athlete at the top of his game, had made everything female in her perk up. Pathetic, but true. Her only excuse was that she hadn't had sex for a very long time.

"Yvonne?" She looked up to see January watching her curiously. "Are you okay?"

"Yes, sorry." She took a seat at the table and accepted a glass of homemade lemonade. "Were you asking about Matt? We had a very nice dinner together at the hotel, and we've been in touch since."

"Awesome." January beamed. "He *really* is a nice guy."

Nice . . . there was that word again. Yvonne smiled. "So everyone keeps telling me."

Matt was everything she thought she wanted. Independently wealthy, intelligent, respectful, *and* pleasant on the eye. He even made her laugh. Did he only *seem* lacking beside the dark-haired, quick-tongued cowboy who stirred her senses in a way Matt could probably never do? But instant lust was never a good thing. She'd fallen into that trap once before and lived to regret it.

It was definitely time to try something new, and Matt checked all the boxes.

"He said he'd be back at the weekend," January chimed in. "He's bringing Jake, and Chase's cat, Jobs, out for a visit."

"Chase has a cat?" Yvonne was momentarily jerked out of the morass of her own problems. "*Your* Chase? The man who hates chickens and is terrified of spiders?"

"He *likes* cats. He thinks they are independent thinkers, and we could always do with another mouser in the barn."

Yvonne tried to picture super nerd Chase Morgan cuddling a cat and failed miserably. "How is Jake doing since his car accident?"

January made a face. "Not so good. He's needed months of rehab and he's fed up living with his parents. Chase thought he might do better out here with some fresh air and company. Sam can help him with his exercise program and provide moral support."

"That's a great idea."

"So you'll come for dinner Saturday night when everyone is here?"

Yvonne studied her friend. "You really are obnoxiously persistent sometimes, you know?"

January grinned. "I know, but will you come anyway?"

Yvonne thought about the cake she was due to deliver to Rio and made up her mind. "Sure. I'll bring dessert."

After another glass of lemonade, and some good local gossip, Yvonne reluctantly turned to business. "It's been lovely visiting with you, but I need to get back to the store. I forgot that Lizzie has to leave at four, and we'll be shorthanded."

She fished in her purse and brought out her notebook. "I need your order for next week."

"I have it right here." January grabbed her tablet and flipped through the tabs. "You know, I could save you a trip and email it to you, but then I'd hardly get to see you at all." She chuckled. "You and your notebooks. Chase would kill me if I didn't adapt to all the latest technology."

"I like writing things down," Yvonne protested. "I remember them better, and I like to talk to my clients. You know? That personal touch thing?"

"Not Chase's strength," January said. "I bet he'd employ robots if he could." She consulted her spreadsheet. "We have no special requests this week, just three times the usual quantities so we can keep feeding the new guests."

Yvonne looked up. "Of *everything*?"

"Is that okay?"

"Yes, of course it is," In her head, Yvonne was frantically rescheduling. "Don't worry about a thing."

"You need to expand your business," January said.

"I need more staff. I can barely manage what I have without giving myself more financial headaches."

"Do you want me to talk to Chase about—"

Yvonne placed a finger on January's lips. "Nope,

not now, not ever. I won't take money from friends. It's a recipe for disaster."

"But it wouldn't just be from a friend. Chase is my husband, and he's a businessman who lends money to all kinds of start-ups."

"I know what he does, January, but I still don't want to risk it." Yvonne put her notebook away. "I love you for offering, but I'll work it out myself, okay?"

January sighed. "Okay. But we'll see you Saturday regardless?"

"Yes." Yvonne rose and kissed the top of January's head. "I'm looking forward to it already."

Chapter Four

Yvonne sank into a chair at one of the small tables squeezed up against the countertop, and took off her apron. She'd barely sat down all morning. Even now, she couldn't escape to her apartment upstairs for a proper lunch and had to hang around in case her staff became overwhelmed again. Popularity was great, but it brought a few headaches with it as well.

What with the increased orders from the ranch, and the three cakes to be finished off, boxed up, and collected, she scarcely had time to breathe.

"Here you go." Lizzie came by with her grilled goat cheese and tomato panini, and a large carafe of coffee. "Eat up. We should be fine now the lunch rush is over. Antonio says he's got things up to date."

"Thanks."

Antonio was a fantastic find and a great lunchtime cook. The goat's cheese was strong and worked well with the local heirloom tomatoes the Morgans had started to grow on the ranch. There was also a hint of the basil she kept on the windowsills of her kitchen. Yvonne mentally catalogued what else she had to do before she could seek her bed and groaned. She also had to squeeze in an interview for two new waitstaff in about half an hour.

"Hey."

She looked up as Rio slid into the seat opposite and almost swallowed her tongue as he smiled at her. The glob of cheese stuck to the roof of her mouth didn't help, and she started to cough. Reaching over, he patted her back until she managed to stop.

"Better now?"

She waved an irritable hand at him, and concentrated on taking a sip of coffee. A glass of water appeared at her elbow and she took a hasty swig.

"Thanks."

"I didn't mean to startle you."

She eyed him suspiciously. "Why are you here again?"

"I told you. I'm getting some summer gear at Maureen's." His innocent brown gaze was definitely too good to be true.

"This isn't Maureen's."

"You're right." He took a lengthy look around and then returned the full glare of his amused gaze back on her. "Sometimes I get confused, and I forget my English."

"*Hmmph.* I don't believe that for a second."

He grinned, displaying that distracting dimple. "I don't suppose you have time to come shopping with me?"

"Nope. It's too busy."

He leaned back in his chair. "You probably need more staff."

"*Really?* Wow, I've never thought about that." She shook her head. "Silly old me."

"I guess it's difficult to get good people out here. HW says they have the same problem up at the ranch.

There's not a lot of housing if you don't want to live in the bunkhouse, the pay is low, and there's nothing to do on a Saturday night."

"That pretty much sums it up." Yvonne sighed. "I also spend a lot of time training kids from the local community college, and as soon as they're proficient, they up and leave."

"That sucks. My father—" He paused and shook his head. "That's not really important right now."

"Your father what?"

Rio raised his eyebrows. "Now who's being inquisitive?"

"Just following your lead. Is your father in the restaurant business?"

"You could say that's where he got his start." He looked over his shoulder. "I'd better be off. I've got a class at two, and I borrowed HW's truck."

Before he could get up, a shadow loomed over the table, and someone spoke.

"Hi, are you the Yvonne who owns this café?"

She looked up. "Yes. Are you here for the interview?"

"Not quite." The woman beamed at her and handed over a card with a familiar logo. "I'm Priscilla Chang from Tasty Treats Productions."

"Should I know you?" Yvonne asked cautiously.

"That probably depends if you watch TV. I was here yesterday and sampled your amazing baking. I wanted to talk to you about an idea I had."

Yvonne flicked her gaze to Rio, who smiled as he vacated his chair and offered it to Priscilla with a flourish. She almost asked him to stick around just so that she'd know it wasn't a weird dream, but decided he'd think she was nuts.

"I'll leave you both to it, then," Rio said.

"Okay. I'll see you Saturday at the ranch with the cake," Yvonne said.

"Great." He tipped his hat and, with a wink, headed out of the store.

"That is a *very* attractive man," Priscilla breathed. "Do you know him well?"

"We're just friends."

"Shame he isn't your boyfriend," Priscilla said. "He'd certainly encourage a certain segment of our viewing population to tune in." She took out her cell, and looked expectantly at Yvonne. "You don't mind if I take a few notes, do you?"

"About what exactly?" Yvonne hated feeling all at sea.

"You and this amazing, out-of-this-world little café of yours." Priscilla lowered her voice and leaned in. "A little goldmine in gold country. I like that! It would make a *great* tagline."

"For what?" Yvonne didn't often feel at sea, and she really wasn't catching on.

"Your TV show." Priscilla shot her an appraising stare. "I see it like this. . . ."

Two days later, and Yvonne still wasn't sure what to think of her extraordinary meeting in the café with Priscilla. She'd got through the rest of the week, delivered all her orders on time, and slept very little while she pondered the opportunity that had opened up for her.

She parked in front of the Morgan ranch house, and retrieved the cake box from the floor of the back seat. The kitchen door opened, and Rio came out. For once, his hat was missing, and the sun caught glints of blue in his crow-black hair. He wore his usual jeans and cowboy boots, but had swapped out his black shirt for a red and white checkered one.

She gave him the once-over as he approached, and he rotated in a slow circle in front of her.

"What do you think?"

"You look like a tablecloth in my favorite Italian restaurant."

"Good enough to eat off then?" His grin made her stomach somersault with pure lust.

"Maybe."

He moved closer, and she held the cake box in front of her like a shield. "Here's the cake."

"Awesome. Can I take a look?"

She opened her car again, and placed the box on the seat. "Sure. It's a dark chocolate and coffee flourless torte, otherwise known as sin cake."

"Sin cake?"

He was suddenly way too near as he stood beside her in the shelter of the car door. Up close, he smelled like sandalwood and saddle leather. He rested one hand on the roof of the car, caging her in.

"That's fantastic." His words vibrated against her throat as he leaned in to take a closer look at the cake, and she shivered slightly. "Thank you so much."

"You're welcome," she whispered, and shut the box.

In her efforts to straighten up, she inadvertently put her hand on his arm. His muscles flexed beneath his shirt, and it suddenly got hard to breathe. His face was an inch from hers, his intent brown eyes staring right into hers. This was *so* not good. She licked her lips.

"Yvonne . . ."

God, she wanted to kiss him so badly. . . . Just a little taste, just—

"Hey!"

They both jumped and moved away from each

other, Rio smacking his shoulder on the door in his haste to disengage as she ducked down to retrieve the cake.

HW Morgan came striding toward them. "What's the big secret?"

Yvonne practically threw the cake at Rio. "Ask him."

Rio grabbed the cake like a lifeline and took a moment to get his bearings. Being that close to Yvonne was intoxicating at some basic caveman level he'd never felt before. He liked sex, he *loved* women, but this need to take, and keep, and *have* was something else entirely.

"You okay?" HW was looking at him strangely.

"Yeah. I'm good." Rio held up the box. "I asked Yvonne if she'd make a special cake for Ruth as a thank-you from me."

HW groaned. "Now she'll be expecting *us* to get her cakes and pointing out how much better you are than her own grandsons."

"Well, she's right." Rio started back toward the house. "I am pretty amazing, and you guys are basically slackers."

HW's snort wasn't a surprise, and both of them were grinning as they entered through the screen door. His old friend was certainly much happier now he'd given up the rodeo and settled back home.

"Where's Chase?" Rio asked, scanning the already busy kitchen. Sam, HW's girlfriend, who was laying the table, looked up.

"He'll be here soon. He just called in to say they landed safely on the ranch airstrip, and Roy's gone to pick them up."

Yvonne came over, and touched his arm again. "Put the cake in the refrigerator before Ruth spots it, and bring it out after we've eaten."

"Good idea. Why don't you distract her while I do that?"

"Sure."

Her smile made him want to cup her chin and kiss all the pretty pink lipstick off her beautiful lush mouth. This wasn't good. He was always in control of his emotions. This was madness, and he didn't know how to make it stop.

She turned away, giving him an excellent view of her excellent ass in her tight blue pants.

"Get a grip, Rio. Cake in refrigerator," he muttered. "Take a lungful of cold air. Maybe chuck some ice cubes down the front of your jeans for good measure."

"Why are you talking to yourself?" HW asked.

"Because no one else understands me," Rio countered as, with a signal from Yvonne, he successfully hid the cake box at the back of the refrigerator. "Right at this moment, I don't even understand myself."

There was a commotion in the hallway, and several people came in at once, including Chase and both his venture capital partners. Jake was using a cane and looked very tired. Matt looked his usual healthy, happy self. Inwardly, Rio groaned.

"Hey!" Matt bounded over toward Yvonne and drew her into a hug. "How's it going?"

"Great, thanks!" Rio noticed she got out of the hug pretty damn quickly. He'd already got the sense that she didn't like being touched that much—except for that moment by the car when she'd looked up at him, and . . .

"Rio! Dude! What's up?" Matt turned to him now.

"I was telling my admin, Tish, about you being at the ranch last week, and she went all fan girl on you. I didn't realize you were so famous!"

Rio shrugged. "Only in PBR."

"But that's a big deal now, isn't it? You're on national TV, and the prize money is into the millions."

Yvonne had moved to stand by Matt, and was listening to their conversation.

"If you're successful, you can definitely make a living these days," Rio agreed.

Matt chuckled. "Well, seeing as she said you were world champion this year, I guess you'd know."

Ruth clapped her hands. "Will everyone please take a seat so we can start the meal? I don't want it to spoil."

In the rush to sit down, Rio found himself on one side of Yvonne with Matt on her other.

"Who's going to say grace?" Ruth asked.

"I will." Rio took hold of Yvonne's hand, and everyone followed suit. "Thank you, Lord, for the good food before us, the family and friends beside us, and the love around this table. Amen."

"Amen. That was lovely, Rio," Ruth said approvingly. "Now, let's start eating."

Rio's cake was delivered to Ruth with great applause, and consumed with the appreciation of people who burned up lots of calories working on the ranch. Yvonne wished she could eat half as much, but despite her hectic schedule, she barely left her kitchen and basically spun in circles rather like a hamster on its wheel.

"The cake is absolutely lovely." Ruth beamed at

Yvonne. "Although goodness knows when you had the time to make it, being as busy as you are."

"I might be getting a lot busier soon." Yvonne considered how the people sitting around the table had become like a family to her and decided to continue. "A woman called Priscilla Chang stopped by the café the other day. She liked my food and the place so much that she wants to make a TV show about me."

"Like a *cookery* show?" Ruth raised her eyebrows.

"I think it's more about me running the bakery, interacting with the customers and throwing the odd recipe into the mix as I go. Sort of like a cakecumentary." Seeing as Rio had been there, she was surprised he hadn't mentioned anything to anyone, but appreciated his restraint. "I don't know what to do. I can barely cope as it is."

"Does this woman work for a production company, or is she just trying to get into the business?" Ruth, an expert on all things reality TV, asked.

"She works for Tasty Treats Productions."

"Well, I never." Ruth looked over at Roy, the ranch foreman, who was shaking his head. They shared a deep love of reality shows that was legendary on the ranch. "Tasty Treats produces all the best cookery shows! We love *Bake the Cake* and *Big Bruno Saves the Restaurant in Ninety Days*, don't we, Roy?"

"Yup, and don't forget *Eat Your Greens*."

"So this company is quite successful then?" Yvonne said cautiously.

"Probably one of the most successful out there." Ruth nodded. "How exciting for you, dear! I do hope you said yes."

"I asked for a few days to think about it," Yvonne confessed. "Priscilla said that was fine as she had to come up with a unique and interesting angle to pitch to her boss anyway. So it's definitely not a done deal or anything."

"But it's a great validation of your amazing baking, and your sparkling personality," Matt interjected. "If you do get to the stage of needing a contract looked over, I'd be delighted to help."

"Matt's almost as good as Chase is at constructing airtight contracts, so you'd better take him up on that offer," January said.

"I'll definitely keep it in mind." Yvonne smiled at Matt, aware of Rio shifting in his seat on her other side.

"Oh! I almost forgot." January turned to Yvonne. "Avery said she wanted to talk to you about some extra staff."

"She has some?" Yvonne perked up. "That would be awesome. Is she at the hotel today?"

"No, she's over at the welcome center setting up a wedding rehearsal dinner for tonight. I said I'd send you over if I saw you."

"Then I'd better get over there." Yvonne blotted her mouth with her napkin and smiled at the assembled Morgans. "Thanks so much for having me. It's always fun."

"And thank *you* for the cake," Ruth replied.

"That was all Rio's idea." Yvonne stood and pushed back her chair. Matt and Rio both stood as well.

Matt's fingers closed around her elbow. "Are you coming back for coffee? I haven't really had a chance to talk to you yet."

"Sure!" Yvonne eased away and ended up plastered all over Rio's chest. "I'll be right back."

Rio followed her out, and she pretended not to notice. She'd almost reached the sanctuary of the welcome center when he called out to her.

"Hey, Yvonne! Slow down."

She paused in the shadows of the barn and turned to face him. "What's up?"

"The cake."

"What about the cake?"

"Firstly, it was excellent, and secondly, I haven't paid you for it yet."

"Oh, right! Yes!" She fumbled in her pocket for the receipt she'd forgotten to give him earlier. It wasn't like her to be so inefficient, but he had the strangest effect on her. "I have the check right here. You can pay me next time you come in the café."

She held out the paper receipt, and he took it from her.

"Thanks."

"You're welcome."

She waited, but he didn't walk away. She found herself talking again, stupidly keeping that tenuous connection between them alive.

"So you're a world champion."

He shrugged one shoulder. "Yes."

"Why didn't you mention it before?"

"Why would I?"

"Most men would."

His smile was sweet. "Maybe I'm not most men."

She could definitely agree with that. "But it's an amazing achievement. I know how hard it is to even qualify for the finals from HW and Avery."

"Sometimes you just have to set your mind to achieving a goal, and then go all out for it. That's what I did."

"And now what?"

His smile was rueful. "I'm the king of the world, and everyone wants to knock me off my throne. I'll do one more year, and then retire when I hit thirty-two."

"That's a good plan. Then what will you do?"

"That's the million-dollar question, isn't it?" He sighed. "At least I have options."

"Because you made some money." Yvonne nodded. "That really helps."

"It's not really about the money. I just want to do something completely different."

"I know the feeling. I started out wanting to get a degree in organic chemistry and then decided I wanted to become a pastry chef. My parents weren't pleased."

"But they must be very proud of you now, right?"

"I'm sure they would be." She hesitated. "They died in a car crash when I was nineteen."

He reached out and gently cupped her chin. "I'm so sorry. My parents hate each other's guts, but at least they're both still alive."

The warmth and strength of his fingers made her shiver. With a soft sound, he grazed his thumb over her parted lips.

"So are you going to give me that kiss now?" Rio asked.

"What kiss?"

"The one you almost landed on me when we were sharing a moment over the cake."

"What makes you think I wanted to kiss you then?" Yvonne desperately parried.

"Because I loved your cake so much?"

She found herself smiling despite herself. "You don't let things go, do you?"

He pointed at his chest. "World-champion bull rider, remember? Focused, tenacious, and successful."

"And I'm your next challenge?"

He studied her for a long moment. "Yeah. I suppose

you are." He sounded almost as surprised by his answer as she was.

"I'm not a prize to be won."

"I get that." He nodded.

"So even if I kiss you because you liked my cake, it doesn't mean you've won anything."

"I understand."

"It's just a kiss." She was no longer sure which of them she was trying to convince.

"Okay."

He moved even closer, his broad shoulders blocking the waning evening sunlight as his mouth came down over hers in the gentlest of butterfly kisses. Even that was almost too much as she reached blindly for something to anchor herself to. Her hand came to rest on his shoulder, and then curved around his neck to keep him exactly where she wanted him.

With a soft murmur, in what she assumed was Portuguese, he kissed her again. This time exploring her willing mouth with a penetrating sweep of his tongue that left her clinging to him like some kind of ridiculous too-stupid-to-live movie heroine. This was *so* not like her. She liked to be in charge, she liked to be worshipped, not swept off her feet. But she still didn't want the kiss to end. Her fingers settled into the crisp dark hair at the back of his neck as she breathed him in.

It seemed forever before he raised his head and studied her, his molten gaze lingering on her mouth.

"Thank you for the cake."

She leaned back against the side of the barn so that she could look at him properly, and maybe stay upright. "Thanks for spoiling our friendship."

"What's spoiled?" He frowned. "We're still friends, aren't we?"

"Friends who kiss?"

"Why not?" He raised an eyebrow. "I still like and respect you. I just like and respect you even more now that I've tasted you."

"You heard what's going on in my life." She crossed her arms over her chest. "I don't have time for a relationship right now."

"And I've got a world championship to defend."

"So I'm right, and that kiss was a mistake?"

"Oh, no. I could never say that." His smile was so wicked her knees almost buckled with lust.

She gathered her composure and raised her chin. "I'm going to speak to Avery, and then I'm going back up to the house to have coffee with Matt."

"Good to know." He nodded and turned away. "I'll drop into the café tomorrow, and pay the bill."

"Aren't you worried about me seeing Matt?"

"After you let me kiss you like that?" He swung back to face her. "Hell, *no*."

"Maybe I'll kiss him, too."

"You do that." He nodded. "Let me know how it goes for you."

She huffed out a breath. "You are *so* conceited."

"No, I just know you. If you really thought there was a real chance with Matt, you would never have let me kiss you in the first place. You're not the kind of woman who plays games."

She opened her mouth to disagree with him, and then abruptly closed it. How come he'd worked her out so quickly?

His smile deepened, and he touched the brim of his hat to her. "That's my girl."

"I am neither a girl nor yours," Yvonne retorted. "I am my own person, and I'll kiss whoever I want to."

"Good for you."

He strolled back in the direction he'd come, whistling, leaving her speechless, turned on, and definitely flustered. None of those things were her style. He was infuriating!

Neither of them wanted a relationship at this point in their lives so why had she agreed to the kiss? Why had he *asked* for it? Now she'd never be able to get anything going with Matt because she had *standards*, and they didn't include kissing other men when in a relationship. She couldn't even say Rio had made her do it. She was the one who'd kept him there having a conversation, and she was the one who'd said yes when he asked to kiss her.

She smoothed down her hair, and gave herself a mental shake. So they were attracted to each other. She had no time to linger on the sensations he aroused in her. She had a business to run, and the possibility of a TV show in her future. *He* had to defend a world championship at venues all around the country where hundreds of women would probably be throwing their panties at him, and begging him to make love to them.

It was just a kiss.

There was no need to make it into anything more.

Chapter Five

Rio grabbed his cell from the bedside table and squinted at the number. His bedroom was dark, the drapes drawn against the encroaching dawn. He'd spent the previous afternoon helping out on a trail ride, and then checked and groomed horses until almost midnight. He'd slept well, his dreams filled with images of Yvonne that had made him purr in his sleep.

It was five in the morning, and he really wasn't in the mood to be disturbed. Even as he pressed delete, the phone started ringing again, and a text flashed up on the screen.

Pick up.

When the heck had his father learned to text? With a groan, Rio sat up and accepted the call.

"What the hell do you want?"

"That's not an appropriate way to talk to your father."

"It's five in the morning. I'm tired. This is the best I can do."

Rio settled the phone against his ear as he pulled

the covers up over his knees. Even though it was summer, the mornings were still cold in the shadow of the Sierras, and he slept naked.

"I told you to come to my office in San Francisco."

"And I told you that I was too busy, and wondered why you were calling me after five years."

"I'm calling because I need to see you."

Rio waited for the rest of that sentence to turn into an order, but there was only silence.

He sighed. "Now you've got me on the phone, why can't you just tell me what you want?"

"Please don't be difficult."

Rio blinked into the darkness. Had his father just said the P word, to *him*?

"Nothing has changed. I don't need your money, and I'm okay about that."

"This concerns your mother."

Rio's gut tightend. "I knew you'd throw out a threat at some point. You can't control me anymore, but you think you can get at me through my *mother*?"

The thing was, the bastard could. Rio supported his mother now, but the land she owned, her house, her goddam *security* was all tied up in his father's wealth.

"I suggest you call and ask her." His father's clipped Bostonian accent came through strongly on the phone. "When you've done that, make an appointment with my secretary. I'll be in town for two more weeks."

He ended the call, and Rio contemplated throwing his cell at the wall. His father was one of the few people who knew exactly how to push his buttons. He hated it, but there was the not insignificant matter of his beloved mother to consider before he went back to ignoring the man again.

Knowing there was no way he would get back to sleep, he mentally checked the time in Brazil. His mother was a few hours ahead of him, so was probably up and about on her ranch. He found her number and listened to the dial tone.

"*Alo?*"

"Hey, *mamae, como yai?*"

"Rio!" She switched to English. "My darling boy. What a nice surprise! Just let me turn down the TV so I can hear you properly."

His mother was as devoted to the daily soap operas as Ruth and Roy were to reality TV.

She chatted away, telling him about her life, asking him how things were going on the ranch, and complaining about his half-sister, Josie, a familiar and comfortable litany that he was well used to hearing. After divorcing his father, she'd returned home to Brazil, married again briefly, and then declared she was done with men and retired to her ranch on the outskirts of Sao Paulo.

She sounded so happy that he almost hated to bring up the reason he'd called, but it had to be done.

"Father called me."

She couldn't quite disguise her gasp or her weak attempt to pretend she hadn't been expecting the question all along. His mother never liked discussing the negativities of life.

"Oh! Did he? Why was that?"

Rio didn't call her out on it. He knew why she preferred not to think about her first and worst ex. "He said to ask you."

"Graham asked me to come to San Francisco."

Rio went still. "But you haven't seen each other for twenty years."

"I know, but he said he wants everyone in his family together in one place because he has several announcements to make about the future."

"Does his fourth wife know about this?"

"She's probably included, Rio."

"But why *now*?" Rio asked. "What on earth does he have to say that has anything to do with either of us?"

He remembered the day she'd been escorted out of their house, her tears, and her fiercely whispered promise that she would come back for him, that she loved him, and that he had to be a big, brave boy until she returned. He'd never forget her face, the scent of her perfume and the way he'd been dragged kicking and screaming from the comfort of her arms and locked in his bedroom.

How could she forgive *that*?

"Knowing Graham, he's probably going to disinherit the lot of us, and give all his money to his favorite charity or his dog, and he just wants to see our faces when he does it."

"Yeah, that sounds about right," Rio agreed. "The thing is—do we really need to see that up-close and personal? We lived it for years."

"I'd like to go."

Even though his mother couldn't see him, Rio frowned. "Why?"

"Because I would. It feels like the right thing to do." She hesitated. "But I won't go without you."

"Which is why the bastard told me to call you," Rio muttered. "I'm so screwed."

"What did you say?"

"I said that if you really want to go, of course I'll come with you."

"Thank you, *meu filho*."

"I want you to remember something when you see him," Rio said sternly. "We don't need him. If he does disinherit us both, I'll buy your ranch from him and make sure you never have to want for anything, okay?"

"You are such a sweetheart, Rio. The only good thing to come out of my marriage to that arrogant pig."

"Thanks." Rio managed a smile. "Let me know when you're due to arrive in San Francisco, and I'll come and meet you."

"Yes, dear."

After ending the call, Rio lay back down on his pillow and contemplated the ceiling. When his parents had met, his mother had been eighteen, and a contestant in a beauty pageant his father had been judging. She hadn't won the crown, but she'd ensnared a rich man who'd married her and impregnated her within days of their meeting. The marriage had gone downhill from there, culminating in screaming rages, threats, and a separation that had left a terrified Rio in his father's hands while his mother went back to Brazil.

He shook off the unpleasant memories. His mom was still his biggest fan, and sometimes more like his big sister than his mother. Her zest for life had survived the worst his father had thrown at her, and she deserved every penny Graham had eventually been forced by the courts to pay her.

So, it seemed he would be going to San Francisco. . . .

He had no intention of calling his father or his admin back. They'd work out he was coming from his mom.

With a groan, he threw the covers back, shivering in the cold, and put on his boxers. The family bathroom was down the hall. He had a quick wash, and promised himself a shower later after he'd mucked out the stalls, and fed the chickens.

A rooster crowed as he drew a warm fleece over his head and tiptoed down the stairs in his socks to the mudroom, where a row of cowboy boots and outer garments filled the space.

"Do you want some coffee before you head out, Rio?"

Rio clutched at his heart as the unexpected voice floated out from the kitchen, scaring the crap out of him.

He reversed direction and went into the kitchen, where Ruth was sitting at the table. She was a tiny woman, but her personality was so big that he often forgot that. In his time at the ranch, she'd made him feel like part of the family and reminded him very much of his own *avo*.

"You're up early." She pushed a mug of coffee over to him.

"Thanks. Yes, I am."

"Everything okay?"

"Just family stuff." He blew out an impatient breath. "I might have to take a trip to San Francisco in the next week or so to see my father. My mother's flying in from Brazil."

"HW said you don't get along with your father."

"That's an understatement. I haven't seen or spoken to him for five years. Now he's demanding me and my mother seek an audience with him."

Ruth sipped her coffee. "Maybe he's making some new choices with his life."

"I doubt it."

"People can change, you know. Look at my son, Billy. He almost lost himself in a bottle, but he found his way home again."

"Probably because there were people like you praying and hoping for his return." Rio smiled at her. "My father isn't like that. He's probably rearranging his business interests to avoid taxes again and wants my mother to sign a new legal agreement or something."

"It's good that you care for your mother and will be by her side."

"She put up with my father for far too long simply

for my benefit. She deserves my one-hundred-percent attention and gratitude."

"You're a good boy, Rio." She patted his hand. "You can tell a lot about a man by how he treats his mother."

"Thanks." He took another gulp of coffee and finally got a nice jolt of caffeine through his system. "I'd better go and start on those stalls."

"That's very good of you. I'm sure my lazy grandsons will join you at some point."

He winked at her as he stood up. "They are good boys as well, you know. Raised by the best—you."

"The cake Yvonne made for me was my favorite flavors."

He paused, taken aback by her sudden change of subject. "I'm glad you liked it."

"She's very talented, isn't she?"

"Absolutely."

"And pretty as a picture."

"I can't say I'd noticed."

"You've noticed all right. You can't keep your eyes off her." Ruth chuckled. "But then she can't stop looking at you, either."

Rio paused. "Really?"

"Ha!" She snapped her fingers. "Gotcha!"

"So I find her attractive." He attempted a shrug. "I can't deny it."

"Then what are you going to do about it?"

Rio thought about the kiss they'd shared. . . . "Nothing. We're both too busy to be in a relationship right now."

"Right, because love can always wait on more important things, can't it?"

He grinned at her. "Your sarcasm is showing."

"It was supposed to." She looked up at him, her chin

resting on her hand. "Sometimes you have to take a chance and grab what's right in front of you."

"I don't think Yvonne would go for any grabbing, do you?"

"How do you know if you don't try?" He opened his mouth to reply, and she carried on speaking. "Don't mind me. I keep forgetting you're not one of my grandsons needing a good kick up the rear."

"I'll take that as a compliment." He put his mug in the sink to rinse it. "My parents met and married in a week. It was a total disaster. That's probably why I'm naturally gun-shy."

"Makes sense, I suppose." She sighed. "I don't know how any of you make up your minds to fall in love and marry these days, what with the Internet, and dating apps, and all that fake stuff. Back in the day, you met a nice boy at school or college or were introduced to him by your friends, and that was it."

"Dating is definitely a dangerous game these days," Rio agreed. "Especially if you're successful or rich."

"So HW tells me." Ruth filled up her coffee cup, and stood up. "I'd better get on. Don't forget to come back and eat after you're done."

"How could I forget your amazing breakfasts?" Rio turned his mug upside down to drain it and dried his hands. "Don't tell your grandsons I've already started the chores or they'll leave me to it."

Ruth put on her apron. "Oh, don't worry, I won't say a thing."

Yvonne wiped her hands on her apron and checked her to-do list. For once, she was on schedule, and it was only just past nine in the morning, which, after her four o'clock start, counted as lunchtime.

Her cell buzzed, and she glanced at a text message from Priscilla.

Are you available at 11? Want to pop by with my producer.

Yvonne bit her lip and contemplated her plans for the rest of the day. Thanks to Avery, she had two new staff members helping Tom so she could leave them to cope if she stayed in the café and was available for any emergencies. . . .

That sounds great. See you at 11.

A smiley face popped up in reply. She put her phone back on her desk and washed her hands. Antonio wouldn't be coming in until eleven to start working on the lunch rush, so she'd have to make her own sandwich.

A knock on the back door of the kitchen had her looking up. She wasn't expecting any deliveries, but sometimes things turned up unexpectedly. Unlocking the door, she discovered Rio smiling down at her. Today he wore his usual black cowboy hat and a thick denim jacket as protection against the early morning Sierra winds.

"Good morning, Yvonne."

She regarded him severely. "Are you sure you don't want a job? You're here every day."

He grinned. "Can't help myself. I came to pay for the cake."

"Come in."

He stepped through the door, and wiped his feet carefully on the mat, his gaze scanning the kitchen through the open door. "Wow, this is twice the size of the café."

"I know. When I can afford it, I plan on leasing the shop next door and having two separate counters and double the seating space."

"Makes sense." He stayed on the mat. "Do you want me to take my boots off?"

"Don't worry. I was just about to take a lunch break so we can walk through to the front. Have you had breakfast yet?"

"Yeah. Ruth fed me about an hour ago. I'm good to go for about a week." He followed her out into the shop. "I got up at five, so it almost feels like it's time for me to have lunch."

"I get up at four to start baking the bread." Yvonne made him some coffee while she added a chocolate croissant to her plate.

"Every day?"

"Except Sunday." She placed the carafe between them, and motioned for him to sit down. The café was relatively quiet now the commuters had gone, and the tourists hadn't yet arrived. "Luckily, I'm an early bird, so it's not too bad."

He poured them both coffee and added cream to his. "Unless you're super human, I guess you go to bed quite early."

"Yes, I'm a real party pooper. Ask my friends."

"Have you ever thought about getting someone else in to bake for you?"

"Why would I do that?" She sipped her coffee. "I love my job."

"Like the best sex of your life, right?" he teased.

She fluttered her eyelashes and gave a breathy sigh.

"Yup, all that pounding, and kneading, and stretching, and . . . *growth* going on."

He choked on his coffee, and she smiled serenely at him.

"What?"

"Nothing." He wiped his mouth with a napkin. "I was just picturing the scene."

"It's beautiful. Poetry in motion. Just like you on the back of a bull."

"I bet it is. Maybe, if you're willing, I can drop by and watch one day."

"Sure." She deliberately licked her lips. "I *love* an audience."

For a long moment, he just stared at her mouth before tearing his gaze away back to his coffee.

"Are you making any special cakes today?"

Oh, she loved it when he backed down first.

"No, I've got Priscilla Chang coming in at eleven with her producer for a chat." She fiddled with her silverware. "I have no idea what to expect at this point."

"Just give them your food to taste and let that do the talking for you."

"I will, but should I have a lawyer with me or something? It's not like they've offered me a contract or anything yet, but I don't want to end up agreeing to things and then regretting it."

He sat up straight. "I could help you."

Yvonne blinked at him. "I don't mean to be rude, but how exactly can you do that?"

"I spent three years working for my father's company. A couple of those years involved liaising with chefs, restaurants, and food critics concerned with his various business enterprises."

"As in?"

"I know how a contract between a brand-name personality and a business venture should be structured. I understand what a company wants from you, and what you should allow them to have." He leaned forward, his large capable hands wrapped around his coffee mug. "Like, say a celebrity chef wanted to launch a range of frozen meals, or own a vineyard, or something."

"You'd facilitate that?" She shook her head. "Wow."

He sat back looking amused. "Wow, what?"

"You're a world-champion bull rider."

"Correct."

"And you work for your father on the side?"

His smile disappeared. "No, they are two completely separate parts of my life. When I graduated from college, I went straight into my father's business. After three years, we had a blazing row, and I went back to Brazil to live on my mother's ranch. That's when I resumed my interest in bull riding."

"How old were you when you graduated?"

He shrugged. "I was a year ahead at school, so I guess I was twenty-one."

"So you were *twenty-five* when you took up bull riding? Talk about a late starter."

"Not quite." He grinned. "Whenever I was allowed to go home to my mother in Brazil, I always rode and competed locally. At twenty-five, I just decided to take it seriously."

Yvonne shook her head. "That's pretty amazing."

He shrugged. "Good genes, I guess."

"And an incredible work ethic."

His smile reappeared, luring out his dimple. "Perhaps, but this isn't about me. I'm just offering to sit in on this meeting if you need me."

She considered him for a long moment. He made no attempt to avoid her gaze, and just stared calmly and steadily back at her. Could she trust him? She hardly knew him, but everything she'd seen and heard about him seemed genuine. The Morgans liked him, especially Ruth, who was an excellent judge of character, so could she trust her gut and accept his offer?

"You're making me nervous here," Rio said. "I promise I wouldn't tell you what to do."

Yvonne rolled her eyes. "As if I'd listen to you anyway."

"I'd just stay quiet, and take notes of the salient points you might wish to consider later."

"Like a secretary?"

"Sure."

"Can I call you that in the meeting?"

He smiled. "If you like."

"Okay, then." She held out her hand. "Welcome on board, Mister . . . what is your last name?"

He shook her hand. "Martinez."

"Then come back just before eleven, and bring a notepad."

After running a few errands in town for Ruth and January and mailing out a letter to his mother, Rio reported back at the café, an old-fashioned yellow legal pad in his hand and a pen behind his ear. Yvonne made him leave his hat in the kitchen, which made him feel vaguely naked.

They settled into a table at the rear of the café, and Yvonne arranged a plate of pastries alongside a cafetiere of coffee on the pristine white cloth. She paused, her teeth caught in her lip, and looked over at Rio.

"Should I make a pot of tea as well?"

"Why don't you wait and see what they prefer?" Rio advised. It was the first time he'd ever seen her look nervous.

"There's Priscilla by the door," Yvonne murmured. "I'll bring her over."

Priscilla wore a bright red pantsuit, which suited her dark coloring, and was accompanied by an older man with a bald head, black-framed glasses, and a single diamond earring. He couldn't have shouted, "I'm creative!" any louder than if he'd shouted it for real.

Rio stood and waited as Yvonne introduced him.

"Priscilla, this is my assistant, Rio Martinez."

Priscilla took his hand in a firm grasp. "Didn't we meet the other day? You work on one of the local ranches, don't you?"

"I'm a man of many talents." Rio turned to the guy. "Hi, pleased to meet you."

"Right back at ya! I'm Greg."

Soon, they were all seated, only to discover that Greg was of course a tea drinker of some fancy decaffeinated stuff that probably stunk of flowers. Rio got up to find the tea, leaving Priscilla waxing lyrical about the food. Luckily, Lizzie knew exactly how to make the right kind and sent him back with it and instructions to let it brew for five more minutes.

As he approached the table, he took a moment to appreciate Yvonne in her sleek French maid work uniform of a black dress and lacy white apron. It was the sort of look that fueled many a feverish dream, and currently owned the top spot on his own personal fantasies. Her black hair was drawn up into a bun on the top of her head with just a few wisps framing her high cheekbones.

He almost forgot what he was supposed to be doing

as he imagined unpinning her hair and watching it
fall down on her shoulders before he buried his hands
in it and brought her mouth to his in a searing, searching kiss. . . .

"Rio?"

Yvonne was staring at him, and he hastened over to
the table, glad that the tint of his skin wouldn't show
he was blushing.

"Here's the tea."

He sat back and listened as Priscilla sketched out
her idea of bringing a camera crew in to watch Yvonne
bake, operate the café, and make her signature cakes.
She stressed that they weren't looking for drama and
wouldn't try to manufacture it. Greg was wolfing down
pastries, and nodding occasionally, which seemed like
a good reaction to Rio.

"I like the idea." Greg finally stopped eating long
enough to contribute to the conversation. "I think our
viewers would respond really well to the less extrava-
gant, get-back-to-basics, hometown kind of vibe you've
got going on here."

Priscilla winked at Yvonne. "I told you he was going
to love it."

"So what's the next step?" Yvonne asked.

"We'd like you to come to our office in San Francisco and meet the entire production team, including
the boss. By then, we'll have sketched out some pre-
liminary guidelines, and can talk specifics such as
length of series, financial remuneration, and all that
kind of interesting stuff."

"I'd need plenty of notice for that meeting," Yvonne
said. "I'll have to find someone to mind the café for at
least a day or two."

Rio admired her calm firmness. She certainly wasn't
overawed by the idea of being on TV and she wasn't

going to rush into anything headlong. Despite loathing his father, he'd learned a lot from watching him work and knew that maintaining a relaxed front during a negotiation process always put you in a more powerful position.

He wasn't quite prepared to admit to enjoying himself, but it was interesting doing something so different from his current day job. After leaving his father, he'd sworn never to pick up a business book or watch the stock market ever again. Until now, he'd kept that promise, but his brain was ticking over, his business instincts were reigniting, and he wasn't sure how he felt about that at all.

Priscilla and Greg left, both carrying boxes of pastries. Yvonne came back to the table with a fresh pot of coffee and set it in front of Rio.

"That went okay." She let out her breath. "I still don't see it happening, but it's kind of fun to imagine what it might be like." She looked around the café. "This place is so tiny, I can't imagine a camera crew fitting in, can you?"

"I'm sure they'll make it work somehow." Rio consulted his notes. "I didn't get any negatives from them at all, did you? But this *is* the honeymoon stage. It sounds like Greg is onboard, and now they'll just punt the proposal up the chain of command, and see whether it sticks."

Yvonne poured the coffee. "Wow, for a cowboy, you sure know your way around a business cliché."

Rio grinned. "It's all coming back to me. I can't decide if that's a good thing or a bad thing."

She rested her elbow on the table and leaned her chin into her hand. It had been nice having him sitting there, watching her back, and true to his word, he hadn't interfered at all. "Why did you and your father end up fighting?"

He sighed. "Years of mistrust and resentment on my part, and a need to control me on his?"

"How did he mistreat you?"

"My parents got divorced." This time, his smile was definitely of the keep-out variety. "You know how that goes."

For some reason, she kept going. "Usually, the mother gets to keep her child, but you ended up with your father, correct?"

"Yeah. He remarried the day the divorce came through so I had a new eighteen-year-old stepmother. She was supposed to take care of me."

"Did your Mom just up and . . . *leave*?"

"No. She was forced out. My father had all the power back then."

She tried to imagine how that must have felt, because he wasn't giving a lot away. "How *old* were you?"

"Seven." He looked down at the legal pad in his hands and ripped out the first two pages, his mouth a stern line. "I've got to get back. Here's a summary of the meeting. Let me know if I missed anything, or if you want to discuss any of the points I raised."

Before she could say another word, he handed her the notes, and headed back to the kitchen, presumably to retrieve his hat and make a quick escape.

She didn't glance at the notes, but continued to stare at his empty seat. So Mr. Easy Going did have some secrets after all. She couldn't imagine how it must have felt to have his mother replaced by a teenager, but it had obviously left its mark.

The thing was . . . it only made her more curious about him, and that wasn't supposed to happen right now. She had a new business opportunity, he'd offered to help her, and that was as far as she needed to go with him. But for one second, she'd seen the hurt behind his confidence. That made her want to hold him and tell him that she'd make everything all right again, which was, quite frankly, ridiculous.

He had a mother he loved. He certainly didn't need another one. She smoothed a hand over the sheets of paper. The trouble was, she didn't feel motherly. Her making him feel better involved getting naked and kissing every inch of his hard, muscled body. . . .

"Hey."

She jumped and looked up into the face of her best friend, Nancy, who worked at the Red Dragon Bar in town, and helped out her mother at the general store. This week, Nancy's hair was dyed black and orange to celebrate her favorite baseball team, and her nose ring was gold. Nancy took Rio's empty seat, and helped herself to coffee.

"How did the meeting go?"

"Fine. They want me to come to San Francisco, and meet the whole team."

"Awesome." Nancy drank her coffee with cream and lots of sugar. "So why are you looking so worried?"

"I'm not," Yvonne defended herself. "I was thinking about someone—I mean something else."

"Like that cowboy guy who's practically moved in here these days?"

"He was very helpful this morning."

"I bet he was." Nancy helped herself to a cream slice. "He wants to get in your pants."

She was always direct—usually a positive in Yvonne's eyes, but not today.

"As I've already told you, it's not like that. We've agreed to be friends."

Nancy just looked at her, one pierced eyebrow raised.

"You are *so* not helping here," Yvonne grumbled. "I need you to remind me of all the reasons why I *can't* get involved with anyone."

Nancy pointed her finger at Yvonne. "Ha! I knew it! He is hot though."

"And he's only here for a few weeks before he goes off on tour to beat off challengers to his world championship. You know how I feel about long-distance relationships. They never work."

"One bad experience doesn't mean you give up altogether," Nancy argued. "Sure, your ex was a dirt bag, but not all men are the same."

"Says the woman who won't go out with a guy more than once," Yvonne countered.

"We're not talking about me." Nancy was never one to back off from a problem, especially when it involved one of her besties' love lives. "How long is it since you went out with *anyone*?"

Yvonne looked anywhere but at her friend. "I can't quite recall."

"Well, I'll recall for you. Every single, living, breathing male in the county who has asked you out comes into the bar to cry into their beer when you turn them down."

"I went out with Matt," Yvonne said weakly, appalled that she'd forgotten already.

"To the hotel for dinner. That hardly qualifies as a date. Don't be lame. When was the last time you got laid?"

"None of your business."

"Which means not since Mr. French Fry left."

"I—" Yvonne sank down into her seat. "So what if that's true?"

"It's just a damn waste of prime womanhood," Nancy

said. "Do you think Paul has remained celibate for the last four years?"

Yvonne guiltily recalled the pictures she'd Googled of her ex earlier in the month. He'd had an arm around a different woman in each shot. "I doubt it."

"Then isn't it time to move on?"

Yvonne groaned. "Why are you bringing this up now? You've always been incredibly supportive of my choices to stay single before."

"Because I've never seen you take an interest in anyone before." Nancy's gaze softened. "You like this Rio guy, don't you?"

Yvonne replayed Rio's kiss in her head. "He's . . . okay."

"I suppose that's a start." Nancy finished her coffee. "If he asks, will you go with him?"

"Who are you, my *mother*?" Yvonne asked. "He won't ask me. I told him not to."

She'd also told him not to kiss her, and he'd gone ahead and done that anyway. . . .

"But if he does?"

"I'll think about it," Yvonne said firmly.

"You do that." Nancy nodded. "And remember, I'm doing this because I love you."

"Now you sound *just* like my mother," Yvonne groused.

"Good." Nancy gave her an unrepentant grin and blew her a kiss. "I've got to get back to work. Jay's off today, meeting Erin's plane, so I'm in charge."

"Words to terrify every single man who ventures into the Red Dragon Bar tonight," Yvonne murmured.

Nancy rolled her eyes. "They love me. God knows why when I treat them all like idiots, but they do."

"Probably because the vast majority of them *are*

idiots, which is why I don't want to go out with any of them."

"Good point." Nancy hesitated by her chair. "Any chance you can come by the bar tomorrow night?"

"Why?"

"Because Jay's going to ask Erin to marry him, and it should be epic."

"Are you going to cry?"

"Probably. Jay's been through hell, and the thought of him getting married and having a family is just *so* awesome. I like Erin. She's the perfect match for him."

"True love strikes again in Morgantown." Yvonne rose as well, sticking the papers in her apron pocket, and gathering up the coffee things. "What next?"

"Hopefully you'll be getting some," Nancy said.

Yvonne tried to ignore the bolt of lust that ran through her. "And how about you?"

"I don't fancy Rio, so I'm good."

Yvonne pointed at her friend. "One day you'll meet a man you want to go on a second date with."

"I can't see it happening, but you know what? If I do, I give you permission to double down on me until I get with the program."

"Like you're doing with me?"

"That's what friends are for, right?" Nancy blew her a kiss. "See you tomorrow night, babe, and don't forget to bring Rio."

Chapter Six

"You're coming with us, right?"

Blue Morgan, retired Marine and all-around badass, fixed Rio with his penetrating blue stare. He'd arrived at the ranch during dinner, and had eaten enough for two men before raising his head to speak.

"Where?" Rio asked cautiously. He'd partied with the Morgan twins in the past, and had learned to be wary.

"Down to the bar in town. My friend Jay Williams is going to propose to his girlfriend, and he's nervous as shit."

"Language, BB," Ruth admonished him.

"Sorry." BB winked at Rio. "They've been shacking up together for a while and, now Jay's feeling better, he wants to make it all official."

"He's been sick?"

"Wounded during the war in Afghanistan and invalided out of the Navy SEALs." Blue grimaced. "He had a hard time getting his sh—I mean getting himself back together."

"Of course I'll come." Rio smiled and finished his coffee. For once, it was only the Morgan brothers sitting around the table. All the women apart from Ruth had gone out to the movies.

"He's asked me to be his best man." BB grinned. "Second time in a year."

"Maybe third if Ry gets around to asking Avery to marry him," Ruth piped up.

Ry shoved a hand through his blond hair. "I'm in no rush to get hitched, and neither is Avery. It should be you next, Blue Boy."

"I'm already on it." BB leaned back and stretched until the chair creaked in protest. "As soon as our house is completed, I'm going to ask Jenna."

"What if she says no?" Ry asked.

"She won't." BB's complete overconfidence made Rio shake his head.

"And what about you, HW?" Rio had to ask. "Any plans?"

"Not yet. I'm still working my way into Sam's good books." HW winked. "She sure is hard to please."

Rio looked over at Roy, the ranch foreman, who was probably in his late seventies, but still worked like a youngster half his age. "Looks like we're the only two sensible men left at this table."

"Sensible?" Roy snorted. "I'd marry Ruth if she'd take me, but neither of us can be bothered with all the fuss."

"He's just kidding," Ruth said. "He's terrified I'll take him up on it."

Roy opened his mouth as if to dispute that, but Ry was already speaking. "That just leaves you, Rio. And a little bird tells me that you've got something going with Yvonne."

"Would that little bird be called Avery?" Ruth wondered. "Yvonne would be perfect for you, Rio, but you already know that."

"I'm just helping her out with this business proposal," Rio said mildly. "We work well as a team."

"Yeah, right. I've seen the way you look at her." Ry grinned. "Boy, were the women ever wrong thinking to pair her up with Matt. I can't wait for them to eat some crow."

"Everyone looks at her like that. She's beautiful," Rio said.

"True," Ry acknowledged. "She'll probably be at the bar tonight for the great proposal. The ladies are planning on ending their evening there, and seeing as Erin went with them to the movies, they have to get her back for the grand finale."

"Sounds like a great evening."

Rio finished his coffee and got up to clear his place. The thought of seeing Yvonne again made his heart beat faster. He couldn't keep denying it. Despite all his mistrust of relationships in general, Yvonne made him want things he couldn't have and maybe didn't deserve. In his limited experience, love hurt, and waiting for it to end or be wrenched away from you wasn't worth the risk.

But he couldn't keep away from Yvonne. So what did that make him—a fool or a liar?

By the time they reached the Red Dragon, it was almost nine o'clock, and Yvonne was beginning to tire. She was usually in bed by now, and not contemplating a noisy end to her night in the only sports bar in town. But she'd promised Nancy, and she liked Erin and Jay, so seeing them get their happy-ever-after was a must.

The bar was unusually full for a midweek night, and Yvonne had to push her way through quite a crowd to get to the bar, where Nancy was working alongside her boss, and another guy.

"Hey!" Yvonne shouted over the din.

"Hey." Nancy looked up. "We reserved a table for you ladies by the back wall. Would you be a love and take some drink orders for me? It's crazy in here tonight, and Jay's too scared to go over there in case he blows it with Erin."

"Like I don't get to take orders all day?" Yvonne fake grumbled as she winked at Jay, who was looking rather pale. "I'll be right back."

She threaded her way back to Erin and company, directed them toward the table, fished a pen and pad from her purse, and wrote down everyone's drink preferences. By the time she'd done that, someone had put the jukebox on and was attempting a line dance in the very limited space.

Skirting the group of shufflers, she bumped into a warm body and took hold of an arm to steady herself.

"Sorry."

"Not a problem. You can grab any bit of me you like," Rio murmured close to her ear.

"And rip it off?"

A shudder rang through him, and then he chuckled, setting off a slow burn in her stomach.

"Hey, not nice." Rio grinned. "Be gentle with me."

She looked up into his eyes, noticing his laughter lines and the soft curve of his mouth. He really was pretty to look at. . . . She reluctantly let go of his arm.

"Did you come with the Morgans?"

"Yes. I understand there is a big event planned."

It was Yvonne's turn to smile. "If Jay can get over his nerves."

"I can totally understand how he feels."

"Have you been married before?" Yvonne asked.

"No. You?"

"Yes." She angled her head in the direction of the bar. "I've got to give these drink orders to Nancy before my friends start complaining."

"Then I'll come with you."

"There's no need." She gave him her brightest *go away* smile before turning on her heel, and plunging into the melee.

She really didn't want to discuss her marriage in the middle of a bar and wished she'd avoided answering the question so honestly. She already knew Rio wouldn't let things go, although why he'd be interested in her failed marriage was beyond her.

To her surprise, after she'd collected the tray of drinks and distributed them to her friends, Rio made no attempt to come over and take up the conversation again. Maybe the idea that she'd been married before had put him off. A lot of people didn't like getting involved with someone who had *baggage*.

She snorted into her cocktail. Like most people who'd almost reached the age of thirty *didn't* have baggage. Her restless gaze returned to Rio, who was chatting to HW and laughing like he didn't have a care in the world. If he'd avoided a serious relationship his entire life, then maybe that said more about him than about her. Or with willing buckle bunnies and fans to choose from every night on the road, had he ever had the chance to settle down and *attempt* a proper relationship? Or even wanted to?

"Why do I care anyway?" she murmured to herself.

"What did you say?" January leaned in. "It's really loud in here. I hope Jay makes his move soon because I want to go home to bed."

"Me, too."

"Should I ask BB to encourage him along?"

"Why not?" Yvonne finished her cocktail. "If it doesn't happen soon, I'm going to fall asleep right here at the table and miss it all anyway."

January patted her shoulder. "Don't worry. I'll wake you up." She walked over to where Blue Morgan was chatting to his brother Ry. There was a lot of gesticulating and pointing, and then BB set off toward the bar.

Moments later, a piercing whistle echoed through the room, and BB jumped on a chair.

"Everyone, listen up! Jay's got something to say."

As the bar fell silent, Jay emerged from behind the bar and headed straight for Erin, who was sitting at the table next to Yvonne. He awkwardly got down on one knee and held out a small blue velvet box.

"Erin, will you marry me?"

It felt like the whole room held their collective breath as Erin stood up, her cheeks flushing with color, her hands clasped to her chest.

"Yes. Yes, please. I'd *love* to marry you, Jay Williams."

And then there was chaos as Jay swept the future Mrs. Williams into his arms and kissed her like there was no tomorrow. Yvonne dabbed discreetly at a tear and saw January doing the same. They grinned at each other in solidarity.

"I love a wedding," January sniffed. "Especially if they choose to have it at our ranch."

"Me, too," Yvonne agreed as she attempted to conceal a yawn behind her hand. "Excuse me. I'm just so tired. I'll congratulate the happy couple and then I'm off to bed."

She hugged all her girls good-bye, kissed the bride-to-be on both cheeks in the approved French fashion, and made her way out onto the sidewalk. The town was quiet now, the traffic almost nonexistent. Strings of fairy lights decorated the fronts of the shops and buildings, giving the street a nostalgic look that never failed to make Yvonne smile.

Rio was sitting on one of the steps that led down off the boardwalk, talking on his cell in Portuguese; his head was bowed, exposing the crisp line of his black hair. He eventually switched to English.

"Yes, I'll see you then. Thanks for letting me know."

Yvonne considered her options. The bar was on the corner of Main and Morgan so she could cross the other way to get back to her café. But when had she turned into the kind of woman who was afraid to talk to a man? Banter and flirting came as easily to her as baking. But, with Rio, something deeper was stirring, and that was making her wary.

Just as she hesitated behind him, he finished the call and stood up, his gaze level with hers because he was on the bottom step.

"Hey."

She pointed in the general direction of her store. "I was just leaving."

"I'll walk you."

"There's really no need. It's literally right over there." She pointed out her shop.

He shrugged. "You never know who might leap out at you from a dark alley."

"An enraged customer who hated my croissants?"

"Maybe."

"Or the soufflé strangler?"

His appreciative wicked grin made everything female in her sit up and beg. She decided not to make a big deal out of his protective instincts.

"Okay."

He held out his hand, and it seemed like the most natural thing in the world to take it. They crossed

Main Street, went past the post office and the bank, and arrived at the front door of her café. The outside chairs and tables were stacked inside the locked shop at night for safety, leaving the sidewalk bare.

"I usually go in the back."

He didn't break stride, just carried on walking right beside her around the end of the row and back along the service road that connected all the shops. There was a security light over her door that flared into life when she stopped to find her keys.

She unlocked the door and quickly punched in the key for the alarm before turning back to her unusually silent companion.

"Is everything okay?"

"It will be." His smile was perfunctory. "My mother is coming to San Francisco."

"That's good, right?" Yvonne said cautiously. "You'll get to see her."

"She's only coming because my father wants to discuss her financial arrangements again." He sighed. "And that means I've got to be there as well, which is the last place I *ever* want to be."

She snapped on the kitchen lights and retook his hand. "Why don't you come in and have some hot chocolate?"

He stared down at their joined hands. "Are you sure about that?"

"Letting you in my place?" She smiled. "I think you'll behave yourself."

His expression stilled. "I'm not as confident as you are."

"Then we'll stay down here, have some *chocolat*, and if you get fresh with me I'll stab you with one of my very sharp kitchen knives."

"Sounds like a plan." He cupped her chin. "You're driving me nuts, you know."

"How come?"

"Because I can't stop thinking about you."

Yvonne allowed herself a moment to enjoy the intensity of his words before returning to the matter in hand.

"We've agreed that this is a lousy time for either of us to get involved with anyone," she reminded him.

"I know that." His smile was crooked. "It doesn't seem to be helping much." He hesitated. "Is it just me?"

"No." She sighed. "You're a terrible distraction."

"Good." He let his victorious smile speak for itself.

"No, it's not good. We are sensible, rational people who have weighed the risks and realized there is no future for a potential relationship."

"Agreed. Then why do I still want to kiss you?"

Now she was staring at his mouth. "I don't know."

He bent his head, giving her all the time in the world to duck away before he gently set his mouth over hers.

This time, she welcomed him in, his taste already familiar and wanted. She hummed as he gathered her in his arms and deepened the kiss, giving back everything he offered her with each stroke of her tongue against his. At some point, his hat hit the ground, but neither of them cared as he kicked the door shut behind him, and they just kissed like desperate teenagers making out in the schoolyard.

He was the first to pull out of the kiss.

"This is not helping me maintain my cool."

She bit his lip, and his whole body flexed against hers, making her all too aware that he was aroused and ready to take things further. And, oh God, she wanted to do that *so* much. . . .

"Cocoa," she murmured while he kissed her nose, her eyes, and her cheek, and as his hand cupped her breast, and thumbed her nipple.

"Yeah."

She didn't want to let him go. She *had* to let him go.

"We've got to stop together, okay?" she said firmly. "Or this isn't going to work. We're adults, not over-sexed teens."

"Sure feel like a randy teen right now," he muttered roughly as he reluctantly moved his hand away. "Just hope I don't embarrass myself."

Her fingers clenched on his hip, wondering whether she dared explore the possibilities of the hardness contained in his jeans. He was like some roller-coaster ride she couldn't get off. She forced herself to think about Paul, of the way he'd seduced her, of how she'd felt so addicted to touch, and sex, and . . .

"Okay. I'm calm now." She put both hands on Rio's chest and pushed him away. "We're stopping."

He didn't attempt to take her back in his arms, but she could see the need in his brown eyes. He was breathing hard, one hand clenched into a fist. He took another step back.

"Hot chocolate it is then."

Rio sat at the table while Yvonne made the cocoa the old-fashioned way in a pan on the stove with proper milk and added whipped cream and shaved chocolate on the top. It was soothing watching her work, and gave him a much-needed moment to tell his aroused body to knock it off and get back into the friend zone.

He was thirty-one, and no longer a horny teenager, but he sure felt like one. He'd never met anyone in his life who affected him so intensely. Was this how his parents had felt when they'd met and "fallen in love" within a week? If it was the same, then all the more reason to be wary of such wasteful false emotions. He didn't trust lust and instalove. How could he?

"Here you go."

"Thank you."

She put the hot cocoa in front of him and took the seat opposite, folding her hands together on the table. She was wearing her favorite navy-blue striped top, and had her hair caught up in a messy bun on the top of her head that somehow still looked sophisticated. She yawned and immediately covered her mouth with her hand.

"Sorry. It's way past my bedtime."

He checked his watch. "Mine, too. Don't worry. I won't keep you long."

Her smile was warm and slightly skeptical. "Under other circumstances, I might *want* you to keep me up all night, but now I'm a responsible business owner and you're a professional bull rider, and we have commitments."

"I know. It sucks." He sipped his drink, which was delicious. "When did you get married?"

She gave him a sharp look. "I knew you wouldn't let that go." She sighed. "I was nineteen, living and studying in Paris, and I fell in love with a French guy."

"So how did you end up back here alone?"

"Basically, after living in California for a while, he

decided he didn't like it and wanted to go home to France. I didn't agree."

She spoke lightly, but he could see the residual hurt in her green eyes.

"It's a shame that he couldn't reach a compromise with you."

"Like six months here, and six there? He wanted to start a new business, and argued that he couldn't give it his all if he wasn't there year round. I got it. I felt the same way."

"Do you stay in touch?"

Rio wasn't sure he wanted to know the answer to his question, but he just had to ask.

"Not really. He's moved on and made quite a reputation for himself over there."

"Well, if you become a celebrity chef on TV, you'll be way more famous than him."

She regarded him gravely over the rim of her mug. "I hadn't thought of that." A slow smile emerged. "He'd probably hate it."

Rio clinked his mug against hers. "Atta girl. My mom always says revenge is a dish best served cold, and she should know. It took her years to extract a divorce settlement from my father."

"I think I'd like to meet your mother."

"She'd love you," Rio said promptly. "If things go smoothly with my father, maybe I can persuade her to come out to the ranch for a few days."

"That would be lovely."

He grimaced. "If I can tear her away from the shops."

"I like her more every minute." Yvonne licked cream and grated chocolate from her spoon, and he couldn't look away. "Stop it."

He raised his gaze to hers. "Can't help it. You just press all the right buttons for me."

"Why is that?"

"I don't know." He sat back and tried to regard her dispassionately. "You're beautiful, you're funny, and you're smart as a whip. What's not to like?"

She smoothed her hair back from her face. "I wish we weren't both so busy."

"Or so scared of relationships—for very good reasons on both sides."

"Am I scared?" she asked, her green eyes serious. "I suppose I am. There's nothing like discovering the love of your life is an illusion."

"Or that your parents hate each other's guts," he agreed.

"I can never understand how some people just forget the past and let themselves go through all that hurt again and again," Yvonne confessed.

"Me neither. Not that I've ever risked trying it in the first place."

She sat up straight. "You've never had a long-term relationship?"

He shrugged. "I've had lots of girlfriends, some of them long term, but I never thought of any of them as likely to become permanent."

"I bet that went down well." Yvonne rolled her eyes.

"Not really. They fell into two camps. The ones who worked it out fast and just enjoyed our time together, and the others. . . ." He hesitated, but she waved him to go on. "The others who'd start dropping hints about engagement rings, or leaving wedding magazines around the apartment."

"Even though you'd made it clear that you weren't in it for the long term?"

Rio nodded. "I'm not trying to make myself out to be a hero here, but I always tried to be upfront about it."

"It's okay. I'm not getting at you." She sipped her cocoa. "Some people think they can change someone's opinions if they just keep working away at them. It rarely works. Especially in a marriage." She sighed. "I thought Paul would want to stay in the USA forever, even though all the signs were there that he really missed his homeland. I ignored them because I was young, stupid, and in love. I thought I could persuade him to change who he was."

"See, that's the thing, isn't it?" Rio agreed. "Even with the best of intentions, someone always gets hurt."

"But getting hurt also teaches you what you don't want," Yvonne said. "If I ever get into another serious relationship I won't be so naïve or allow myself to be hurt so badly." She gathered the empty mugs together. "That's why I thought Matt might be the best option for me."

Rio tried to stay neutral while wondering why the hell he was having to discuss Matt right at this particular moment. "He's definitely a good guy."

"But?" Yvonne asked.

Rio shook his head. "You can't expect me to defend my competition, or badmouth him."

"I suppose not." She stood and looked down at him, her gaze uncertain. "Lately, a lot of my good friends have gotten serious with men, and even married them." She paused. "And some of them have overcome far greater problems than I have ever done."

"So?"

"It's made me doubt myself." She hesitated, biting her lip. "Maybe we *aren't* the sensible ones who avoid relationships so we don't get hurt. Maybe *we're* the cowards."

He held her gaze. "Yeah, maybe we are."

She turned away to put the mugs in the sink, and he got to his feet.

"Would you like me to wash those for you before I go?"

She looked over her shoulder as she ran the faucet. "That's really sweet of you, but I like to clean up my own kitchen. I'm fussy like that."

"So I've heard." He walked over to the sink, and dropped a kiss on the top of her head. "Thanks for the cocoa."

"You're welcome."

He studied her perfect features, noticing the tiredness in her eyes even as the words slipped out. "I don't want to go."

"Even if you stayed, I'd still be asleep in about three seconds flat."

"Luckily for you, I'm not that desperate, but it's damn close." He smoothed his thumb over her mouth. "I'd much prefer you awake and willing."

"Then you'll have to start going to bed around eight in the evening."

"Eight?" He leaned in for a slow, careful kiss. "I was thinking six at the latest."

She gently pushed him away. "Go home."

"If I must." He turned toward the door. "Don't forget to arm the alarm when I've gone."

"I won't."

She followed him to the door, and he snatched another quick kiss before she finally shut him out. The town was quiet around him, the night air still cold even in the early summer. He considered walking back to the bar, where things were still hopping, but wasn't in the mood for company.

He crossed the street, taking his time to get to his truck, which was parked in the lot behind the bar usually filled with tourists in daylight hours. Was Yvonne right? Was he a loser who was afraid to commit to a relationship? At least she had tried. He had never made the attempt or put in any effort in his love life.

He stopped to find his keys and clicked to open the door of his new truck. Well, if he was a coward, at least he was in good company.

Chapter Seven

"Okay, everyone, settle down, and welcome to the quarterly meeting of the Morgantown business and community liaison project."

Chase Morgan smiled at the assembled townsfolk and local ranchers who had gathered in the church hall, and clicked to reveal the first slide of his Power-Point presentation. Rio, who was sitting beside BB near the back of the hall, heard a groan.

"Jeez, Chase is going to talk for hours, isn't he? How many slides do you think he's got queued up this time?"

Ruth, who was sitting on Blue's other side, nudged her grandson. "Be quiet, BB, and listen to your brother."

"I've been listening to him for years, and he still makes no sense," BB grumbled, and settled further into his seat.

Rio had to disagree. Chase was obviously used to addressing meetings and was moving rapidly through an update of all the plans Morgan Ranch had set in motion, and how they were affecting the local community. From what Rio could remember, some of the locals, including the Hayes family, who owned the hotel, had been worried about loss of revenue when the guest ranch opened its doors.

If Chase's graphs and charts were correct—and knowing his technical abilities, Rio had a sense they probably were—it looked like the ranch was adding to the prosperity of the area rather than diminishing it, offering more employment, local produce, and visitors who liked to shop and dine in the town.

After his summary, Chase looked around the hall. "Any questions?"

A young man stood up. "I've got no issue with what you've said, Chase, but can we talk about the increase in traffic down Main Street? I know gasoline is my business, but I hate seeing all those coaches and huge trucks trying to force their way through the parked cars. Someone's going to get hurt one of these days."

"I agree with you, Ted." Chase nodded. "How about the rest of you?"

A spirited discussion about loss of revenue if the town was bypassed developed between several of the shop owners, including Maureen, who owned the local store, and Daisy at the flower shop. There was also some question if the town would lose its historic route moniker if the highway no longer went through it.

Chase took notes, and nodded as everyone talked things out, and then summarized every point.

"He's good," Rio murmured to January, who was sitting on his other side. "He's *really* good."

"I know." She sighed happily. "And he's all mine."

"I suspect we're going to need to talk to the county about this. And maybe get an independent traffic study done." Chase nodded. "Are you all okay if I go ahead, or does anyone have any leverage at county level? Shall we take a vote?"

The majority went with exploring their options, and Chase suggested they break for coffee, which won a round of applause. Out of the corner of his eye, Rio noticed Yvonne coming through the door. She still wore her work uniform, and was doing something with her phone, her expression distracted.

Beside him, January waved and pointed to the empty seat beside her. Yvonne came around the back of the hall and slipped quietly into the row.

"Thank you. Did I miss much?"

"I'll catch you up, later," January said. "Why don't you move next to Rio while I go and help Ruth and Chase with the coffee?"

Rio happily breathed in the scent of vanilla and chocolate that always clung to Yvonne's slender frame as she took the seat next to him. He hadn't seen her for a few days. Roy had hurt his back chasing his pigs, and Rio had stepped up to help out. Not that he'd stopped thinking about their very adult conversation in her kitchen, and their admirable ability to admit they didn't have time for a relationship.

It still sucked, though, but he couldn't ask her to hang around and wait for another year or so while he finished out his career. She deserved better than that after being deserted by the French idiot. Not to say that he didn't understand the pull of home. He'd been desperately unhappy when his mother had moved back to Brazil, and left him with his father in Boston.

On several occasions, he'd tried to run away and been brought back by the police. In the end, his father had set a bodyguard on him and threatened to stop him ever seeing his mother again if he kept escaping. Seeing as the thought of being with his mom was keeping him alive, it had been enough to stop him in his tracks,

He'd been actively discouraged from speaking Portuguese, and his mother's staff appointments who had spoken it with him had been dismissed by Wife Number Two, who didn't like people speaking "foreign" around her. Not that she'd been around him long enough to hear him say anything. . . .

"Hey, stranger." Yvonne nudged him in the ribs.

"I thought you'd be pleased I'd stayed away," he joked.

"To be honest, I've been too busy to notice your absence."

"You wound me." He placed his hand over his heart. "What's up?"

"Lizzie's pregnant and suffering from terrible morning sickness so every so often she has to rush away from the counter, leaving yours truly to manage everything." Yvonne sighed and leaned slightly against his shoulder. His fingers flexed with the effort not to put his arm around her. "I'll just get started on something in the kitchen, and then I have to run and take over."

"Get someone in to cover for her."

"I'm not sure it's worth it." She chuckled. "The funny thing is, she's fine ten minutes later, like nothing happened, and she assures me it won't last long."

"So I understand. My mother was as sick as a dog when she was carrying me. That was when my father started to regret his decision to marry her."

She wrinkled her nose. "The more you tell me about your father, the less I like the sound of him."

"There's nothing to like. He's a bully." It was his turn

to sigh. "And I've got to go see him next week with my mom."

"Next week?" Yvonne dug out her phone. "What days?"

He gave her the dates, and she checked something on her calendar. "That's the week the production company has asked me to come in. Maybe we could travel to the city together?"

"Fine by me." He winked. "Hey, we could save money and room together."

"Nice try." She gave him an amused look. "They're paying for my room."

"Even better. I can go for free."

"Won't you be staying with your mom?"

"There is that," he conceded. "She'd probably wonder what the hell I was doing if I didn't show up."

"Then we're all set." She put her phone away in her large purse.

"I'm not. I'm mourning lost opportunities."

She studied him for a long minute. "You're hoping that fate will throw us together somehow?"

"Why not? I'm a great believer in a higher power."

"So that we can't resist our mutual attraction?"

"Yes."

"Lame."

At that moment, Chase called the meeting to order again and January came back to sit on Yvonne's other side, leaving Rio to contemplate what Yvonne had made him reveal. Was he that desperate? Was he really hoping something would push them into bed together?

Yeah, he was.

Then why couldn't he man up and find a way to make things work through the usual channels? Like asking her out on a date again, or taking her to the movies?

. Chase closed his laptop and called out, "Any other business?"

"Yes."

To Rio's surprise, Yvonne stood and smiled at Chase, who motioned for her to speak.

"I have a question. I know the ranch is struggling to fill jobs, as are a lot of small business owners in town."

Chase nodded. "Yes, we definitely have more jobs than applicants at the moment."

Several people in the audience murmured in agreement.

"So what can we do as a community to persuade people to come and work here?" Yvonne asked.

Nate Turner, the deputy sheriff, stood up. "One of the problems is the lack of housing around here. Some of my siblings would love to stay in the town where they were born, but there's nowhere for them to live except at home." His grin widened. "And, for some reason, they don't always want to do that."

"So we need more affordable housing?" Chase blew out a breath. "That's a big issue."

Ted Baker raised his hand. "There are several older buildings around the town that could be converted into apartments. We'd just need someone to finance the project."

"And administer and manage it after construction," Chase said, his gaze going toward his business partner, Jake, who was sitting in the front row. "That's something we can definitely look into."

"What about all that land up at the ranch?" Margery Hoffa, the woman who managed the Realtors next door to Yvonne's café, added her voice. "You Morgans are rolling in money, and seeing as you caused this problem in the first place, then maybe you should be willing to have all those low-income folks on *your* doorstep."

Chase frowned. "I'm not sure how offering local people jobs is a problem, Margery, but—"

"Maybe you should pay them more? Then they could commute in from the larger towns," Margery persisted.

Chase, to his credit, didn't allow her to get a rise out of him. "Ranch work doesn't really work to a nine-to-five timetable, but I take your point."

"I hope you do, because I don't want outsiders changing *my* town and ruining the housing market for the discerning buyer."

"Discerning buyer? How about first-time buyer?" Nate Turner asked. "There's almost nothing here for those guys. And what about my family, Margery, and maybe even yours, if they want to come live here again?"

"You know that's not what I meant, Nate." Margery looked defiantly around the room. "Who *knows* what type of people you will attract if you offer cheap lodgings? And what happens when Morgantown has to deal with a whole new set of problems?"

"We're hardly talking about putting in thousands of new homes," Chase objected. Rio was impressed by his calm tone. "Just enough to house local families who can't afford to buy around here anymore, and our new workers."

"That might be how it starts," Margery said darkly. "But who knows what might happen in the future? If the prices go down, my Realtor company will not stay in a *ghetto*."

A chorus of voices broke out, both agreeing and disagreeing with the subject, until Chase had to call the meeting to order again.

"How about we find out more about this before we

all go off the deep end? We can discuss it in depth next time we meet."

"Agreed," Nate Turner said. "You asked the original question, Yvonne. Are you okay to do that?"

"Absolutely."

She sat down, and Rio immediately noticed she was trembling.

"Are you okay?"

"I'm fine, thanks. It's just sometimes people can be so narrow-minded." She glanced over at Margery, who was still holding forth to a small group of people now gathered around her.

"Is property expensive around here?" Rio asked.

"It's not cheap. We're close enough to drive to San Francisco, Sacramento, and up to the ski resorts. All those places command a premium. I've known people who have commuted into one of the bigger towns every day for years. The main problem here is there just isn't enough actual property, especially at the lower end. Lots of ranches, small towns, and inaccessible mountains."

"That's a problem when you need to employ people at local rates."

"If all the kids grow up and have to leave to afford a place somewhere else, what happens to the town? Services vanish, schools close down, and the sense of community and family that Morgantown has provided for around one hundred and fifty years disappears."

"BB said that Maria will have to be bussed to school in Bridgeport because there's no high school here anymore."

"Exactly. So encouraging people to stay and work within their local community is a *good* thing."

Rio smiled. "You don't have to convince me—not

that I ever got to go to school locally, but I understand the need for it."

"Where did you go to school, then?" Yvonne asked.

"After my mother left, I was sent away to boarding school."

"When you were *seven*?"

"Trust me, it was better than staying home with my father and his new wife."

Marginally better, but he wasn't going to start spilling details of that ugly episode of his life in the middle of a town meeting.

She grabbed his hand in a fierce grip. "Some people should never be allowed to have children."

Surprised and touched by her support, he kissed her fingers. "I survived."

"The childhood from hell."

"It wasn't that bad. I was never abandoned. I knew my mother was out there somewhere, and that one day I'd be reunited with her."

"When did you first see her again?" Yvonne asked.

"About five years after she left. My father's lawyers blocked all her applications to see me, insisting she would take me back to Brazil with her. My father managed to find a judge who agreed with his viewpoint." He smiled. "And he was right about that. My mother would've fought like a lioness to get me back over that border. At first, she had to agree to see me in San Francisco at my father's apartment."

A gentle cough sounded behind Rio and he looked up, realizing that almost everyone apart from the Morgans had left the building.

"Hey, Rio, are you coming back to the ranch, or do you and Yvonne have something else to do?" BB asked.

Yvonne hesitated and met Rio's gaze. "I did want to

talk to you about this meeting coming up with Tasty Treats."

"Then I'll walk you home, and work out how to get back to the ranch when we're done," Rio said as he stood and nodded at BB. "Thanks for the ride down, and I'll see you later."

"Billy will be coming back to the ranch from his AA meeting around ten, so if you do need a ride, catch him in the parking lot right here." BB winked at Yvonne and walked away.

Yvonne let Rio into the kitchen, and waited as he carefully wiped his boots on the mat, and took them off.

"Come on up." She headed up the stairs and unlocked the door at the top. She'd knocked almost all the space above the café into one long, L-shaped room with a bedroom, its en suite taking up the remaining corner. The dual aspect meant the apartment was always full of light, and being above the street and traffic made it quieter than most dwellings in the town.

She gave the place a quick once-over and grabbed a T-shirt that hung on the back of one of the dining room chairs. She'd left a bra air-drying in the bathroom, so she'd retrieve that in a minute.

"Make yourself at home."

Actually, in his black cowboy hat and dark clothing, Rio looked very out of place in the pink and floral décor.

"How about you go shower and change out of your work clothes while I make us some coffee?" Rio suggested.

"I'd completely forgotten I had this on." She glanced ruefully down at her black dress. "It's been that kind of day."

"Then go and change." He headed toward the kitchen. "I'll figure it out."

"Okay, thanks!"

Seeing as she had one heck of a fancy coffee machine, she wasn't so sure he'd manage, but she was too tired to doubt him, and too impressed that he'd thought about her comfort to put up much of an argument.

She took a quick shower and washed her hair, which always smelled of roasting coffee by the end of the day in the café. It would be much more convenient if she cut it short, but she wasn't prepared to give up on her long hair just yet, even if the only person who ever saw it down was her.

She put on a pair of pink cupcake pj's and a white T-shirt without any underwear and went back through to the kitchen. The smell of coffee greeted her like a siren, and she inhaled appreciatively.

Rio had taken off his coat and rolled up his sleeves to display strong forearms and the hint of a tattoo that disappeared beneath the edge of his shirt.

Yvonne zeroed in on it. "What's the tattoo?"

He glanced down at his right elbow as he poured her a mug of coffee. "It's a quote in Portuguese from Ferdinand Magellan."

"The guy who proved the Earth wasn't flat?"

"That's the one."

"Saying?"

He grimaced and looked adorably embarrassed. "It's kind of long, but when I was eighteen, it had a lot of meaning for me."

"Tell me," Yvonne encouraged him.

He cleared his throat and started to recite. "*The sea is dangerous and its storms terrible, but these obstacles have never been sufficient reason to remain ashore . . . Unlike the mediocre, intrepid spirits seek victory over those things that seem impossible . . . It is with an iron will that they embark*

on the most daring of all endeavors . . . to meet the shadowy
future without fear and conquer the unknown."

She blinked at him. "Wow, that is long, but very powerful."

"It worked in several ways—that I wouldn't let the space between my mother and I divide us forever, and that I would succeed in whatever I chose to do even if my father said it was impossible." He grinned. "He also forbade me to get a tattoo."

Yvonne let her gaze travel up his arm. "Do you really have the whole thing on you?"

"Yes, do you want to see?" He undid the top three buttons of his shirt and, in one quick motion, pulled it and his T-shirt over his head.

For a long moment, all Yvonne could do was stare at the muscled perfection of his chest, his defined biceps and abs, and hope that she wasn't actually drooling.

"It's mainly on my back."

He obligingly turned around to reveal how the quote went up his arm and over his shoulder, and covered the right upper quadrant of his back.

"I like the fact that when I'm on a bull, my free hand is over my head giving my father the proverbial F you every time I ride."

Yvonne moistened her lips. "Makes sense."

He turned to face her. "You okay? You sound a little strange."

"Your body . . ."

He looked down at himself. "What about it?"

"It's perfect."

"Yeah?" He sauntered around the counter and came close—way too close, so she could feel the heat radiating from his skin.

"You can touch it if you like."

As if in a daze, she reached out, and stroked the taut heat of his shoulder. "Oh God . . ."

"What's wrong?"

She met his gaze. "You know what we talked about? About how sensible we were not getting involved and all that?"

"Yes?"

"Well, do you think we could just give into lust just this once?" She was babbling now, but she didn't care. "We could agree upfront that it still meant we weren't ready for a relationship, and just make this a one-off, and—"

His mouth descended on hers, and words didn't matter anymore as he sat her on the top of the table, and moved between her spread knees, fitting her softness to his hardness. One of his hands wove in her hair, and the other wrapped around her hips, holding her tight against him.

She wasn't being shy herself, her fingers scratching down his spine, and over his shoulders, making him groan into her mouth. Emboldened, she wound her fingers into his belt loops, and eased the buckle free. He smelled delicious, he tasted even better, and the feel of him under her hands was short-circuiting her exceptionally practical brain.

"Bedroom?" he managed to mutter. "Or right here?"

"Bedroom," Yvonne said. "Because—"

He simply picked her up and took her there, easing her onto the bed and following her down a second later, scattering the throw pillows everywhere. His hands were all over her, easing down her pajama pants, and sliding under her T-shirt, his thumbs settling over her already hard nipples.

"Oh . . ." Yvonne shoved a hand down inside his

jeans to find what she guessed would be the most perfect ass in the universe.

He firmly removed her hand. "You first."

"That's very sweet of you."

He captured both of her wrists over her head and smiled down at her. "I have to tell you that I'm not feeling particularly sweet right now."

"That's—" Her words ended as he kissed her again with a slow, possessive thoroughness that focused her scattered thoughts on the amazing sensations he was arousing in her.

"Mmm, you taste like coffee," he murmured, nibbling on her lower lip. "I want to eat you up."

"Don't let me stop you."

His grin was wicked as he kissed his way down her throat and over her stomach and ended up between her legs, his hand releasing her wrists, and settling on her breast.

"Rio . . ."

She clenched her fingers in his hair as he delicately tongued and licked her; the hint of his stubble added a delicious element to her building arousal. Then he added his fingers, and sent her over into an intense and deeply satisfying climax.

When she opened her eyes, he was smiling down at her, the dimple on his cheek clearly visible.

"Good?"

"Not bad." She tried to sound nonchalant, but wasn't sure she was successful. "Come here." She reached for the button of his jeans, and he froze over her.

"Wait." He sounded even more desperate than she felt. "I don't have protection."

"Dammit!" She gazed up at him and wanted to cry. "Neither do I."

With a groan, he rolled off her, and buried his face in her frilly pink pillows.

She shakily pushed the hair out of her eyes and sat up. What on earth had she been *thinking*? She was almost thirty. How could she have been so irresponsible?

"What time is it?" Rio asked.

Bewildered, Yvonne glanced at her bedside clock. "Just before seven, why?"

"Stay there." He rolled off the side of the bed, grabbed his shirt, and headed for the door at a gallop.

"Where are you going?"

"I'm taking your keys!" he shouted out to her.

"But . . ." She flopped back on the pillows and stared up at the ceiling, waiting for her body to calm down and stop wailing at the loss of the finest specimen of manhood she had ever been privileged to see up close and personal.

Had he gone back to the ranch? Yvonne considered her current position. Had she scared him off for good? Did he really expect her to just lie there like a maiden in distress, and wait for his possible return? After the climax he'd given her, she had no inclination to go anywhere anyway; her body was humming and sighing with joy. She consulted her clock. She'd give him fifteen minutes. If he didn't turn up again, she'd get more coffee and call him.

Rio pulled his T-shirt on, checked that his jeans were at least still buttoned, and ran down the stairs to the kitchen. He put on his boots and was out the door and heading diagonally across Main Street, to the corner of Morgan, before he really drew another breath.

The Red Dragon was open. With a prayer of thanks,

he ran straight for the restrooms and made a quick financial transaction with the machine before hurrying out again.

By the time he reached the top of the stairs of Yvonne's apartment, he was breathing as if he smoked sixty cigarettes a day and wheezing to match. He realized he still had his boots on and kicked them off before heading back into the bedroom.

He paused at the door to admire the luscious sight of Yvonne sprawled out on the bed and instantly felt better. He'd been expecting her to be sitting up and asking him all kinds of pointed questions. Instead she looked like a beautifully rumpled princess it would be his pleasure to awaken with a kiss. A slight rattling sound had him advancing closer to see that she was fast asleep and snoring lightly.

So much for kissing her awake . . .

He glanced at the condom packet, and then back at Yvonne, and made his decision. She needed her sleep more than he needed to get laid, and at least this time he'd managed to get her almost naked. His dick disagreed with his mature decision, but he drew the sheets over her, placed the pack of condoms on the pillow, and tiptoed out into the hallway.

He took a moment to go into the bathroom and wash before he placed her keys on the countertop, drank his coffee, and turned off the machine.

Next time he'd live up to his Boy Scout motto and be prepared.

Chapter Eight

"Yvonne! I'm glad I caught you!"

Margery Hoffa came into the café with a professional-looking clipboard clasped to her bosom and a militant gleam in her eye. She wore her usual blue "I'm a Realtor" uniform of a well-cut skirt suit and blouse with high heels that Yvonne couldn't imagine were comfortable to walk around in all day.

"Hi, how can I help you?" Yvonne wiped her hands on her apron, and stepped up to the counter. Lizzie had disappeared off to the bathroom again.

"I wanted to know if you and your staff will sign this." Margery handed over the clipboard. "It's a petition to the town council and county board of supervisors to prevent the Morgans from building cheap housing in Morgantown."

Yvonne took her time reading through the call to action, and then handed the clipboard back to Margery. She was surprised to see that there were already quite a few signatures on it.

"I'm sorry. I can't sign that, but you're welcome to ask any of my clients in the café."

"Why can't you sign it?" Margery asked.

"Because we *do* need more housing here to keep young families around, and to house our increasing workforce."

"But what about property values?"

"That's your line of work, Margery. I just feed people, and the more people who come through my doors, the better."

"It's unlikely that the kind of people who exist on ranch wages or in minimum-wage jobs will be able to afford y*our* prices." Margery's gaze swept the glass-fronted display counter. "I mean, *three dollars* for a croissant? I can get a dozen at the supermarket for twice that."

"And they will taste like it." Yvonne tried to remain pleasant. "Just think about it this way. A lot of those new families might expand, earn more, and end up buying bigger and better properties from you."

"I suppose that might happen." Margery didn't look convinced. "But I still don't like it."

"No one likes change, Margery. I get that, but on this occasion, reviving old buildings within the town, and maybe adding some affordable housing, would be a good thing for the community."

"I thought you'd say that." Margery's gaze swept the coffee shop. "But you don't mind if I put a copy of the petition up on your community noticeboard, do you?"

"Be my guest." Yvonne tried not to monitor what went up on there too much.

"Thank you." Margery hesitated, her gaze lingering on the lines of cream cakes. "I must be off. I have a client coming in at eleven."

Yvonne took the sheet for the petition and smiled at her neighbor. "Then have a great day!"

Margery left, and Yvonne walked over to the notice-board just inside the door and spent a few minutes removing old stuff and repositioning the new items. It was an eclectic mix of local classes, lost pets, baby-sitters, and community outreach programs. The petition didn't sit well with any of it, but she'd promised to put it up there, and she was a woman of her word.

She stood back and reread the heading. It seemed as if Chase Morgan might have a fight on his hands for the future of Morgantown after all. . . .

"So what gives, girlfriend?" Nancy handed Yvonne a ten-dollar note, and accepted her change and coffee. Today her hair was blue and silver, but Yvonne was fairly certain it was a new wig. "The other evening, your Rio ran into the bar restrooms, and then out again like the hounds of hell were pursuing him."

"Oh, *that's* where he went," Yvonne said. "I suppose it makes sense."

She'd woken up to her alarm going off at four in the morning, and discovered that not only was she alone, but that her stealthy seducer had left a packet of condoms on her pillow, and disappeared.

"What do you mean, that's where he went?" Nancy asked.

Yvonne checked to see who was around in the café, and lowered her voice. "Things got a bit hot and heavy between us, and then we both realized we didn't have protection, so he disappeared on me, and I . . . fell asleep."

Nancy slowly closed her mouth. "You fell *asleep*?"

"I'd had a long day," Yvonne said defensively.

"But did you fall asleep before, during or after?"

"I suppose during, but only just." Yvonne gave Nancy her best stare. "I'm not sharing the details, so don't ask."

"So basically he didn't get any?"

"Possibly not," Yvonne said diplomatically. "He certainly didn't come back and take advantage of me in my sleep."

"Did you get some?"

"I might have." Yvonne tried not to smirk.

"Poor guy." Nancy shook her head.

"What about poor *me*?"

"You fell asleep!" Nancy's chuckle was hard to resist. "That's kind of hilarious."

"Okay, I suppose it is," Yvonne agreed. "But what do you think I should do about it?"

"He hasn't called you?"

"He texted me to say he had gotten a ride back to the ranch with Billy, and hoped I had a good night's sleep."

"And what did you say to that?"

"I haven't replied to him." Yvonne sat down at the small table nearest the counter. "I don't know what to say."

Nancy sat opposite her, her sandwich forgotten in its bag. "*You* don't know what to say? What the hell is going on in this world?"

"We talked about not being in the right place to have a relationship, and we agreed that was the plan," Yvonne said. "It all came out of nowhere. He was just showing me his tattoo. . . ."

Nancy snorted.

"He took off his shirt, and things just got a bit out of control due to his extreme hotness, and my inability to control my lust for his body. The next thing I know, I'm practically devouring him on my kitchen table, all practical thoughts wiped from my brain."

"By his sheer hotness, go on." Nancy nodded.

"So what do I do now?" Yvonne asked. "It was a

moment that came from nothing, so we should go back to just being friends who can't commit, right?"

"It depends."

"On what?"

"On whether you *want* to take things further again."

"But we agreed not to do that for Very Good Reasons." Yvonne groaned. "It was a *spontaneous moment.* Not a planned seduction, which is a different thing entirely."

Nancy studied her intently. "Okay, I'm confused. What's the problem here? Spontaneous sex is okay, but having a relationship with sex *isn't*?"

"*Exactly.* And I can't be spontaneous again."

"Why not?"

"Because then it would be *premeditated sex* because I now know how hot he is, and I want more."

"And premeditated sex means you're in a relationship." Nancy slowly shook her head. "You know that's nuts, right?"

"I am aware of that," Yvonne agreed. She'd spent several precious hours of her life already trying to make sense of everything and gotten nowhere.

"How about you have another honest conversation with the man, and see whether he *wants* to have a relationship with you?"

"Because we can't have a relationship right now!" Yvonne almost raised her voice. "Nothing has changed apart from his hotness factor and my lust. Last time I gave into lust, I ended up married to someone who didn't really care for me after the sexual attraction burned away."

"You were a lot younger then, and grieving because you'd just lost your parents," Nancy reminded her gently. "You know yourself better now, and you know what you want."

"I thought I did," Yvonne said miserably. "But maybe I was wrong."

"If he really is a good guy, then you need to tell him what's going on. You can't just hope that another situation will arise that will just fling you together so you can have sex with no strings attached." Nancy sipped her coffee. "It's not like you're leaping in and *marrying* the guy like you did last time. You'll still be an individual and you won't have to go through the pain of divorce again."

"*Mon Dieu.*" Yvonne brought her hand to her mouth. "I just had a terrible thought."

"Why? Did you accidentally marry Rio in your sleep?"

"I hope not." Yvonne let out her breath, her happiness deflating like a soufflé. "Because, if I did, that might make me a bigamist."

"*A what?*" Nancy gulped down her coffee.

"I left Paul handling the divorce in France." Yvonne stared wide-eyed in horror at her friend. "I'm not sure he ever got back to me with the legal paperwork."

Half an hour later, Yvonne was sitting at her desk, staring blindly at the screen. Did she even have a current phone number for her ex? He'd moved around a lot in the past four years, and she wasn't sure she'd kept up.

"Don't panic, Yvonne," she murmured to herself. "There is a perfectly straightforward way to solve this. You just call Paul, ask him what's happening, and simply drop a casual question as to the whereabouts of the paperwork for the divorce into the conversation."

She bit her lip. Like he wouldn't be immediately

suspicious if she called him after four years of nothing. Hell, she'd freaked out when he'd emailed her on their anniversary.

Email.

That would be a lot easier, and she'd have the excuse that she was replying to the message he'd sent her a couple of weeks ago. She clicked on his email, and brought it up on the screen.

Thinking of you . . She considered his words again. Did he want something? Was there a reason why he'd emailed out of the blue? Maybe there was some negotiating room after all. She took a deep breath and started typing in English.

> Hi Paul, hope all is good with you, and that the restaurant business is treating you well. AND, BY THE WAY, YOU COMPLETE IDIOT, WHERE ARE MY DIVORCE PAPERS??

Yvonne hastily deleted the part in caps, and considered if she could phrase it better. Then she deleted all of it and tried again.

> Hi Paul, thanks for thinking about me on what was once our special day. I can't believe it's been four years since you callously walked out leaving me heartbroken and alone! Did you ever get around to filing for divorce like you promised me you would, or is that yet another thing you let me down on?

It was better without any caps, but still not quite the sentiment she was trying to get across.

> Hey Paul, funnily enough I was thinking about you on that special day myself because my accountant

was asking for details of our divorce for tax purposes.
I realized I didn't have a copy of the legal docu-
ment. Can you send me one? Thanks a million.
Yvonne

She grimaced at the screen. It wasn't good, but in
her present state of agitation, it was the best it was
going to be. They'd been married in France and, according to the laws of that country, she had to petition
for divorce there.

She hit send. He'd probably be asleep at the
moment, so she didn't have to worry about a reply
until the next day. Which meant she'd only have to
worry herself to death for a short while.

A reply icon flashed up on her screen, and she
almost died from shock.

Hey, thanks for getting back to me! The divorce
thing got a bit complicated, but it's back on track
now, so I can get you all the paperwork you need.
I'm currently in New York talking about setting up
a new restaurant here, so maybe we can get
together before I leave? I wanted to talk to you
about something anyway.

Yvonne stared at the message. He'd probably forgotten to file for the legal separation when he'd returned home. He might not have had the funds or
delayed just to annoy her. Either option could be true.
She Googled the French divorce laws again to remind
herself of the criteria, and realized they'd been apart
long enough now to fit the standards to legally separate without having to appear before a judge. If Paul

didn't sort things out, she might be able to assist him. She typed a reply.

> Meeting up sounds great, but I'm not sure if you are aware that I live on the West Coast, so I'm quite a long way from New York!

She hit send and sat back, resisting the unusual urge to bite her nails.

> I'm flying into San Francisco in a couple of weeks. Can we meet there or at your place?

> Sure! Yvonne typed.

> Then I'll be in touch when I have more concrete plans. Au revoir. Paul

Had he really sorted out the divorce? Yvonne considered her ex-husband's amazing ability to charm and lie himself out of any corner. Was it possible for her to check the status of her marriage through the French system? They were probably online *somewhere*.

Yvonne sighed and got out of her chair. She'd already been away from the kitchen for too long, and even though Tom was improving nicely, the work was mounting up. If she couldn't work out how to access the French legal system online, she knew a man who could. Chase Morgan had never met a software system he hadn't conquered, and she knew January would offer her husband to help out her best friend.

The thought of actually seeing Paul again made her pause. Would he bring back some of the worst memories of her life? After her parents had died so unexpectedly, she'd been looking for someone to love, and

Paul had seemed perfect—until she'd realized he was all about his own needs and incapable of considering hers. . . .

He hadn't liked her strength of purpose and ambition, so she'd muted her personality, tried to become the wife he wanted, and lost him anyway because she was no longer a challenge. It had taken her years to reclaim her confidence and appreciate her own adventurous nature again. Seeing him would put everything she'd achieved since he'd left to the test.

Yvonne pushed in her chair and turned off her laptop. When she thought about it like that, she was actually looking forward to it.

Rio checked his cell again, and pushed open the door into Yvonne's café. The sweet smell of chocolate and coffee flowed over him, and he inhaled appreciatively. For once, the place wasn't packed, which meant Yvonne wasn't behind the counter and Lizzie was. He'd kept to the ranch for almost a week, waiting to hear from her, but apart from a generic glad you got back safely text, she hadn't suggested they meet up.

It was an unusual experience for him to be the one doing the chasing, but he was enjoying it immensely. A month away from the rodeo circuit was a good reminder that, to most people, he was completely unknown, and just another guy in a cowboy hat. Unlike HW, who had really enjoyed the whole celebrity aspect of being at the top of the standings, Rio had endured it in order to do the thing he loved—ride bulls.

He'd hated the fact that being in the public eye again meant his father could track his movements. Not that the old man had ever indicated that he cared enough to do that, but it still made Rio feel exposed.

The publicity surrounding his parents' long-running and acrimonious divorce had given him a dislike of being thrust into the spotlight, and caused him endless problems at school.

"Hi, Rio!" Lizzie waved at him. "Do you want coffee?"

"That would be great. Is Yvonne around?"

"She's in the kitchen. Do you want me to give her a shout?"

"If she's not too busy." Rio accepted his coffee and leaned against the countertop idly, considering whether he could squeeze in an éclair and regretfully concluding that Ruth's shepherd's pie had filled every crevice in his body.

"Hey."

Yvonne emerged wiping her hands on her apron. A curl of her hair had escaped her bun, and was hanging over her nose. Rio couldn't help but brush it to one side and anchor it behind her ear.

"You look busy," Rio said.

She crossed her arms over her chest, which was never a good sign. "I'm always busy."

"I just wanted to check in with you about our travel arrangements for next week."

"Oh right! That!"

She sounded way too bright for his liking, as if she'd expected him to talk about something else. He had a fairly good idea what that was, but he wasn't averse to keeping her in suspense for a few moments longer.

"You sound like you'd forgotten," Rio said.

"That we're traveling together in Chase's plane on Tuesday? I got your text, thanks. I can meet you up at the ranch."

"Is everything okay?" Rio asked slowly.

"It's all good." She huffed out a breath. "It's just been a busy week and—"

"Maybe you need more sleep?" He nodded gravely. "I can see that."

She met his gaze. "Are you going to be obnoxious about what happened?"

He tried to look innocent. "Which part?"

"You know darn well which part."

He smiled. It was glorious seeing her all ruffled and flustered.

"If I'm going to be honest, Yvonne, there *are* some parts of me that still haven't recovered, but thanks for asking."

She took hold of his hand, dragged him through her kitchen and then out into the hallway.

"You disappeared on me!"

"*You* went to sleep," Rio protested.

"I didn't *mean* to go to sleep. Maybe if you'd told me you were in hot pursuit of some protection I might have managed to stay awake."

"Who told you I was doing that?" Rio frowned.

"Nancy, of course." Yvonne sniffed. "You think no one noticed you charging around town like a stallion feeling its oats?"

"A stallion?" He gave her his biggest smile. "I appreciate the compliment."

"You—" She flapped her hand in his general direction.

"I what?"

"You confuse me!"

"Good." He kissed her knuckles, and then turned her hand over to kiss her palm. "And right back at you."

She reluctantly disengaged her hand from his. "I have to work. As I'm going to be away for a few days, I have a lot of extra baking to do so that the café won't run out of supplies."

"I understand." He nodded. "We can talk about this more when we get on the plane."

"Talk about what?"

"You falling asleep." He backed away, his hands held up like a hostage. "Next time, I'm going to come prepared, and I'm not leaving until you are one fully satisfied customer."

"*Next* time?" For once, she didn't smile at his lame joke. "Okay, we really do need to talk. I'll see you on Tuesday."

She went back into the kitchen, and he didn't attempt to follow her. He just stood and stared at the swinging door. Had she just shut him down?

He went back through the entire conversation in his head, wondering when it had come off the rails. Had he *assumed* she wanted him back in her bed? Was she pissed at him because of that, or was it because she'd immediately regretted what had happened and never wanted him to touch her again?

"Ouch," he murmured. "Was I that bad?"

And why had he even said such a stupid thing in the first place? He didn't want a relationship with anyone, and yet he'd suggested they carry on where they'd left off. He resisted the temptation to kick something. Maybe Yvonne was on the right track, and the only person who had careened off the rails was him.

Chapter Nine

Yvonne eyed her companion as he strapped into the seat next to her. Chase had the luxury of owning his own plane and had offered her and Rio a seat for the trip back to San Francisco. It was the first time she'd flown on such a small aircraft, and she was slightly nervous.

Chase had taken a seat in the front, and the moment they took off, he opened his laptop, put on his headphones, and got to work. Rio had chosen to sit with her, but was staring intently at his phone. He hadn't spoken or contacted her since his last visit to her shop. It was hardly surprising, seeing as she'd panicked and walked away from having that *meaningful conversation* she needed to have with him.

And she had panicked. Seeing him smiling at her had shaken her resolve to either tell him to back off or take things further. She knew things needed to be said—especially now she had to deal with Paul again—but she'd lost her nerve, and that had rattled her even more.

Rio deserved better. From the pleasant but bland

expression on his face, it looked like he'd decided he'd take himself out of contention anyway.

"Which hotel is your mother staying in?" Yvonne asked brightly.

He glanced over at her. "The Ritz-Carlton."

"*Nice.*"

"Yeah, my father's paying for it." He looked down at his cell again. "She has a suite, so I'll be staying with her."

"Great." She waited, but he didn't ask her any of his usual considerate, thoughtful questions. "I'm at the Omni. Is that close?"

"I'm not sure. I don't know the city very well. You're probably better off asking Chase."

"Okay, I will. Thanks."

He returned his attention to whatever it was that was so important, and she worried her lip. When had she become used to him being the one to make conversation?

"Is your father staying at the same place?"

This time, he took longer to respond, his calm gaze searching her face before he answered. "I have no idea. He has an office somewhere, and probably an apartment. From what I understand, we're supposed to meet him at his office complex."

She reminded herself that this was what she wanted. No flirting, and no involvement while they both concentrated on their respective careers.

For a long while, they both remained silent, the only sound in the cabin the soft click of Chase's fingers on his keyboard.

"When is your meeting with Priscilla?"

Rio's soft question made her jump. "It's tomorrow for lunch at my hotel, and then she's taking me to their head office for an afternoon of talks."

He looked down at his cell again and frowned. She had a strange desire to grab it out of his hand, and throw it out the window. Not that you could actually do that on a plane, but she could still fantasize. . . .

"I don't think I can manage lunch, seeing as I'm taking my mother and half sister out, but if you give me the address, I can probably meet you at their offices for the actual meeting itself."

Yvonne gaped at him. "You're still going to come?"

"If you want me to."

"But we've been *fighting*."

He raised his eyebrows. "As far as I'm aware, we haven't actually *had* a fight."

"Then why aren't we talking to each other?"

He shrugged. "Well, for my part, I was trying to respect your obvious wish for me to back off."

"Oh." That shut her up pretty damn fast. "Okay then."

Did she need him? She'd never negotiated a deal involving her own persona and business before, and certainly nothing in this league. Was she going to let her feelings destroy the advantage he might bring her? She took a deep breath.

"I would really appreciate it if you could come with me."

"Then I'll come." He added something to his calendar. "Can you shoot me the address?"

"Sure. And, thank you."

"You're welcome."

At the airport, they were shuttled through a discreet and secure exit that made Yvonne feel like a celebrity. Chase spoke to his pilot, and then turned to her and Rio. It was strange to see Chase without his cowboy hat on, morphing into a hard-eyed Silicon Valley millionaire.

"I'm going back to the ranch on Thursday. If either of you want a ride, text me."

Yvonne stood on tiptoe to kiss him on the cheek. "Thanks so much for this."

"You're welcome." He patted her shoulder. "Now, do you need a taxi to the hotel, or do you want my chauffeur to take you?"

As Yvonne hesitated, Rio joined the conversation with a smile, and a handshake for Chase.

"If it's okay with you, Yvonne, we can share a cab, and let Chase get on."

"That would be great," Yvonne agreed.

"Then that's settled." Chase nodded. "Take good care of her, Rio, or my wife will kill me."

"She can take care of herself, but I get your point." Rio tipped his hat to Chase and grabbed hold of Yvonne's carry-on. "Thanks again, and I'll see you on Thursday."

Even carrying two bags, Rio was halfway to the taxi rank before Yvonne caught up with him. But then he wasn't the idiot wearing heels. He glanced back and slowed down, his appreciative gaze taking in her whole frame.

"Sorry. I'm not used to you being all glamorous."

She grimaced down at her poor cramped toes. "I'm obviously not used to it either."

The one good thing about her heels was that she was now at his eye level. Or was it good because now she had no excuse not to stare at him?

He helped the cab driver get the bags in the trunk and came to sit beside her in the rear of the taxi.

"I'll get the driver to drop you at the Omni first, okay?"

"Thanks." She wasn't that familiar with the city, having mainly spent time at the tourist spots and in the excellent shops. "If your mom wants to go shopping before I leave, let me know and I'd be happy to take her around."

"That's very kind of you. I'll see what she wants to do."

Yvonne looked out of the window as they exited the airport and approached the mass of moving cars on the freeway. She'd once enjoyed living in a city, but she couldn't see herself doing it again. She'd come to appreciate fresh air, and the value of a settled community.

Rio eased one arm along the back of the seat as they bumped over some unfinished pavement. He smelled his usual delicious self. Yvonne had to fight the urge to lean in and nuzzle his neck, maybe even lick or bite him just a little bit. . . .

She was so hosed. . . . She heaved a sigh and tried to ease away from temptation.

"Are you okay?"

He was sitting so close that his mouth brushed her ear, sending tremors of sensation down her neck.

"I'm good, thanks." Yvonne just managed to speak.

"Look at us being so polite."

"It's better than fighting or ignoring each other."

"Yeah, I know." He looked out his window. "The traffic isn't too bad today. We should be there soon."

"I really do appreciate you agreeing to come with me to the production company."

"It will be interesting to visit that part of my life again and see if I remember how it works."

"I can't quite imagine you in a suit working in a city," Yvonne confessed.

"I was a different person back then. I was still trying to impress my father. Eventually I learned that would never happen, so I stopped trying and walked away from it all."

"Was it hard to do that? Did you miss anything?"

"It wasn't as easy as I'd thought it would be." He hesitated. "I disappointed some people along the way—people who'd helped my career, and who supported me despite my father. I didn't make my decision and take the time to wind things up properly—I just up and left one day. That wasn't fair."

"Sometimes you have to break things to get to be the person you need to be," Yvonne said. "That's what my ex, Paul, told me anyway."

Rio glanced down at her. "Did he break you?"

"At first I thought he had. But, as time went by, I realized a weight had been lifted from my shoulders and that I was finally free to be myself."

Rio frowned. "He stopped you from being yourself? I can't imagine that."

"Paul didn't like me being too bossy, or opinionated, or too . . . determined. He wanted a wife who would put him and his needs first." She paused. "Not that there is anything wrong with that if both partners agree."

"He sounds a lot like my father."

"For a long time after he left, I felt like it *was* all my fault. That I'd signed up for that life with him, and then I'd changed and wanted more. He said that when we moved back to California I became more demanding and argumentative. Maybe I did. Maybe when I reached my home state I felt more sure of myself than I did in France."

"According to my mother, marriages are, or should be, a series of compromises where both parties are willing to step up or step back in order to keep the other partner happy."

"Your mother sounds a lot like Ruth Morgan."

"Yeah. I think they'd get on like a house on fire." His fingers trailed over her shoulder until they cupped her cheek. "You are an amazing person. Paul was a fool not to recognize that in you, and appreciate your strength."

The quiet sincerity of his words sank into her soul, and she hurriedly tried to keep things light.

"You don't think I'm bossy and opinionated?"

"In my eyes, those are some of your plus points."

"Then what don't you like about me?"

A smile kicked up the corner of his mouth. "Your determination and resolve?"

"You mean my resolve not to get involved with you?"

"That's the one. For the record, I also admire your extreme adulting skills." He glanced out of the window. "We're almost at the hotel. Make sure you've got all your stuff."

After settling Yvonne in her room, Rio decided to walk to his mother's hotel, which was on Stockton and, according to the map on his cell, not that far away. Sitting in a plane and a cab up close and personal with the woman of his dreams meant he needed some exercise to clear his head. It was supposed to be warm in the city, but the shadows from the higher buildings sometimes made the streets below both cold and dark.

It was amazing how quickly he adapted to the rules of the city again, speeding up his pace, dodging oncoming pedestrians, and crossing the busy roads where the trolley car cables beneath the ground hummed and rattled their own unique San Francisco song. He'd spent his last six months in the United States working in the city before he'd bailed.

Despite that, he hadn't lied when he'd told Yvonne he didn't know the city well. When he'd worked for his father, he'd barely taken any time off, and regularly spent eighteen-hour days at his desk or in meetings. He shuddered at the thought of returning to that life now. Sure, he'd earned a fortune, but he'd been so busy he'd never had time to enjoy the money or even have a social life.

Risking his neck on a bull was way more exciting and required every drop of his courage, ability, and luck. Crushing business competitors and dirty tricks had never sat well with him. His father had jeered at him for having a conscience, but he didn't regret that part of him at all—the honest part his father had tried, and failed, to break.

He entered the fancy lobby of the Ritz-Carlton and made his way to the concierge. Within minutes, he was on his way up in the elevator to one of the penthouse suites at the top of the building. His father must really want something badly if he was willing to treat his first and most hated wife so well.

"*Meu filo*. My son!"

His mother, Isabelle, was waiting for him at the door of the suite, her arms flung wide. For a moment, he allowed himself to be held, petted, and fussed over, even though these days he had to bend down to receive his blessings. She smelled of her favorite Chanel perfume and home.

"*Mamae.*"

He kissed the top of her head, and she took his hand, urging him inside, asking him a million questions and not bothering to wait for a single answer.

"Slow down," he joked. "Speak English—I've forgotten my Portuguese."

She took him through to the sitting room, where a coffee table was covered with opened plastic boxes.

"I've brought you *pacoquita* and *pao de queijo*. You're

looking thin. Sit down, and eat something, for the love of God."

"Cheese and candy? I love you, *Mamae*."

After years of his father's cold remoteness, his mother's dramatic tendencies had taken a while to get used to again, but had definitely enlivened his adult years. She wasn't the kind of woman who held things in. If she had a problem, she'd let you know, which was one of the reasons why his early childhood had been such a screaming match.

She brought him a cup of coffee, a glass of water, a napkin, a plate, and silverware.

"Eat."

He knew it was pointless to resist so he meekly ate a few of the treats that had survived the trip from Brazil. To his surprise, he was suddenly hungry. The homemade food and candy reminded him of his mother's windswept ranch and the gauchos who, much to his mother's horror, had taught him how to become a bull rider.

He suspected they'd thought he'd fall off once and go running home crying to his mother, but that hadn't happened. From the first moment on the back of a bull, he'd known he wanted to be good at it—wanted to follow in the footsteps of the famous Brazilian riders like Adriano Moraes and Silvano Alves who had gone and conquered what became the PBR.

His mother sat down on the couch opposite him, and clasped her hands to her bosom. Her style was firmly stuck in the Joan Collins *Dynasty* era. She was currently wearing a flowing pink satin robe over matching pajamas. She was also a fan of big hair.

"So, I will practice my English with you before I have to speak to your father." She smiled encouragingly. "Now, have you anything important to tell me?"

"Well, I did win that PBR world title." Rio grinned at her.

She reached over to pat his knee. "And I was very excited for you, and boasted to *all* my friends about how clever you are. They were very impressed. Anything else?"

"More important than that?"

"Yes, like have you met a nice woman yet?" She pretended to pout. "I'm the only woman I know without a single grandchild."

Rio raised an eyebrow. "You think I want to get married after watching what happened with you and my father?"

She waved his objections away, making her many gold bracelets jangle. "Don't be silly, Rio, darling. That's all in the past. I survived it, and so can you."

Sometimes he wasn't so sure about that. He'd never had her airy view of life. "But you married another idiot."

"True, but I did have an ulterior motive for that marriage."

"What?" He put his cup down on the table.

"Getting you back." Her smile was triumphant. "How do you think I was able to take your father to court? Arturio, the old sweetheart, funded everything for me."

"I didn't realize that." Rio frowned.

"Believe me, he was happy to help."

"So that wasn't the reason you got divorced?"

"No! He was in love with his secretary, poor woman. She'd waited years for his first wife to die, and then I appeared and spoiled her plans. When I realized that Arturio really did care for her, I had a chat with her, and—"

"Wait," Rio interrupted. "You chatted to your husband's *lover*?"

Isabelle opened her brown eyes wide at him. "Well, what else was I supposed to *do*, darling? It was silly for all of us to be unhappy when there was an easy solution. She got the man she loved. I got my darling Josephina and a decent divorce settlement, which helped me continue to fight your father every time he tried something devious to stop me from seeing you."

Rio shook his head. "You are incorrigible."

She raised her chin. "I certainly don't give up on those I love. Now, are you *quite* certain that you haven't met anyone new?"

Rio hesitated, wondering whether it was wise to venture into the whirling maelstrom of his mother's romantic fantasies. "I have a friend in town with me who would love to take you shopping if you have time."

"A male friend?"

"No, a female one." Ignoring his mother's hopeful expression, he continued on. "Her name is Yvonne Payet, and she runs the French bakery in Morgantown near where I'm currently staying."

"With that bad boy HW, yes?"

"That's the one."

"He is such a charming boy, and so handsome!" His mother sighed. "He quite makes me wish I was ten years younger."

"Try twenty, and you might be on to something." Rio grinned. "And by the way, haven't I told you not to ogle my friends?"

"Age is just a number, Rio." She patted her curly hair. "I can't help it if all your friends think I am beautiful."

He and his mother had an unconventional relationship. Seeing as she'd had him so young, she acted and looked more like his older sister than his mother and sometimes he treated her accordingly.

"You are beautiful, *Mamae*. I think you'll like Yvonne a lot."

"Then tell her I would be delighted to accept her very kind offer. In fact, why don't you ask her to have dinner with us tonight so that I can tell her myself?"

"She's only just arrived in the city. I think she'll be too tired to come out tonight," Rio said.

"How about lunch with us tomorrow?"

"She can't do that either. She has a business lunch, and then a meeting, which I'm going to attend with her."

"Then let's do dinner in the evening."

Rio resigned himself to the inevitable. "I'll ask her, okay?"

"This Yvonne is smart, then? Is she pretty?"

"I think so."

His mother beamed at him. "You like her, don't you?"

"We're good friends."

"She's married?"

"No."

"Then you cannot be friends," Isabelle stated. "Men and women are not *capable* of being friends except when they are old and gray, and even the idea of sex has disappeared."

Rio rolled his eyes. "Don't be so old fashioned. I have many friends of both sexes. It doesn't mean I want to jump into bed with them."

"You have many friends because you are a delightful well-brought-up man. They *stay* friends because you don't believe in love." She fixed him with her fondest stare. "Don't argue with your mother. It is the truth—we both know it—and it means that I will never get to be a grandmother."

One of the interior doors in the suite opened and a voice came floating out.

"Wow, thanks, Mom. What about me? I might give you a grandchild or two one day."

"Josie!"

"Hey, *mano!*"

"*E ai? Como vai?*" Rio jumped to his feet as Josephina, his half sister, came into the room.

He swung her up into a big hug, lifting her off her feet and twirling her around while she squeaked at him to put her down. She'd been born when he was seven, during his mother's brief marriage to the sainted but ancient Arturio. When he'd finally been allowed to visit his family in Brazil, he'd fallen in love with his tiny sister and, despite the usual sibling moments, had remained her slave ever since.

She thumped him on the shoulder. "Put me down, you great big lug."

He obliged, but kept an arm around her, monitoring all the changes since he'd seen her last. She wasn't very tall, and had their mother's black hair, and her father's blue eyes.

"I hear congratulations are in order, *mana.*" He kissed her cheek. "Double major, eh? Now what are you going to do with all that knowledge?"

"I'm going to copy my big brother, dump my Ivy League education down the toilet, and run away to the circus."

He pretended to sigh. "No circuses to run to anymore. Maybe you should get a real job."

"Like you have?" She grinned at him. "Staying put on a bull for a measly eight seconds while flapping your arm around your head?"

He shrugged. "I enjoy it."

"That's because at heart you're an exhibitionist like Mom."

"Maybe," he admitted. "Did you come with Mom for moral support, or are you looking for a job out here?"

"Both, really." She sat beside him on the couch. "I was also thinking of coming to visit my brother first, and taking a couple of weeks off."

"That would be great. Did Mom tell you I'm staying with the Morgans?"

"Yes. How's hot HW?"

"Getting hot and heavy with another woman."

She sighed. "Typical."

Rio mock frowned. "And he's too old for you, anyway."

"He's the same age as you."

"Exactly. None of my friends are good boyfriend material."

"But I bet there are a few hot cowboys on that ranch?"

Rio groaned. "Don't you get enough of that at home with Mom?"

"They've all known me since I was born." She smiled. "They treat me just like you do. I need fresh blood."

"I'll check in with Chase and January Morgan, and see if they can squeeze you in."

"Nice." She pecked him on the cheek. "As long as I don't have to share a room with you, I'm not picky as to where I stay."

"I'll talk to them after dinner," Rio promised. "I'm sure they can put you up in the barn or something."

"Very funny." She made a face at him. "Are you looking forward to seeing your father? Mom isn't. Sometimes I'm glad the Sainted Arturio is dead."

"He was a good man," Rio said diplomatically.

"He was an old man who certainly didn't expect to

have a new baby when his oldest child was almost the same age as Mom. I think my arrival hastened his demise."

"I cannot help being irresistible," Isabelle chimed in. "He fell in love with me at first sight and pursued me for months."

Rio nodded at his sister. "That is actually true."

"So *are* you looking forward to seeing your father?"

Rio sighed. One thing his sister shared with their mother was her persistence. "No, of course I'm not."

"What do you think he wants after all this time?"

"I have no idea."

"When are we seeing him?"

"Tomorrow morning at his offices," Isabelle said. "And you aren't coming, Josie."

She pouted. "Are you sure? I'd quite like to meet him."

"No, you wouldn't." Rio quashed that idea immediately. "He isn't susceptible to charm and intelligence."

"But he does like them young," his mother chimed in. "I think his new wife is just out of her teens, and Graham is over fifty."

Rio shuddered, and Josie made a face as Isabelle went off to the small kitchen to brew some more coffee.

Josie leaned in and lowered her voice. "Ugh. Maybe I don't want to meet him after all. He might take a fancy to me. I'll just spend my time touring the city and looking for jobs instead."

"Good idea." Rio caught her eye. "Trust me, you really don't want to get involved with this."

"But I'm worried about Mom."

"I'll take care of her. I promise you that. Whatever happens, she'll be safe and well on her ranch, with his money or without it. Nothing can take that away from her."

Josie grabbed his hand and squeezed it hard. "Thanks, big brother."

"Nothing to thank me for. Think of it as payback for all the years my father made her life miserable."

"What are you two muttering about over there?" Isabelle inquired as she came back with the pot of coffee. "Is he telling you about his girlfriend?"

"What girlfriend?" Josie fixed him with an accusing stare, and Rio sighed. He could only hope that, when Yvonne did get to meet his inquisitive family, she wouldn't regret it.

Chapter Ten

"Thank you."

Rio tipped the guy who'd brought his dry-cleaned suit up to the suite, and let him out of the door. There was no sign of his mother or sister yet, and breakfast had been delivered ten minutes ago. If they didn't appear soon, he'd go bang on their doors and threaten to eat everything.

That usually worked.

He took the new suit through to his bedroom, removed the plastic cover, and hung it in the bathroom to catch some of the remaining condensation. He hoped it would fit. After taking up bull riding professionally, he'd changed the definition and bulk of his muscle distribution. He'd hate to look like some kind of muscleman bursting out of his shirt like the Hulk. Although, the idea of popping a few buttons and turning green in front of his father did hold some appeal. . . .

After a good breakfast, for which his mother and yawning sister eventually joined him, he sent a text to Yvonne confirming he'd meet her at the production company's offices on Market. She replied with a smiley face. Even that was enough to help calm his nerves as he approached the meeting with his father.

Predictably, his mother was late, but as he'd had to struggle into his suit, and remember how to knot his tie, he hadn't been ready too early himself. He caught a glimpse of his reflection in the hall mirror and didn't even recognize himself without his cowboy hat.

"You look very handsome, Rio."

His mother came into the entrance hall, her handbag over her arm, her coat unbuttoned. She was wearing high heels Yvonne would probably approve of, but still barely reached his chin.

"So do you." Rio offered her his arm. "Now, remember, don't lose your temper and let me handle this, okay?"

She sighed. "I'll try, but Graham does have the ability to get under my skin."

"Which is why you'll let me do the talking," Rio said firmly. "Now, do you have the address for his new office ready?"

The offices of Howatch International occupied a whole floor, providing spectacular views over the city and the Bay Bridge beyond. The receptionist led them along a long hallway, past glass-sided cubicles, and meeting rooms that made Rio break out in a cold sweat. The place smelled like bad coffee and money, so not a lot had changed.

Rio stood back to allow his mother to precede him into the end office, where his father's executive assistant stood to greet them.

"Good morning, Mrs. Howatch, Mr. Howatch."

"That's Mrs. and Mr. Martinez," Rio replied. "Good morning."

Looking slightly flummoxed, the young man went to knock on the inner door.

"Mr. Howatch? Your visitors have arrived."

"Thank you. Send them in."

Again, Rio ushered his mother in front of him, aware that she was already tense, and not feeling much better himself. He was reminded of when he'd been a small boy cowering next to her on the couch while his father yelled at them both for some minor transgression. Sometimes things had gotten even worse. . . .

"Isabelle. How good of you to come."

"Graham."

His father came around his desk, a pleasant smile on his face. He wore his usual bespoke, made-in-London pinstripe suit with a plain tie and a pale blue shirt. His hair was almost as grey as his eyes now, and he'd lost some weight. Rio had never looked much like him, and had fervently prayed at one point that he wasn't really Graham's son. Only the relative lightness of Rio's skin compared to his mother's revealed his shared heritage with his father.

Graham took Isabelle's hand, and leaned in to kiss her on both cheeks before turning to Rio.

"Son."

Rio nodded, but didn't say anything.

"You're both looking well. Please take a seat. My admin will bring us some refreshments. What would you prefer?"

"Coffee would be fine." Rio finally found his voice.

He was surprised his father's lawyers weren't already present. The man usually never moved a step without them. With an empire spanning the entertainment and food service industry, he was usually involved in litigation for something. The absence of even one lawyer made Rio even more suspicious of his father's motives.

After the coffee arrived and was dispensed, Graham returned to sit behind his desk. He drew two folders from the stack to his left, and placed them in front of him.

"I have decided to make some adjustments to my current holdings, and as some of your income derives from shares in these companies, Isabelle, I will need your permission to realign your portfolio."

"Why did you need to see my mother in order to do that?" Rio asked. "You could have asked her over the phone."

"He's right, Graham." Isabelle nodded at Rio. "As you say in America, what's the catch?"

His father didn't smile. "I need your signature on a few documents. Knowing how much you hate technology, I decided it would be simpler if you came to sign them in person rather than me attempting to get classified documents delivered to the middle of nowhere."

"Sao Paulo is hardly that," Isabelle protested.

"She's not signing anything until we've had a chance to read it through," Rio said.

"Naturally." His father looked over at him. "You might have decided to throw away your career, but I certainly didn't raise a fool."

"You didn't raise me. I had a succession of nannies, your young wives, and boarding school to do that for me," Rio said. "Are we done?"

"Not quite." Graham folded his hands together on his desk, and looked down at them. "I would like to invite you both, and your daughter, Josephina, to dinner with me tonight."

Isabelle and Rio shared a quick, startled glance.

"Why?" Rio asked slowly. "What do you have to gain from that?"

"Is it so difficult to believe I might wish to spend some time in your company?"

"Yeah, actually, it is," Rio replied evenly.

"Isabelle?" Graham looked directly at his ex-wife. "Please?"

Knowing both his mother's tender heart, and her extreme love of drama, Rio wasn't surprised when she capitulated.

"Oh, I'll come then." She sighed. "But Rio doesn't have to if he doesn't want to."

Like he'd let his mother walk into that lion's den without him.

He hesitated. "We do have a prior engagement with Yvonne, Mom."

"Yvonne?" Graham asked.

"Yvonne Payet. She's a friend of Rio's—a good friend," Isabelle said.

"Then please, bring her along, too." Graham sat back. "My admin will give you the address."

Rio went across to take the folders from his father's hand. "Thank you."

Graham didn't quite let go of them. "I'd prefer the papers to be signed before you leave town."

"That depends on what they say, and whether my mother needs to speak to her lawyers," Rio said.

"I have no desire to cheat your mother out of anything."

"That'll be a first." Rio jerked the folders out of his father's fingers.

"It's a shame that seven years away from civilized society have obviously tarnished your manners, son."

"You think this is being uncivil?" Rio met his father's gaze head on. "You have no idea."

"Rio." Isabelle put her hand on his arm. "Let's go."

With a sharp nod at his father, Rio acceded to his mother's unspoken plea and left the room with her. He still needed to process what had just happened. The non-event somehow didn't ring true, or was his father right, and had his ability to behave in a civilized manner disappeared?

No. Graham Howatch was a devious snake who could not be trusted. He'd had that lesson rammed into his head at a young age, and he wasn't going to forget it.

He waited while Isabelle got the details for the dinner party, and then walked her back to the elevators. After checking his cell, he realized he would probably have time to meet Yvonne for lunch after all, but decided he'd better stay with his mother and at least make an attempt to go through the paperwork with her.

"Graham looked thinner, didn't he?" Isabelle said. "But still quite distinguished."

"For a despicable human being, I suppose he did."

"Oh, Rio. Don't be so hard on him."

"*Me*?" He looked down at his mother. "You once threatened to cut his throat, and bury him in the desert so the coyotes could dig him up and eat his bones."

"I was *annoyed* with him!"

"You were in a court of law! Why do you think he ended up getting full custody of me? Nothing's changed, Mom. He's just better at hiding it."

She bit her lip. "I suppose you are right. But, maybe he's just lonely, and wants to reconnect with his family?"

"Mom," Rio said gently. "I know you love happy

endings, but this isn't one of your soaps. Dad treated you appallingly. He had an affair right under your nose with my *nanny*!"

"Yes, he did, but I didn't behave very well either."

"You were a saint compared to him."

"Yes, but still, I was very young, and I didn't always—"

"Shall we go?" Rio interrupted her.

The elevator doors opened, and they got in, and were whisked down to the lobby. Outside, the sun was shining, and the roar of the city traffic permeated even the thick glass doors. Rio contemplated getting a taxi versus persuading his mother to walk a block or two.

"Please listen to me." Isabelle put her hand on his arm, and he looked down at her.

"What is it?"

"I *wasn't* a saint, Rio. I behaved very badly and refused to compromise with Graham about *anything*. That's why I lost you. I'll regret that for the rest of my life."

"You *weren't* at fault," Rio said firmly. "You were played by a master. How else were you supposed to behave when he had all the power on his side?"

She sighed. "That's very sweet of you, darling, but I wasn't a fool. I knew what I was doing when I married him. I thought being beautiful meant I could have everything I wanted in life. I was spoiled rotten, and that should've ended when I had a child."

Rio looked over her head toward the street outside. "Can we talk about this some other time? I'd hate for one of Graham's minions to overhear us."

"You never want to talk about it." Isabelle patted his arm. "But you are right. We really should be getting on."

As they approached the exit, a uniformed man sitting by the door sprang to his feet.

"Mrs. Martinez? I'm one of Mr. Howatch's drivers. He told me to offer you a ride back to your hotel."

Isabelle smiled in delight and spun around to face Rio.

"That would be lovely, wouldn't it, darling? How kind of Graham to think about us."

Rio sighed, and followed his mother and the driver outside. He didn't trust his father at all, but he wasn't stupid enough to antagonize his mother and this would save her a long walk or a long wait for a cab.

Was she right? Had her behavior contributed to the breakdown of his parents' marriage? He'd always hated his father and idolized his mother, but was there more to it than he'd imagined? He shrugged off the thought. That was the trouble with seeing his father. The man looked so innocent that it was almost impossible to believe what a monster he could become when he was thwarted.

After all these years, Isabelle might be willing to forgive Graham and accept her share of the blame. Rio still wasn't sure if he would ever be in that position. He'd never told his mother how bad things had gotten once she'd left. He'd been afraid that she'd get so angry that she'd literally go for his father's throat, and then he'd lose her forever.

He'd go through the documents with her during lunch, and then leave her to make her decision. After that, he'd go and meet Yvonne. With the mood he was in, he wasn't going to let anyone give her shit.

Yvonne glanced at her cell, and worried her lip. It was almost two o'clock, and there was still no sign of Rio. He hadn't texted her since his initial confirmation that he'd meet her at the Tasty Treats Productions offices. Which was where she was now, sitting outside the conference room, waiting. . . .

"Yvonne?"

She looked up at the man striding toward her and did a slow double take.

"*Rio?*"

He halted in front of her. His usual smile was absent. "Sorry, I couldn't get a cab. Am I late?"

She pointed at his chest. "You're wearing a suit!"

He looked down at himself. "Yeah. Is that a problem?"

"No, you just look . . ." She tried to frame words. "*Delicious.*"

His eyebrow went up. "Better than my cowboy look?"

"Just different." She rose to her feet and walked a slow circle around him. The suit was very dark with a tiny pinstripe, and he'd paired it with a white shirt and grey tie. "It fits you like a glove."

He shrugged, creasing the fine wool over his broad shoulders. "I was just glad it still fit me." His gaze traveled over her. "You're looking pretty good yourself."

She fiddled with the floppy bow of the white silk blouse she'd worn underneath her pale blue pantsuit. "It feels weird not to be dressed in black."

He grimaced. "You and me both."

"Did you cut your hair as well?"

Now he was looking embarrassed. "No, you're just not used to seeing me without my hat. How did lunch go?"

She glanced around the empty space. "Okay, I think. It was just Priscilla and Greg. Their boss and the other members of the team are going to be in this meeting. They are already in there, talking things through."

"Okay." He sat down and patted the seat next to her. "So what do you want to get out of this?"

She stared down at him. "What do you mean?"

"Money, fame, a line of your own cooking products? What's important to you?"

She blinked at him. "Wow, put you in a city, and in a suit, and you become a totally different person, don't you?"

"I'm just trying to make you think about what you want. Having some kind of game plan before we go in there is always useful."

"I think I'd like the money, and the business opportunities," Yvonne said cautiously. "I'm not sure about the fame bit."

"Unfortunately, it often comes with the territory." His smile finally emerged, and it was so full of sympathy and warmth that she wanted to grab him and kiss him stupid. "But we can talk about that, and put certain caveats in place if need be."

"Are you okay?" Yvonne asked.

"I'm fine. Why?"

"You look a bit fierce."

"This is my game face."

She sensed it was more than that; he was tenser than she'd ever seen him before.

"How did it go with your father?" Yvonne asked.

"How about we talk about that later, and keep this discussion about you, and what you want to achieve in this meeting?" he countered.

Okay, so he was definitely pissed about something, but it wasn't her. She'd never seen him look so determined before. It was interesting to see his more competitive side coming out to play. For the first time, she could see why he'd become a world champion.

"Do you want me to ask questions, or would you prefer to handle everything yourself and have me just listen, and give you feedback later?" Rio asked.

"If I look like I'm floundering, or not asking the right questions, please feel free to join in."

"Got it." He took out a pen from his inside pocket. "One last piece of advice. Don't show your hand too early. Make them work for this, okay?"

She was just about to reply when the door into the conference room opened and Priscilla came out.

"Hi, Rio! So glad you could join us!" She beckoned them both over. "Come on in."

Yvonne glanced over at Rio as they waited for the elevator.

"You were awesome."

He winked at her. "You weren't too shabby your-self."

"Do you have time to come back to my hotel and talk this through?" Yvonne asked. "I've got *so* many questions. I'll even buy you dinner if I keep you too long."

"Sure." He hesitated. "Dinner might be tricky."

The elevator arrived, and they got in.

"Why's that?"

"As my mom and sister would love to go shopping with you, I was planning on asking you to come to dinner with *us* this evening so you could meet them."

"That sounds like fun."

"Which, it would have been." He sighed. "The thing is, my father invited us over to his place."

She had to admit to a throb of disappointment. "Oh well, I'll meet your mom tomorrow anyway, when we go shopping."

"My father invited you to dinner as well," Rio said. "My mom made the mistake of mentioning you, and he suggested we bring you along."

She searched his face, noting the lines of tension around his mouth that made him look older and harder.

"I'm quite willing to come, but only if it's okay with you." She paused. "I get the impression that you and your father aren't 'sit down together and have a meal' kind of people."

"We're not. But my mom wants to go, and I can't let her deal with him alone."

"She is a grown woman who can make her own decisions, Rio," Yvonne pointed out as they walked out of the lobby, and into the street.

"Yeah, I know I'm being overprotective." His smile was crooked. "But she's my *mamae* and I love her." He grimaced. "And he wants to meet my sister, Josie, too, which he's never done before, and she's dying to go."

"Sounds like you're not the only determined one in the family." Yvonne turned to face him and cupped his cheek. "I'm fine to come if you want me to. At least then I'll have met your whole family in one hit."

"True," he acknowledged, turning his head until his lips met her thumb and he kissed it. "Let's walk back to your hotel, shall we?"

"Easy for you to say in your flat shoes," she grumbled.

"Hey, I've been wearing cowboy boots for the last five years. My feet are in agony." He took her hand and set off. The sunlight was dazzling, and the streets were crowded, but it didn't seem to faze him.

"I thought you said you didn't know the city well." Yvonne had to yell above the traffic to be heard.

"I know the business district, but that's about it." He glanced up at the tall buildings surrounding them. "Jeez, it's hot. I wish I had my hat. In fact, I wish I was back on the ranch, period."

They arrived at her hotel, and went straight up to her room. She pointed him in the direction of the coffee maker, and went to freshen up in the bathroom. She carefully hung up her pantsuit and blouse, and put on her yoga pants and a baggy T-shirt, leaving her feet bare. She'd have to get dressed up again for dinner, but she might as well be comfortable for a few hours.

The smell of coffee greeted her as she entered the room, as well as the sight of Rio, shirtsleeves rolled up to the elbow. He'd draped his tie and jacket over the back of one of the chairs.

"Take your shoes off if you want," Yvonne invited him.

He glanced down at his feet. "I might take you up on that, but I'm scared once they come off I won't be able to get them back on again."

"Hey, take everything off." She winked at him, relief at having gotten through the meeting making her giddy and maybe a bit flirty. "I wouldn't complain."

"But then we wouldn't get any work done."

"True." She pouted. "Naked meetings aren't really a thing, are they?"

"Maybe only in Scandinavia."

He brought two mugs of coffee over to the desk, and pulled up a second chair. "I took notes, so fire away with your questions, and I'll see what I've got."

"Well, firstly, they seem to be moving pretty fast on this. Is that normal?"

"No. Shows can be in production for years, but I did some research last night. Apparently, one of their regular shows is coming off the air because the lead couple is going through a nasty divorce. The producers don't want all that emotional stuff spilling out and overshadowing the show. They need a quick and cheap replacement, and I guess that might be you."

"*Cheap*?" Yvonne raised an eyebrow.

He grinned. "I meant inexpensive. You could never be cheap."

"I suppose that makes sense." Yvonne nodded. "But does that put us in a better or worse bargaining position?"

"You're a newbie, so they won't be paying you anywhere near what an established star would be getting, which they'll like, but you could also be a complete flop, so there is some element of risk."

"Gee, thanks."

"When I say *you*, I mean the concept presented in the show. They might go for a particular angle that just doesn't work with the viewers."

"Like what?"

"Like a 'city-girl cake maker in small town full of hilarious yokels who don't know one end of a croissant from the other' vibe, or something like that."

"Oh, I see what you mean." Yvonne considered her next question. "How will we know what tack they are going to take before they start filming?"

"That's a great question and a difficult one to answer. From what I remember, they don't usually *know* what angle they are going to take, beyond choosing the presenters, and the venue, and making a few general assumptions. They usually like to see some audience reaction first. But sometimes they do have an agenda and get things wrong, or try and force the action to go a certain way."

"I wouldn't like that. Is there anything you can put in the contract which says I have control over the final content?"

"That's almost impossible to get." He made a face. "It's certainly something we can talk about." He typed in a note on his cell. "I know a couple of people who might have a better idea about how that might go. I'll get in touch with them tomorrow."

"They didn't really go into specifics about money at all, did they?"

"Not yet. Greg said he's going to bring John, the boss of the parent company, and Sara, the finance person, out to Morgantown in the next few weeks to get a feel for the place." He checked his notes again. "Then they'll have to draw up a profit and loss statement, discuss timing, reimbursements, and all the legal stuff to make sure they are good to go."

Yvonne leaned back in her chair and stretched, pointing her toes and arching her back. "This is way too complicated, you know?"

"Not if we break it down into manageable steps," Rio reminded her as he helped himself to more coffee. "And if it's something you want to do."

She straightened up and stared at him. "Do *you* think I should go ahead?"

"Yeah." His brown eyes narrowed in amusement. "Why do you think I'm sitting here helping you out?"

"Because you like me?"

"Maybe I just want to get rich, and run off with all your money?"

"Like you need it," Yvonne scoffed.

"Some people are never satisfied."

"But you're not one of those people."

He raised an eyebrow. "What makes you say that?"

"Because you've already walked away from one lucrative career. I don't see money as a motivator for you."

"Hey, I'm motivated. After I left my father's business, I had to work out a way to keep my mom at her

sn't far to his father's new place, so they wouldn't
te.

e wished he'd taken Yvonne up on her offer of a
ver because something about being in a city always
de him feel grimy. But he figured that if he got
ed they might not be going anywhere ever again.
e'd looked glorious today in her blue pantsuit with
r hair piled high on the top of her head, displaying
e elegant length of her neck and her beautiful face.

"Sorry, I took so long, Rio. Can you help me with
e clasp?"

He looked up from his cell to see her backing toward
im, one hand grasping the ties of her dress. For the
first time ever, he was completely bereft of speech. She
wore a clinging black dress with a halter neck that left
most of her back exposed.

"Rio?" She tried to look over her shoulder. "It's just
a hook and eye and pearl-button thingy, but I can't get
my fingers around it."

"Sure."

He swallowed hard and approached her. She smelled
like a flower garden underplayed by the subtle scent
of vanilla that never seemed to leave her. She bent her
neck, offering herself, and he fought the urge to kiss
is way down her spine.

"I've got it. You can let go."

Jeez, his fingers were trembling so much he almost
uldn't fasten the tiny hook and eye. The pearl button
s even harder.

He stepped back before he did something foolish
 fall to his knees and worship her.

Thanks." She turned around, and he was treated

ranch if my father decided to stop payir
the bills."

"Did he stop?"

Rio paused, an arrested look on his fac
didn't."

"Why does that surprise you?" Yvonne ask

"Because I hadn't thought about it befo
father *had* threatened my mother's financial
I would've come back to work for him imme
with my tail between my legs." He put down his
cup. "Why didn't he do that?"

"Maybe he didn't want to upset your mother.

"He spent three years fighting her for sole cus
bribed judges, and used every dirty trick in the b
to show my mother in a bad light so she wouldn't e
get to see me again."

"Maybe he's changed."

"You sound like my mom." He shook his head. "I
can't see it, myself. And, anyway, we're supposed to be
talking about you."

He was good at that—redirecting the conversation
away from the personal. She'd noticed it before, an
here in San Francisco, where he had to deal with
parents in person, it was even more apparent.
where did the truth lie? Was his Mom a saint an
dad the devil? In her experience, things were
that simple. . . .

Rio checked the time, and waited for Yv
come out of the bedroom. They were goin
the suite in the Ritz-Carlton, where Yvonne c
his mom and sister while he got changed

to the front view, which was not as swooping as the back, but still spectacular. "Are you drooling?"

He wiped an unsteady hand over his mouth. "Probably."

"Good." Her mischievous smile flashed out. "This is my favorite dress."

"It's rapidly becoming my favorite, too," Rio murmured.

"I really need better shoes, but I couldn't get any more pairs in my bag."

He looked down at her black, spiked-heel sandals. "They look pretty good to me," he said hoarsely.

"You're obviously a lost cause." She did a pirouette in front of the mirror, making her short skirt ripple around her. "Do you think your family will approve?"

"I don't care."

She gave him an exasperated, but fond look. "Are you ready to go?"

"I've been ready for the past half an hour."

And, if he didn't leave pretty damn soon he'd be tearing that dress off her, throwing her over his shoulder, and taking her to bed. Considering the evening ahead of him, that idea sounded better with every second.

She picked up her wrap and purse, and headed for the door.

"Come on, then. I can't wait to meet your mom."

Chapter Eleven

Isabelle Martinez was a delight. Yvonne could easily see whom Rio had inherited his charm from. And his half sister, Josie, was funny as hell and super smart, even if she delighted in telling Yvonne all the horrendous things Rio had ever done to her.

Yvonne was sitting with them while Rio got changed, and he was totally unaware of what was going on. Yvonne enjoyed every second of the gentle teasing, and filed a few things away for future reference.

"So, Yvonne, you run a coffee shop and patisserie, yes?" Isabelle asked.

"That's right. I trained in France, and then came back home to set up my own business."

"That was very brave of you," Isabelle said approvingly. She had a delightful, lilting accent. "And why did you pick Morgantown? Do you have family there?"

"No, I just fell in love with the place. When I realized there was no eatery catering to the locals and tourists, I knew I'd found my home."

"And you've been successful?" Josie looked up from her cell. "I know how hard it is to start a new restaurant."

"It was something of a struggle to begin with," Yvonne

admitted. "We didn't have the money to pay any staff, so at first we did all the baking, and all the serving. It was exhausting."

"We? Did you have a business partner?" Josie asked.

"Well, yes and no. I was married when I first came back, so I started the café with my husband." She fixed on a bright smile. "But that didn't work out, so he went home to France just before our official opening, and I kept plugging away at it."

Isabelle's eyes softened. "That must have been very difficult for you."

"It certainly didn't help. I was lucky enough to make some good friends in Morgantown who helped me find new staff and keep going."

"Where is your husband now?"

"My ex returned to live in Paris. He's a chef. We met at pastry school."

"You are divorced then?"

"Yes." Yvonne mentally crossed her fingers and helped herself to more coffee. At least she hoped she was divorced. When she saw Paul, she'd make darned sure of it.

"Good." Isabelle clapped her hands and leaned closer. "And what do you think of my lovely son?"

"He's been very kind to me," Yvonne replied. "I will certainly miss him when he leaves the ranch."

"I think he'll miss you, too. You are the first woman he has ever introduced me to."

"Really?" Yvonne tried to conceal a smile. From the hopeful expression on Isabelle's face, she was attempting a little unsubtle matchmaking. "Maybe that's because you're based in Brazil, and Rio hasn't been able to bring anyone down there to meet you."

Isabelle waved that idea away with a flick of her

beringed fingers. "If a woman was important to him, he would bring her to my ranch."

Josie cleared her throat. "Mom, stop fishing. It's embarrassing." She winked at Yvonne. "She's just desperate for grandchildren."

"Oh God, not that again." Rio entered the conversation, and Yvonne turned to look at him.

He'd abandoned the suit in favor of his usual PBR shirt, black jeans, and cowboy boots. His hat twirled through his fingers. She couldn't decide which Rio she preferred. They were both pretty hot. But which one was the authentic version? Could a man really separate out his life so cleanly?

"Don't listen to either of them," Rio recommended as he came to sit beside her on the couch. "They just love making stuff up about me."

"Actually, your mom was telling me how great you were." She tried to look innocent. "I should've known not to believe her."

"Hey." His smile was for her alone. "You already *know* how great I am."

Her first answer was not fit to be uttered in front of his mother so she settled for an enigmatic smile.

"You're not that bad."

Josie chuckled. "Yeah. I can get behind that statement. Wow, bro, you really know how to charm the ladies." She glanced at the clock. "After all your primping, are you ready to leave now? I can't wait to meet your father, Rio."

"Sure, let's go."

Yvonne noticed Rio wasn't looking quite as thrilled with the idea as his sister. He opened the door of the suite and stood back to allow all the womenfolk to go past him.

"Are you okay?" Yvonne murmured as they headed for the elevator walking behind his chattering mother and sister.

"I'll survive." He looked like he was bracing himself for a storm. "He doesn't scare me anymore."

She linked her arm through his and patted his biceps. "Good. Because you are a remarkable person, and if he gets into anything with you, I'll be the first to stand up, and tell him a few truths."

He paused to look down at her, his brown eyes crinkling at the corners. "You'd do that for me?"

"Sure. I like you."

"Yeah?"

His slow smile made her knees wobble.

He bent down, his hat shielding his face from his mother and kissed her. "Thank you."

"You're welcome," Yvonne breathed.

They went down in the elevator, and Rio was just about to find a taxi when a uniformed man came toward them.

"Mr. Martinez? The boss told me to come back and collect you all this evening. I hope that's okay."

Isabelle rushed forward to take the chauffeur's hand. "How lovely to see you again, Dominic! How is your wife today? Did she have the baby?"

"Not yet, Mrs. Martinez . . ."

Rio glanced down at Yvonne with a wry smile as Isabelle went out chatting to the chauffeur. "My mother loves getting to know people."

"She's a sweetheart."

"Yeah, she is." He took her hand. "Come on. We might as well enjoy the luxury of a limo for the night—especially at my father's expense."

* * *

It seemed that Rio's father didn't own an apartment but a whole house among the famous San Francisco painted ladies on Steiner Street. Or maybe he was just renting it for the week. Rio had said his business was based in Boston.

They were ushered inside by a butler-type person, divested of their coats, and led through into the drawing room. which seemed to go the length of the building. The house was furnished in a lush, rich Victorian style that went well with the age of the house and its proportions. A couple stood waiting by the far window. The woman was beautifully dressed and looked about the same age as Josie. Her smile was less than enthusiastic. Yvonne could detect no likeness to Rio in the older man who came toward them. He wore the typical Californian uniform of a golf shirt and ironed chinos.

"Isabelle, how kind of you to come tonight."

He drew his ex-wife into an embrace and kept his arm around her waist as he swung around.

"This is my wife, Jennifer." After the two women exchanged an awkward hello, his attention moved quickly on. "And you must be Josie. Please call me Graham."

Josie, who was wearing a pink and black striped tunic and flowered leggings, stuck out her hand. "It's nice to meet you, Graham."

"The pleasure is all mine." Graham nodded as he leaned in to kiss her cheek. "I hear you just graduated from college with a double major."

"That's right." Josie grinned at him. "Any jobs going at your place?"

"Josie!" Isabelle remonstrated. "There's a time and a place for business, and this isn't it."

"Sorry, Mom." Josie didn't look sorry at all and had the audacity to wink at Graham and mouth, "Call me," which made Yvonne want to laugh.

Graham turned to Yvonne. "By default, you must be my son's friend, Yvonne."

"That's correct." She shook his proffered hand. "Thank you so much for allowing me to tag along tonight."

"It was my pleasure." He didn't release her hand, his gaze traveling over her from head to toe in a leisurely fashion that made her raise her chin and stare right back at him. "Any friend of my son's is welcome here."

She thought Rio, who was standing behind her, might have snorted.

Detaching her hand, she stepped back, and almost collided with Rio's chest. He was obviously in protective mode tonight.

"Good evening, son." Graham nodded at Rio. "Glad you could make it."

"Mom wanted to come, so I made the time."

Yvonne glanced uncertainly up at Rio's face. Gone was her charming, warm cowboy, replaced by the cold, clipped businessman she'd encountered earlier. The dislike emanating from him was palpable.

As Rio turned away to shake hands with his father's wife, Graham's faint sigh caught Yvonne's attention. He met her gaze and grimaced.

"He doesn't like me very much," Graham murmured. "It's quite understandable, but it still hurts."

"That's really none of my business," Yvonne said firmly.

He took her by the elbow and walked her toward a bar, where the butler was now polishing glasses. Graham was obviously the kind of man who was used to getting his own way. She could either go with him or cause a scene, which really left her only one option.

"Would you like a glass of wine or a cocktail?" Graham asked.

"Sparkling water would be fine, please."

"No wine?" Her companion raised his eyebrows. "Yet I believe you have a French surname."

"I'm not technically French, although my mother had French citizenship through her mother. I just lived and studied there for a few years."

"And didn't pick up the habit of drinking wine? Now that I find hard to believe."

Yvonne took the glass of sparling water adorned with a slice of lime, and thanked the butler. "I'll definitely enjoy a glass of wine with my dinner. I'm sure you'll have something nice for us to try."

"I do hope so." Graham smiled. "I own a vineyard in Napa Valley that produces a very good chardonnay. You should get Aurelio to take you out there one day. He knows it well. He helped set it up."

"Aurelio?" Yvonne asked.

"That's 'Rio's' real name. I can't abide nicknames. Hasn't he mentioned it to you?"

"Why would he?" Yvonne shrugged. "We're just good friends, and everyone in Morgantown calls him Rio, which suits him just fine."

She looked around to see where *Aurelio* had gotten to, but he was talking with Graham's young wife, who had suddenly found her smile, just for him. Luckily, Isabelle was bearing down on them, so there was some hope of escape. She didn't like the intensity of Graham's scrutiny, and his attempts to be charming.

"Ah, Isabelle. Do you still drink cocktails?" Graham asked. "Johnson, my butler, knows how to make about a hundred different kinds."

"How lovely! I shall try and give him a challenge then," Isabelle replied.

Josie came up too, and gave Yvonne an encouraging smile. "He's not as awful as I thought he'd be. And I'm pretty sure he'd give me a job if Mom and Rio got their noses out of my business. He seems to like you, though. Maybe he's dying to be a grandparent just like my mom and thinks you and my bro are a couple."

That wasn't the vibe Yvonne was getting, but she didn't argue. Graham was certainly used to being in charge, and being listened to. She took a sip of her water, and tried not to notice how Rio was now making Wife Number Four laugh.

Josie nudged her in the ribs. "Guess how old Jennifer is?"

"Thirty?" Yvonne guessed.

"No, she's twenty-two. Graham is thirty years older than her."

"Wow." Yvonne glanced over at Jennifer, who was listening intently to whatever Rio was telling her. "She's very beautiful."

"Not as beautiful as you, and don't worry, Rio would never take up with one of his father's exes."

Yvonne went to reply, and then realized that Josie was grinning. "You're so not funny."

"Dude, the fact that you actually care who my bro is speaking to is even funnier."

"I'm just worried about him, period," Yvonne said. "He didn't want to come tonight."

"Well, Mom seems to have gotten over her dislike of her first husband, and is having a lovely time. Maybe Rio will loosen up, too."

Rio came up to talk to his mother while Jennifer got a drink, and then he stopped beside Yvonne.

"You doing okay?"

"I was just about to ask you the same question," Yvonne said.

"I'll survive."

His dimple appeared, and for one glorious second,

she contemplated grabbing his hand, and running for the hills. And San Francisco definitely had a few challenging slopes.

Unfortunately, the butler cleared his throat.

"Dinner is served. Please come through to the dining room."

"Would you mind bringing your brandy through to my study while the ladies enjoy their coffee so that we can have a moment in private, son?"

Rio looked down the table to where his father was sitting. The dinner had been perfectly prepared, and the accompanying wine had impressed his discerning palate. Conversation had remained reasonably polite, and his father had displayed a dry sense of humor Rio had never noticed before.

Isabelle turned toward him. "*Converse com ele. Por favor.*"

Rio gave his mother a long stare and then reluctantly stood up. "*Tá bem.*"

He laid his napkin on his plate, and carefully avoided Yvonne's gaze. The sense that his father wanted something from him had only grown during the evening. He was now at the point where he just wanted the suspense to be over, which was probably exactly what his father wanted.

As he followed Graham along the hallway and up the stairs, he reminded himself that he was an independent adult, and that there was nothing his father could do to hurt him.

The study was wallpapered in dark green silk and contained rows of bookcases and a large oak desk that took up half the space. It smelled faintly of the cigars his father had always imported from Cuba—a scent that brought back several unhappy memories.

Rio waited until his father sat down and switched on his laptop before sinking into the chair in front of the desk. He'd wait him out. He had nothing to say right now. A clock ticked on the mantelpiece, and Rio sipped his excellent brandy.

"I wanted to talk to you about your future plans," Graham said.

"My future plans?" Rio asked. "With all due respect, what do they have to do with you?"

"Do you intend to keep riding bulls?"

"I'm the current world champion," Rio said. "Believe it or not, I have obligations to my sponsors and management team to keep competing."

"Ah." Graham sipped his brandy. "How long do you believe you will remain competitive? From what I understand, it is a sport with a high attrition rate."

"I'm not intending to keep it up until I'm forty if that's what you are asking. I'd be a fool to do that. I'd like to retire with all my bones intact."

"And after that?"

"I don't know." Rio paused. "Why does it matter to you?"

Graham put his glass down. "It might have escaped your notice, but you are my only child."

"I'm well aware of that."

"Then you must also be aware that at one time I was training you to be my successor."

"I walked out on that life. I walked out on you," Rio pointed out. "You disinherited me."

"I *assumed* I would have other children." Graham interlocked his fingers, and stared down at them. "Unfortunately, that didn't happen."

Rio had a horrible sense he knew what was coming next.

"So, by default, that brings me back to you," Graham said. "You are my only son and heir."

"Whom you disinherited, and by the way, I'm quite okay with that," Rio said evenly.

"I'm offering you a seat on the board and enough stock to keep you invested in working to improve the company."

Before his father finished speaking, Rio was already shaking his head. "I'm sorry, but I'm not interested."

"What financial arrangement *would* be enough to interest you?"

"It *isn't* about money. Don't you get that? Look, you're not that old. Keep trying for son number two, or even daughter number one, and keep running everything until he's old enough to take over."

"It's not that simple. I—"

Rio finished his brandy in one swallow and stood up. "It's been a nice evening. Let's not end it with a pointless argument, okay?"

Graham looked up at him. "I'd like you to at least consider the idea."

"Why?"

"Because, despite everything, you are still my son. I would prefer my business interests to be kept in the family."

"A son you banished from your house at the age of seven and barely bothered to acknowledge until I was old enough to work for you. A *child* you kept from his mother in your vicious little divorce battle until you won and then never gave me another thought. Why the hell would you think I would *want* to work for you?"

"Because you have the talent and ability, and you're refusing to use your skills."

Rio shrugged. "I have other talents."

"Riding a bull?" Graham made a dismissive gesture. "Anyone can do that."

"Yeah? You've tried it yourself? You wouldn't last a damn second."

"Probably, but as you said, it's hardly a lifetime career, is it?" Graham sighed. "Look. Your mother has forgiven me. Why can't you? Maybe the problem isn't me, Aurelio—maybe it's you. Maybe *you* are the one who is incapable of moving forward, and letting go of the past."

"I'm quite happy to be the problem," Rio said. "I've let go of the past. I just don't see myself in your future. Is that so difficult to understand?"

"Yes."

Rio stared at his father. "You're *kidding* me, right? And while we're talking, because I doubt I'll be seeing you again, how about you sell me Mom's ranch?"

Graham's slow smile made all the hairs on the back of Rio's neck stand up.

"So you *do* want something from me after all."

"If you make this about my mother, I will do everything in my power to bring you down," Rio warned.

"Bring *me* down?" Graham chuckled. "Unlikely, with your financial resources—and yes, I do know what you have in the bank, son. But I don't actually want to fight with you either, so let's do this. You consider the proposal I'll send you about coming onboard, and I'll consider selling you the ranch."

"What's the point? I'll still turn it down," Rio countered.

"You'll read the proposal, and respond to it in a way that ensures I know you have at least read it through. If you do that, I will open up negotiations on the sale of your mother's ranch to you." Graham stood and held out his hand. "Deal?"

Rio considered walking out for at least thirty seconds, and then reluctantly shook his father's hand.

"Deal."

Inside, he was furious with himself for allowing his father to use his mother against him, but he'd been the stupid ass who'd brought her up.

"Then why don't we rejoin the ladies? Your friend Yvonne is very nice."

"A, she's too smart to be fooled by you, and b, she's way too old for you." Rio glared at his father as he opened the study door.

"And, c, you like her very much yourself, don't you?"

"We're just good friends," Rio said calmly. "She's not really into dating right now."

"I'm sure you could convince her otherwise."

"Nope." Rio headed down the stairs. "And we'd better be going soon. Yvonne has some work to finish up tonight."

"Then why don't you take her back to her hotel, and I'll make sure your mother and Josie get back safely?"

"It depends on what Mom wants to do," Rio said. "Let's check in with her first."

Chapter Twelve

Yvonne unlocked her hotel door and turned to Rio, who was standing right behind her. He'd been unusually quiet on the taxi ride back, and she wasn't quite sure why.

"Would you like to come in for coffee, or are you heading out?" Yvonne asked.

He looked at her as if he'd never seen her before. "Coffee? Yeah, that would be great, thanks."

He followed her into the room, where she immediately kicked off her shoes. "I've just got to text Avery, and make sure everything's going okay in the café, so make yourself at home."

"Will do."

He removed his jacket and walked over to stare out over the city while she texted away, and received all the reassurance she required from Avery and her very efficient sister, Marley, who was basically running the place.

"Seems like everything is going well." Yvonne breathed out a huge sigh of relief. "Even Tom's behaving himself."

"Good to hear."

She walked over to where Rio was standing and put a tentative hand on his rigid shoulder.

"Are you okay?"

"I'm . . ." He sighed. "I'm sorry, I've got a lot to think about. I'm not the best company right now, am I? Do you want me to leave?"

"How about we have that coffee, and you can tell me what's up?"

"I'm not sure—"

Yvonne poked him in the chest. "Don't go all male on me."

He almost smiled. "I *am* male."

"Yes, but you shouldn't clam up when you have something on your mind, and think that jamming it down inside you will make it go away."

"Men do that?"

"You know they do." She looked him right in the eye. "We're supposed to be *friends*. Friends *share* things."

He shoved a hand through his hair. "Okay, let's start with the coffee and see how it goes from there."

She went to the bathroom, and then tended to the coffee Rio had started while he did the same. She decided to leave the drapes open, as the city view was quite spectacular, and curled up on the couch.

"Thanks for this." He set his cup on the coffee table beside hers, and took up position on the other end of the couch.

"Where do you want to start?" Yvonne asked, sitting forward, her hands wrapped around her mug. "I assume this has something to do with your father, who, by the way, was quite charming to me."

"He's always charming, and he never loses his temper."

"Really? Mind, you don't lose your temper either, do you?"

"I learned early on that he wouldn't tolerate it." A shadow darkened his eyes and was quickly replaced with a smile. "Trust me, he can still do damage with a smile."

"I suspect he's used to getting his own way," Yvonne said cautiously. "And he probably hates that you're independent of him."

"Yeah, that about sums it up." He took a sip of coffee and stared off into space again until Yvonne sighed.

"You're not very good at this."

He raised an eyebrow. "What do you mean?"

"You're supposed to be *sharing* with me, remember?"

"I *am*."

"No, you're prevaricating."

"That's not allowed?"

"Nope." She waved him on. "Come on, spit it out. What happened?"

"Can't you guess? As I'm his only son, he wants me to come back and work for him."

Yvonne put her coffee down on the table. "He's been married four times, and he only has one kid? What's *wrong* with him? That's getting toward Henry VIII territory."

"Now who's changing the subject?"

"I'm not changing the subject. I'm just commenting on an *aspect* of it—keep up! So you told him to get lost, right?" She looked expectantly at him.

He was studying his coffee mug as if it was full of flies. "No. I . . . agreed to look at his proposal."

"*Why?*" Yvonne demanded. "What could he possibly have said that made you backtrack like that?"

He shot to his feet and walked away from her. "This talking stuff out obviously isn't working. Maybe I should go."

Yvonne got off the couch in a mad scramble, and went after him. "Don't you *dare* stop now."

He swung around to face her. "Why, when you obviously can't be bothered to give me a fair hearing, and have jumped to all kinds of conclusions?"

"The only person jumping to conclusions here is you!" Yvonne glared at him. "What's *really* going on inside your head?"

"Maybe I'm just sick and tired of people trying to tell me how to live my life!"

"I merely *asked* why you would even listen to him! That's a *perfectly* reasonable question! You just over-reacted, which usually means you know you're in the wrong." She poked him in the chest. "*You* are the problem here, not me."

"Wow, now you sound *just* like my father." He grabbed hold of her wrist. "Thanks for nothing."

"If I was in my kitchen right now, I'd go for you with my rolling pin or a nice iron-cast pan to knock some sense into you," Yvonne said fiercely.

"Yeah? Like you could hit me. I'm *way* stronger than you are."

"So now you're making this into a pissing contest?"

"Nope." He bent his head and snatched a savage kiss. "I am thinking about hog-tying you to that bed though."

"What?" Yvonne's words were muffled as his mouth again descended, stilling all her rational thoughts. She managed to wrench her mouth away. "This isn't *helpful.*"

"It's damn well helping me." Rio wrapped an arm around her waist, and jerked her hard against his body. "Kiss me."

"But—"

"Kiss me. *Please.*"

"Oh, for goodness sake." Yvonne cupped the back of his head, and brought his lips to hers. "I can see I won't get any more sense out of you right now."

His arm tightened until she was plastered against him from knee to shoulder while his hands made a leisurely tour of inspection over her uncovered back. He kissed her like it was his last day on earth, with so much pent-up need and heat that she luxuriated in the sensations and gave them right back to him. She wanted to protect him, to offer him everything she was to take the hurt from his eyes.

He backed up against the nearest wall and slid his knee between her thighs raising her almost off her feet as she rubbed herself shamelessly against him. As his fingers flexed against her skull, her hair fell around her shoulders and he made an approving noise as he fanned her hair.

"I want you," Rio murmured against her lips. "I want you first and then we'll talk, okay?"

"What about all the reasons why that's not a good idea?" Yvonne gasped.

"To hell with those reasons." He hesitated. "I . . . need this. I need you."

Something inside her responded to that need, and she stroked an unsteady finger over his mouth.

"Do you promise to talk to me afterward?"

"If I can still breathe, yes."

"Then, okay."

With a murmured prayer, he swept her up into his arms, and headed for the bed, laying her gently on the cover, and following her down a second later. She braced herself, but he did nothing but stare down at her.

"What?"

"You are so damned beautiful," he said hoarsely. "I don't even know where to start."

She touched a fingertip to her lower lip. "How about here?"

With a stifled sound, he bent down, and kissed her gently on the lips. "Yeah, that's definitely working for me."

She pointed to her throat. He made a leisurely journey down past her jawline, nipping her earlobe, which made her shudder, and then kissed her neck. The slight abrasion of his stubbled chin made her stomach do all kinds of somersaults. She reached for him, only to have both her wrists caught within one of his strong hands.

"Hog-tied, remember?" he whispered in her ear.

"Not happening."

He drew her wrists over her head. "This okay?"

"If you must."

"Oh, I must." He scraped his teeth down her throat, and she squirmed against him, her hips rising to meet the hardness in his jeans. "I like this."

With his free hand, he undid the halter neck of her dress, and drew it away from her skin, his breath hitching as he stared down at her.

"No bra."

"Duh."

"Thank you, Lord." He leaned in and kissed the swell of her breast, capturing her nipple in his mouth and drawing on it until she was writhing against him. His hand moved lower, gathering up the soft folds of her skirt to explore underneath.

Eventually, he went still again and muttered something against her breast.

"No panties." He raised himself up on his elbow to stare into her face. "Were you like that *all through dinner*?"

"Would you have liked that?" Yvonne asked innocently.

He just about managed to nod, his pupils turning black with what she concluded had to be sheer lust.

She decided to leave him guessing, not wanting him to know she'd actually spent precious moments wrangling with her spandex in the bathroom when they'd got back. Her dress was very unforgiving of the slightest curve.

He cupped her mound, and she forgot about teasing him as he gently played and stroked her with his long, strong fingers. She was more than ready for him as he drew her dress down over her hips and threw it onto the floor. With a growl, he finally released her hands and kissed his way down over her belly and the jut of her hip, to just where she needed him most.

She tangled her fingers in his hair as he pleasured her, pressing shamelessly against him until his teeth grazed her throbbing center, and she climaxed. He made a humming sound against her thigh, and started again, which should've been unfair, but somehow just doubled her enjoyment.

"Take this off." She yanked at the back of his shirt loosening it from his jeans. "*Now.*"

"Do it for me. I'm busy."

She pulled his hair.

"Ouch!" He reared back onto his knees.

She helped out anyway, practically strangling him when she didn't open quite enough buttons to allow her to pull the shirt over his head. His torso emerged, the soft gleam of his tanned muscled skin an enticement to lick, and kiss, and . . .

"Now the belt."

He fumbled with the large silver buckle and eased open the top button of his jeans so slowly that Yvonne batted his hands away.

"Faster!"

"Not happening unless you want this show to be over before it starts." He breathed out so hard his abs flexed, and Yvonne had to pause to admire the amazing sight. "Let me do it."

He slowly lowered the zipper, and Yvonne pounced, shoving his jeans away from his hips, and closed in on her target. She licked the damp cotton that barely contained his hardness.

"You wore boxers."

"Yeah." He sounded like he was breathing through his teeth. "Don't do that."

"What, this?" She curled her tongue around him, and he groaned. "Don't you like it?"

A second later, she was flat on her back, and he was holding her in place with his hips.

"Next time, you can do what you want with me, but this one is all for you."

Yvonne sighed. "Again?"

He shucked his jeans, socks, and boots so fast she blinked.

"I figure that if I get first go, you won't have time to fall asleep on me."

"Maybe you'd better do it fast then."

He glanced down at his aroused body. "Don't think I have a choice about that."

She leaned over to the bedside table and showed him her makeup bag, which she'd brought through from the bathroom. "Condoms in here."

"Thanks."

As he covered himself, his smile was somewhere between grateful, blissful, and desperate, which did all kinds of good things to her. Then he was moving over her, and she forgot everything except the heat and scent of him, the surge of power as he filled her, and the two seconds it took after that for her to start coming.

* * *

Rio gritted his teeth and hung on like the world-champion bull rider he was. If he wasn't careful, he'd be lasting eight seconds, but he didn't think Yvonne would be very impressed by his score. It was hard not to let go when the woman of his dreams was thrashing and moaning beneath him as she climaxed in long, shuddering waves that drew him in, and kept him chained deep inside her.

Breathing through his nose, he counted backward from a hundred, enduring the little aftershocks and clenches until Yvonne lay still beneath him again. She raised a languid hand, and touched his cheek.

"Okay, you can stop now. I'm going to sleep."

"Not happening." He deliberately rolled his hips, and her eyes flew open. "We've only just begun."

He began to move, savoring the way her flesh clasped and released him with every stroke. He cupped her breast, and she gasped his name, her fingers digging into his shoulder as she rocked with him in perfect harmony. He could keep this rhythm up all night, but his body had other ideas and was way too excited to last much longer.

Pressure built at the base of his spine, and he increased his pace, his breath shortening as Yvonne grabbed hold, and held on with a strength that surprised and humbled him. He shifted positions slightly, coming higher up on his knees so her back was against the headboard, and rocked into her.

"*Louvado seja Deus,*" Rio gasped as he came hard, and collapsed over Yvonne, face-planting into the pillow beside hers, his body suddenly a dead weight.

Eventually, she stroked his shoulder.

"What did you just say?"

He was still trying to remember who he was, let alone what he'd shouted out in his moment of release.

"It was in Portuguese," she said helpfully.

"Praise God," he managed to mumble into the pillow.

"Well, that's a new one on me."

He rolled off and gave her the eye. "What did your Frenchman say then?"

"*Mon Dieu*, of course."

"Same thing then."

"I suppose so."

He eyed her cautiously. "Are you always this chatty right after sex?"

"I suppose I am. Why?"

"Because maybe next time I'll try harder to reduce you to adoring, exhausted silence."

She snorted. "Good luck with that."

"Well, at least you stayed awake this time."

"And you stuck around."

They smiled at each other. He had a desperate sense that if they could just keep it light, happy, and friendly, then nothing bad would ever happen to him again.

"Aurelio, eh?"

Some of his happy disappeared. "Who told you that?"

"Your father. He said he doesn't approve of nicknames. Does it mean anything?"

"Gold, I think."

She stroked his cheek. "That's lovely, and very accurate for you."

"Yeah? Because I'm solid?" He winked at her.

Her voice softened. "No, because you're good, and pure, and precious."

Not so light either then . . .

He rolled away from her. "I have to use the bathroom. You okay if I go first?"

What had she said to send him running for the hills? Yvonne studied the bathroom door, her sense of unease growing. He'd made love to her like a dream, and had been everything she'd imagined he'd be times ten. Strength, elegance, and power, all captured in one adorable, sexy man.

Maybe he'd panicked because she'd said something nice about him . . . something that had come from her heart.

Was he afraid she was going to get all clingy and ruin everything between them? Did she *want* to get clingy with everything going on in her life at the moment? After her parents had died so suddenly, she'd done that with Paul, and it hadn't ended well. They really did need to talk. She was quite prepared to lock the door and swallow the key to make sure that happened.

He came back into the bedroom, a towel wrapped around his lean waist, water dripping down his torso. He hesitated, and she pointed silently at the bed.

"You promised you'd talk to me."

"I will, but maybe we should get dressed first?"

"You're done having sex with me?" For some reason, that hurt.

"I'm trying to be sensible here."

"Okay." She held up her hands. "I'll take a quick shower, and you'd better still be here when I get out."

* * *

True to her word, she was back ten minutes later, wrapped in her dressing gown, her wet hair in a high ponytail. She'd given herself a stern talking-to in the bathroom mirror, and was resolved to remain calm and pleasant regardless of what happened. Had she let herself give in to lust again just like she had with Paul? Ten years on, hadn't she learned *anything*?

Rio was sitting on the only chair, fully dressed apart from his boots and jacket. He'd also made more coffee, which mellowed her a little. He poured her a cup and pushed it across the coffee table to her.

"Thanks." She cuddled up on the couch, drawing her feet up under her, and wrapped her hands around the mug.

"I'm sorry." Rio looked down at his linked hands. "You're right. I shouldn't have talked you into bed. I used your concern for me as a lever, and that wasn't fair."

She took a moment to digest what he was saying. Had she really been that obvious? It felt more like a slap in the face than she had anticipated.

"So you think I'm a pushover, right?"

"*No!*" He looked up. "Not at all. This is on me."

"Because you're that irresistible?" Yvonne nodded. "Makes sense."

"Not that either." He held her gaze. "Come on, you know that's not what I meant."

"Okay, so let's just say we both made a mistake and move on." Wow, she sounded so calm and mature. And everything she'd said made perfect sense for both of them. She offered him a bright smile. "Not that it wasn't lovely, but we can still be friends and business partners, right?"

He studied her for a long moment. "You sure you're okay with that?"

"Why wouldn't I be?" she said airily. "Neither of us is in the right place for a relationship right now. Let's just chalk this one up to mutual lust and hope we've got it out of our systems."

Like she'd ever get the best sex of her life out of her system, but sometimes you just had to fake it until you made it.

He still looked worried, which she supposed was better than him grinning with relief and high-fiving her as he disappeared never to be seen again.

"Yvonne—"

She ruthlessly interrupted him, not sure if she could keep on adulting for much longer. "So are you going to tell me why you considered accepting a job from your father?"

His eyebrows shot up. "You really want to talk about that *right now*?"

"Sure! Why not?" She shrugged. "We're supposed to be friends." And it gave her time to recover from the unexpected pang of hurt his agreement to go back to just being friends caused her. But that was what she'd asked for, so she could hardly fault him for going along with it.

His pause before replying this time was even longer than the first.

"Okay, I've been trying to buy my mom's ranch property from my father for the last three years. He's refused to even discuss it until now."

"So he used it as a bribe to get you back working for him?"

"Kind of. I agreed to read a proposal as to my potential role in the company, and the benefits I'd accrue if I take the job. In return, he'll consider a bid for the ranch from me." He shoved a hand through his still-damp hair. "It was my stupid fault he even came up with the idea. I mentioned buying the ranch, and he was all over me."

"Your mom is very important to you, isn't she?" Yvonne asked.

"Yeah, and she deserves to live the rest of her life without worrying about being beholden to my father."

"Excuse me if this sounds rude, but Josie suggested that your mother is quite wealthy in her own right," Yvonne asked tentatively. "Why hasn't she bought the ranch back herself?"

"Because my father's lawyers tied it up too tight, which meant she'd have to take him back to court, and potentially lose the whole place paying the legal fees."

Yvonne nodded. "Then I take it back. You obviously did the right thing."

"Thank you." His smile emerged for the first time since they'd made love. "This sharing stuff is hard, isn't it?"

She hid a yawn behind her hand, and finished her coffee. "It has its moments."

"I should go. You look worn out." He rose to his feet, and took both the cups back to the coffee maker.

She got up as well and waited until he collected his hat and jacket and put on his boots before walking him to the door.

"Thanks for all your help today." Yvonne managed another chirpy smile, but it was getting harder every time.

He hesitated and looked down at her. "I still feel like I've messed up somewhere, and I'm not sure how to fix it."

"You haven't." Damn, there was a catch in her voice he was bound to notice. "Tell your mom I'll see her at ten in the lobby of the Ritz-Carlton, okay?" Then she wouldn't have to go up to the suite and see Rio at all. "I'm just tired. It's been a long day."

He put on his hat, and she opened the door and practically pushed him out, her throat aching with unshed tears.

"Night then, Rio."

In his usual stubborn-ass way, he refused to budge an inch, and now her hand was pressed against his chest, and that wasn't good. He took her fingers and gently kissed them before returning her hand to her.

"I want you to know that making love to you wasn't a mistake. It was both an honor and a privilege. I'll never regret it."

"Great, thanks for the input." Was she babbling now? She didn't want to be that person, that stupid girl with her ridiculous need to be loved. Paul had fought to escape that need, and she didn't want to have to watch Rio do the same thing. Why was she so bad at relationships even when she wasn't in one? "See you Thursday on the ride back to Morgantown."

This time, she shoved harder and managed to catch him off balance. Stepping smartly back, she shut the door in his face and locked it. Holding her breath, she waited to see if he'd try and reconnect with her. There was a very long silence, and then the sound of his boots walking away.

She went back to the couch and sat down, wrapping her arms around herself. Okay, it could have gone better at the end, but she'd done a pretty good job of refusing to be clingy or demanding. Common sense said that she'd made a sensible decision, and that Rio was happy to go along with it. It really was for the best. Because she did like him—as a friend.

She raised her head to stare out over the city, and took a deep, steadying breath.

"Hell."

There was no point denying it. She wanted him back in her bed right now, wanted to share herself with him and revel in his frank appreciation of her charms. But he'd agreed with her that it was a bad idea, had willingly allowed her to reinstate the walls between them, but oh, somewhere deep inside her, she really wished that he hadn't. . . .

Rio had reached the hotel lobby before he stopped walking and just stared into space. What the hell had just happened? Why wasn't he still in bed with the most beautiful woman he'd ever met?

"Excuse me, sir, do you want me to call a taxi for you?"

Actually, he needed someone to slap him silly, but he doubted the concierge would be up for that.

"No, thanks. I'm walking."

He went out into the street and took another long moment getting his bearings before turning left. It wasn't even that late. His mother and sister might still be with Graham.

He'd just had the best sex of his life and he was walking away. Yvonne had made it pretty damn clear she was happy to revert to being friends again.

"But only after you bolted from her bed when she got too personal," Rio muttered.

He checked to see that no one had heard him talking to himself and realized that, in such a big city, he probably wasn't going to stand out much.

The question was *why* had he bolted?

"Wrong time, wrong place, right woman."

It was a cliché, but it was still true. Rio crossed the

street, avoiding an oncoming trolley, and turned up the hill. What else was there to say? They'd both given in to the moment. There was nothing wrong with that.

He reached the Ritz-Carlton, went into the lobby and up in the elevator to the penthouse suite. Josie was sitting on the couch in her dressing gown, typing. She held a finger to her lips and pointed at the bedrooms.

"Mom's gone to bed. She had a few too many cocktails."

Rio contemplated keeping on walking into his room, but instead threw himself down beside Josie on the couch.

"How did the rest of dinner go?"

"It was great. Jenny went to bed just after you left. Graham stayed and entertained us for another hour. He was really nice."

Rio snorted. "Right."

"No, he really was, bro. Even Mom said so on the way home. She said he'd mellowed and matured."

"Because she always thinks the best of everyone."

"Well, everyone except him usually, so this was something of a big deal. Why are you still so hard on him?"

"Because this is what he *does*. He charms the pants off people, and makes them think he's this harmless guy. Then, when he's got you all acquiescent, he turns into a fricking shark."

"He's a businessman." Josie shrugged. "That's what they do."

Rio met her gaze. "He's not a good person, Josie."

"Maybe not to you, but that doesn't make him evil personified."

He flung his arms wide. "So basically everyone likes my father, and I'm the problem? *Muito obrigado.*"

"People do change, Rio. You weren't that nice when

you first came back to Mom's ranch, but we all gave
you the time and space to find yourself again."

"You could give my father the whole universe and
he'd still need more," Rio grumbled. "And now he
wants me to come and work for him again."

"What?" Josie sat up. "But you've got a world championship to defend!"

At least, being a PBR fan, Josie got that.

"Yeah, and a life of my own."

"I suppose one day everything he has could belong
to you. . . ." Josie shook her head. "All those people
and companies depending on you for their living."

"Exactly. Who'd want that?"

She frowned. "What would happen to all Graham's
charitable stuff?"

"What charitable stuff?" Rio asked.

Josie showed him her laptop screen. "I was just looking it up. He suggested there might be a job there
somewhere for me."

Rio studied the web page and shrugged even as he
mentally memorized the URL. "It's a tax write-off for
him, Josie. That's all it is."

"It didn't sound like that when he talked about what
he was trying to accomplish. You're determined not to
allow the man a single redeeming feature, are you?"
Josie said.

"Not if I can help it." Rio grinned at his sister, who
didn't look impressed.

She sniffed the air. "Did I mention that you smell
like a bunch of flowers?"

"Don't I always?"

"I hate to tell you, but that's not your normal aroma.
Usually it's a mix of horse and leather." She looked up
from her laptop. "Whose shower gel did you borrow?"

"None of your business."

She rolled her eyes. "I'm not five anymore. Anyone with a lick of sense can see that you've got the hots for Yvonne, which, by the way, I totally approve of because she's lovely."

"Yvonne is . . ." Rio leaned his head back against the couch. "Complicated."

"You mean she doesn't like you back?"

"She . . . we've both got too much on our plates at the moment to get involved with each other."

"Yeah, right," Josie scoffed.

The thing was, the more he said it, the lamer that excuse felt, and the more he agreed with his sister.

"I've got another season of bull riding ahead of me, so I'll be touring the country. Yvonne's got the café to run, and other business interests."

"So?" Josie looked at him as if he was an idiot. "Make it *work*!"

"It's not that easy."

"Only if you don't really want to try."

Rio gave her his best side eye. "You'll fit into my father's company so well. Sometimes things don't work out. That's just the way life goes."

"Only if you give up," Josie repeated stubbornly. "And don't tell me I'm too young to know what I'm talking about. That's *infuriating*."

Rio wisely held his tongue and waited to see where she would go next.

"You've always been like this."

"Like what?" Rio asked.

"Like this with women. You always give up too easily. Why is that?"

"Because I'm not a fool?"

She met his gaze; hers was unusually serious for a change. "Or because you're afraid of intimacy?"

"For God's sake, Josie, don't start that crap with me."

She poked him in the leg. "See? I know I'm right because you're getting antsy."

"Because *you're* way off target. When I find the right woman, I'll know what to do, and I'll do it."

"So Yvonne isn't the right woman?"

He opened his mouth and then closed it again. "She's potentially the right woman, but at the wrong time in my life."

"Well, I suppose that's something." Josie closed her laptop. "For some reason, she seems to like you, so my advice, big brother, would be to get your shit together and close her down before some other guy comes along."

"Wow, thanks for the dating assistance."

She frowned at him. "This isn't about dating—you date all the time. This is about being in love with someone and wanting to be with them for the rest of your life."

"Like Mom and Graham? That worked out just great."

Josie raised her chin. "Sometimes things *don't* work out, but at least they went with their feelings."

"And damaged countless people around them, including me."

"Jeez, Rio, just *let it go, okay*? Stop using your parents' stupid marriage to justify not committing to anyone in your own life. It's totally lame." She stood up and tucked her laptop under her arm. "I'm going to bed. What time is Yvonne coming over?"

"Around ten. She'll call from the lobby."

"Great." Josie blew him a kiss. "Good night, my idiot

brother who can't see a gift horse staring him right in the face."

She went toward her door, and Rio called out to her. "Maybe that's why I prefer bulls."

Her smile was sweet. "Then maybe one of them will kick some sense into your thick head."

Chapter Thirteen

"Come up to the suite, darling! We're not ready to leave yet!" Isabelle said.

Yvonne sighed as her cunning plan to avoid Rio came crashing down around her ears. She'd hoped to meet the Martinez ladies in the lobby, but had obviously overestimated both their timekeeping skills and sense of hospitality.

She'd spent a sleepless night going through every moment of her evening with Rio and working out what she should've done differently. Did she regret making love with him? Even if it went against common sense and everything she held dear?

No, and the worst thing was that, if offered the opportunity again, she'd probably do the same thing. So what did that mean, and where did that leave her and Rio's relationship? The fact that she was even contemplating changing her stance on having a relationship at all was mind blowing.

She got into the elevator, and went up to the top floor. There were only two doors opening off the lobby, and the Martinez one was already open.

"Hey."

Of course it had to be Rio standing there waiting for her. She made herself meet his soft brown gaze and smiled. He wore a tight black T-shirt and jeans, and looked like he'd just gotten out of the shower.

"Isabelle told me to come on up. I hope I'm not interrupting anything."

"Not at all. They are just finishing breakfast."

He held the door open for her, and she resisted the urge to inhale him in as she went past.

"Thanks."

She spotted Isabelle and Josie sitting at the table near the floor-to-ceiling window, and made her way over to them. At least they appeared to be dressed, and almost ready to go.

"Ah! Yvonne, my darling girl!" Isabelle waved at her. "Please sit down and have some coffee. Graham has lent us a driver for the day, so there is no need for us to worry about sore feet or too many bags."

"Nice." Yvonne took a seat and accepted the coffee Isabelle poured for her. Rio hadn't returned to the table, meaning he might be somewhere behind her, which made her nervous. "Do you have thoughts about where you want to go?"

"I'd like to check out some vintage stores," Josie said as she dabbed at her mouth with her napkin. "Mom will want to hit every single brand-name store in the city."

"I don't come to San Francisco very often, Josie," Isabelle said with a smile. "I have a lot of pent-up *need* when I get here."

Yvonne nodded at Josie. "I know some great vintage places that suit my budget. We'll focus on your mother this morning, and then go farther afield to find what you like."

Isabelle looked past her. "And what are your plans for the day, Rio, my dear?"

"I'm going to drop these signed documents back to Graham. After that, I'm not sure," Rio called out.

"Then join us for lunch and come shopping!" Josie shouted. "I'll text you to let you know where we are."

"Okay." He came to stand by his mother's chair, and bent to kiss her cheek. "Have a good day, *Mamae*, and don't bankrupt the ranch."

"As if I would," Isabelle scoffed. "That place means more to me that anything." She patted his shoulder. "Thank your father for lending us his chauffeur, won't you?"

"Of course." Rio kissed Josie on the top of her head and dropped an envelope on her plate. "Graduation money. Enjoy."

"Oh, wow! Thanks!" Josie squealed and jumped to her feet to give Rio a hug.

His amused gaze met Yvonne's, and for a moment, there was nothing else worth doing but sharing a smile with him. Yvonne hastily dropped her gaze to her coffee and took a huge gulp. Okay, so she wasn't getting over him any time soon. Time to think up a plan B.

"I'll see you guys later." Rio picked up his hat and went toward the door. "If you hear anything back from Tasty Treats, Yvonne, don't hesitate to contact me."

"Will do."

With one last cheery wave, he left the suite, closing the door behind him with a definite clunk. Yvonne let out a quiet breath. The first meeting after sex was always difficult, and that had gone okay—apart from the fact that she'd wanted to grab him and do it all over again. . . . She looked up to find both Isabelle and Josie staring at her expectantly.

"So is Rio going to talk to his father about the job offer after all?" Yvonne asked.

Isabelle wrinkled her nose. "What job offer?"

Inwardly, Yvonne cringed even as she tried to sound careless. In her efforts to misdirect conversation away from herself, had she just dropped Rio right in it? "Oh, nothing, I must have misheard what he said."

"No, you're right, Yvonne," Josie chimed in. "I just don't think Rio had mentioned it to Mom yet. Graham did offer Rio his job back. Both of them told me last night."

"Well, why didn't anyone tell *me*?" Isabelle shook her head. "Why is it a secret?"

"Seeing as Rio isn't interested in the job, he probably thought it wasn't worth bothering you about," Josie said. "He hates Graham's guts."

"I know." Isabelle put her coffee down. "And that's my fault."

"How did you work that out?" Josie asked.

"I was very young when Rio was born and I . . . probably shared too many of my fears and anxieties about his father with him. I needed a champion, but I should not have forced my son into that role, or used him against his father."

"Seeing as Graham took full custody away from you, I should imagine Rio feels he has quite enough ammunition of his own to dislike the man," Yvonne pointed out.

"He told you about that?" Isabelle was studying her intently.

"Yes, well, some of it anyway," Yvonne answered. "Why?"

"Because he never usually talks about it." Isabelle's smile returned. "He must like you a lot."

"We're just good friends." Yvonne shrugged.

"Yeah, right." Josie snorted. "My brother is so confused right now that he doesn't know which way is up."

"We're friends, really," Yvonne repeated. "Neither of us is in a good place for a relationship right now."

"Wow, you sound just like Rio." Josie winked. "You two commitment-phobes are obviously made for each other."

Isabelle patted Josie's hand. "Now stop being rude to our guest, dear, and let's get ready to go out." She rose to her feet and smiled down at Yvonne. "I'll call the driver and make sure he's there when we get down to the lobby."

Rio followed his father's admin through the row of cubicles, aware that some kind of buzz, like a slow tidal wave of interest, was following along behind him. Had someone worked out his relationship to Graham and leaked the information to everyone on staff? It was highly likely. No company was without its gossips, and there might still be people around who remembered him from a few years ago.

"Aurelio!"

He turned toward the shout to see a familiar face grinning back at him from one of the offices.

"Frank! How are you doing, buddy?" Rio went over to shake hands. "I'm glad to see you're still working here."

"Someone has to keep everyone in order." Frank smiled at him. "Congratulations on that world championship, by the way. I never thought I'd live to see Graham Howatch's son on the back of a bull."

"Thanks." Rio hesitated. Frank was in charge of the

San Francisco office when his father wasn't around, and had been something of a mentor to Rio. "I owe you an apology for walking out all those years ago."

"I understood why you had to go. Your father was ten times harder on you than on anyone else, and the pressure just got to you."

"Thanks for being so nice about it."

"We all felt for you," Frank said. "Graham isn't the easiest man to work for, period, and with you, he became a tyrant. We were all placing bets on how long it would take for you to rebel." Frank held up his hand. "Not that any of us wished you anything but good, of course."

"It's okay. I get it." Rio nodded. "I still didn't handle it very maturely, and I regret that."

"You're forgiven." Frank smiled broadly and then leaned in. "Especially if the rumors are true, and you are coming back into the fold?"

"Not true, I'm afraid." Rio found a smile. "I only came to help my mother with some legal matters. I'm back on the bull-riding circuit soon."

"That's a shame. The best way to learn how a company operates is to come onboard early so that when you take over, you're familiar with the entire structure."

"I'm not planning on taking over."

Frank looked him right in the eye. "Then a lot of folks are going to be out of work."

"I'm sure my father will find an amazing successor to his throne."

"The thing is, he won't even look. He's determined to pass the company down to you."

"Then he's going to be disappointed." Rio shook Frank's hand again. "It was great to see you again. Give my best to your wife."

"Will do. Nice to see you again, Aurelio, and I do hope you'll reconsider."

Rio carried on walking until he reached the open door that led into his father's private sanctum. During his hectic tenure at the company, he'd gotten to know lots of his father's employees all across the country. Would his father really let them all lose their jobs just because he couldn't settle on a successor? Or would he leave everything to Rio and make him responsible for the mess that would follow?

Graham's admin waved him through to his father's office, and he went on in. His father was sitting behind his desk, typing away on his keyboard.

"Good morning, son."

"Why haven't you trained a successor for your little empire?" Rio asked.

Graham looked up at him over the top of his spectacles. "I beg your pardon?"

"Why haven't you appointed a successor?" Rio repeated the words slowly.

"I'm not stupid. I heard what you said. I just can't believe you require an answer."

"Because you thought you'd have an heir?" Rio sat down in front of the desk. "Surely you made contingency plans?"

"I certainly have considered a variety of employees who have potential, yes, but ultimately none of them felt right."

"If you're considering stepping down, you can guarantee half your staff already know about it. Not having an obvious heir will cause uncertainty, and hurt the company."

"That's true."

"Then why haven't you promoted someone into

that big empty office beside Frank's? It's not like you to risk the future security of a company you built from scratch."

Graham shrugged. "Uncertainty also breeds competition."

"And you're way too young to be considering stepping down anyway."

"You think so?"

"What are you going to do with yourself if you retire?" Rio asked. "You have no hobbies, you never take a day off, and you hate traveling."

"A man can change his habits, Aurelio. When you were a child, I had to work extremely hard to ensure my survival."

"Survival? Don't make me laugh. You were already a multimillionaire in your twenties. You worked because you loved it."

"I worked to support you and your mother."

"Bull crap. You could've supported us on a fiftieth of what you brought home. You just liked making money. Mom and I were supposed to stay in the background and shut up."

"As if your mother would ever do that."

"You didn't know what she was like when you married her though, did you?" Rio argued. "You had no idea she'd hand you your ass rather than be the kind of showcase wife you wanted."

A reluctant smile warmed his father's rather cold features. "She certainly proved to be a fighter."

"But even she couldn't prevail against your wealth and connections, could she? You got rid of her eventually, and kept me just to spite her."

Graham frowned. "That's not true."

"I was there, remember?" Rio pointed out "That's exactly what you did."

"Your mother was . . . very young when we separated and very angry with me. I was concerned that she would struggle to bring you up in a manner in which I approved. I thought she might be taken advantage of because of her newly acquired wealth, and would marry unwisely."

"Wow, you really didn't know her at all, did you?" Rio shook his head. "Instead, she married someone even older than you, and almost as wealthy."

"Which, if you remember, was when I finally let her have joint custody of you."

"You thought Arturio would be a stabilizing influence on her?" Rio half-smiled. "He was like putty in her hands."

"I . . . wanted you to have the opportunity to see your mother," Graham said slowly. "Is that so hard to believe?"

Rio didn't even bother to answer that.

"I also knew Isabelle would use every penny Arturio was worth to fight for you in the courts." Graham hesitated. "I didn't want to put you through that again."

"So I should really be grateful to Arturio for taking my mother on," Rio murmured, still unwilling to give his father credit for anything, but unsettled all the same. Did Graham have a point? Had he attempted, in his own way, to ensure that Rio was protected? "He did at least give me a stable home, unlike you."

"You had a very stable home, staffed by the best money could buy, and the care of my new wife." Graham stared him down. "A woman you attacked and threatened to kill, by the way."

"A *woman* who used to shut me in my bedroom closet in the dark if I made any sound louder than breathing. A woman who beat the shit out of me when she thought no one was looking, and deprived me of food. Yeah. A very stable home. I was almost glad when you sent me away to that appalling school."

Graham frowned. "Vanessa told me you were impossible to control. She showed me bruises and bite marks on her skin."

"*You* might have been impossible to control if you'd been stuck in a locked closet all day, and then were physically attacked." Rio held his father's gaze. "Of *course* I wanted to fricking kill her."

"I had . . . no idea about this." Graham sounded shaken.

"Why would you?" Rio shrugged. "You were never there. She basically had a free hand once she'd replaced all Mother's staff with her flying monkeys."

"I'm sorry." Graham met Rio's gaze. "I truly didn't know."

"It's in the past." Rio shrugged. "I've gotten over it." Eager to change the subject, he tossed the two folders he'd brought with him on his father's desk. "I just don't get why you need me now."

"Is it so wrong of me to want my own flesh and blood to run my businesses for me?"

"In this case? Yes." Rio sat forward. "It's not like you to be sentimental."

Graham looked out of the window. "Maybe I've changed. Maybe I'm concerned about all the people I employ losing their jobs if I don't find a worthy successor or if the business gets sold and split up so that only the most profitable elements of it survive."

"Why would you care? You've spent your life doing those very things to others. Maybe it's time for you to see it from the other side."

Even as he spoke, Rio couldn't help but picture all

the employees he'd met having to worry about their futures just because Graham was having some kind of personal crisis.

"You wouldn't let the business go under just because I refused to play your games, would you?" Rio asked slowly.

"Why would you care, if you turn your back on the opportunity?"

"Because destroying things in a fit of pique has never been your style. You're a cold shark of a businessman, not a bleeding heart."

"As I keep trying to tell you, maybe things are different now."

Rio wasn't getting into that fantasy world. He pointed at the two files he'd put on the desk. "Mom signed your paperwork. It all looks good."

"Thank you." Graham put the file in his outbox. "What's the other one?"

"My proposal for the sale of Mom's ranch to me."

"Excellent. Let's discuss that over lunch."

Rio half-rose from his chair. "I wasn't planning on sticking around—"

Graham met his gaze. "If you want me to consider your offer, then you owe me a few hours of your time. I have some business to take care of. You can accompany me. Then we can sit down together like civilized people, and discuss your offer, and my proposal. If you *insist* on disappearing again, I will not look at anything from you until I return home to Boston."

Rio let out his breath. "Fine. Then let's get on with it."

Yvonne accepted the cup of coffee Josie poured for her and sat back on the couch.

"Take your shoes off," Josie said. "I don't mind. We're practically family."

"Thanks, I will." Yvonne groaned as she kicked off her high heels and stretched out her toes. "Your mother could shop for America."

"I know. She's crazy, isn't she? I'm not surprised she's gone for a nap." Josie grinned. "Thanks for taking me to those great vintage shops. Due to that timely infusion of cash from Rio, I was able to get some awesome things."

"You both did great." Yvonne yawned so hard her jaw cracked. She'd had a wonderful day out with two kindred spirits. If she never saw the Martinez ladies again, she suspected they'd remain friends for life. She really should get back to her hotel, but her body wasn't willing to move yet.

The door into the suite opened, and Josie turned around.

"Hey, Rio. How was your day?"

Yvonne closed her eyes and leaned her head against the back of the couch. She was too tired to make a quick escape. If Rio wanted to talk to her, she'd let him. He was used to her falling asleep around him anyway.

He came into the apartment, his gaze scanning the mountain of shopping bags piled up around the table, and whistled.

"Wow. Mom really went for it, didn't she?"

"Yeah." Josie patted the seat beside her. "We had a ball. Do you want some coffee?"

"No thanks." He grimaced. "I spent most of the day with Graham, and I drank way too much of the stuff." He looked over toward Yvonne. "Hey. I almost didn't see you there amongst all the bags."

"I'm just about to go back to my hotel." She smiled at him. "But for some reason my legs aren't working."

His eyes narrowed with amusement. "Possibly because you spent the day with my mother. She's enough to wear anyone out."

"She made me look like an amateur." Yvonne groaned and struggled to sit up. "I really should get going."

"If you really want to leave now, I'll come with you and help with all the bags," Rio offered.

Yvonne considered him for a long moment. Was that a good idea or not? Her body said yes, and her common sense said no.

"Or if you're really tired, I can load you into a cab and wave you good-bye."

"Take him with you, Yvonne. He's really good at carrying bags and all that kind of manly stuff," Josie said helpfully. "I'll tell Mom where he is if she needs him for anything."

"Okay." Yvonne finally got off the couch and blew Josie a kiss. "Give Isabelle my love, and tell her I'll be in touch before I leave tomorrow."

"Will do. Thanks for today, Yvonne. It was awesome."

Rio winked at his sister, and then came to stand at Yvonne's side. "Which bags are yours?"

"Just these dozen or so."

She really did need a hand. Somehow, she'd forgotten to keep count of her purchases, and now had more bags to carry than she could manage alone.

"Okay." He picked up the majority of the shopping in one capable hand, and then grabbed another load. "We'll probably need a cab."

They didn't talk on the way back. Rio got out of the cab and carried all her bags into the nearest elevator in the lobby. Yvonne assumed he wasn't afraid to come up to her room with her. Which was good, right? It meant they were still okay around each other.

She slid her room key into the slot, and the door opened onto her newly refreshed and housekeepered space. She loved that about hotels.

"Just dump everything over by the window and I'll sort it out later," Yvonne said. "I hope Chase has room on the plane for all this stuff."

"I'm sure he'll cope." Rio carefully put the bags down, and straightened up. "Did you hear anything from the Tasty Treats crew?"

Yvonne fumbled for her phone. "Do you know, I haven't even looked. Between your mom and the noise of the city, I just put my cell away, and forgot about it." She pointed at the small kitchen area. "Why don't you get us both a bottle of water while I check?"

"Sure."

She kicked off her shoes again and sank down on the couch to read her messages.

"Priscilla says she's going to bring the whole team out to Morgantown in the next couple of weeks to really get a feel for the dynamics of the town, and the central part my café plays in it." Yvonne read out the text. "Well, if they stay overnight, the Hayes Hotel will be pleased to get a bunch of guests."

"Anything else?" Rio handed her a chilled bottle of water.

Yvonne made a face. "Greg sent a text asking me out."

"Wow, classy." Rio sat opposite her. "No conflict of interest there at all."

"Actually, I think he's more interested in my cooking than me."

"The way he was stuffing cream cakes down his gullet when he came to visit, I'd agree with you." He took a long swig from his bottled water. "It's been a long day."

Yvonne opened her water as well. "Isabelle said you ended up having lunch with your father. How did that go?"

She was amazed that, despite all the potential awkwardness between them, she still really wanted to know how he was doing.

He made a face. "It was . . . interesting. He made me trail around behind him all morning while he visited various departments and spoke with his staff."

"Interesting in what way?"

"In that he genuinely seemed invested in what they were doing, and they genuinely seemed to like him."

"Just because you don't like someone doesn't mean they are always unlikeable to others," Yvonne pointed out.

"Yeah, but my father always had this reputation. . . ." He stopped speaking and stared off into space. "He keeps telling me he's changed, and I don't want to believe him."

"Why not?"

"That's the million-dollar question, isn't it?" Rio sighed. "Why can't I allow my father to have a good side?"

"Because if he does, that means you might have to reevaluate how you feel about him, and your mother, and what happened all those years ago."

"Yeah. We did talk about that a bit." Rio blew out a breath. "He said he didn't know his new wife was beating the shit out of me."

Yvonne sat bolt upright. "She did *what*?"

"She didn't like kids." He shrugged. "I was a typically annoying kid who played too loud, broke things, and demanded regular meals."

"What did she do to you?"

"Locked me in the closet, punished me by removing my food privileges, and knocked me around when no one was looking. When I finally retaliated, she went running to my father about me being a vicious little bastard, so I was sent off to one of those correctional schools to force some discipline into me."

"That's . . . horrible."

"It wasn't good." His smile was perfunctory. "But it taught me a lot about self-preservation, and self-belief."

Her hands slowly balled into fists, and she knelt up on the seat. "Where does this woman live?"

"Why?"

"Because I want to find her and give her a taste of her own medicine."

He took her balled fist and gently unfolded her fingers. "It's okay. She's not worth worrying about."

"You're being way too nice about her," Yvonne growled.

"No, she really isn't worth your time. She's an alcoholic with anger issues who lives off her divorce settlement from my father, and continues to make spectacularly bad choices."

"So you keep tabs on her then?"

He smiled. "Not really."

"Liar."

"Okay, maybe I Google her once a year just to check she's still hanging in there screwing things up."

"Karma's a bitch, right?" Yvonne met his gaze.

"Yeah, it is."

He was still holding her hand, his thumb caressing her palm. And he was way too close. . . .

"My father also has this massive charity foundation."

Yvonne blinked. "He does?" Rio was really getting into this "friends share stuff" thing.

"Yeah, Josie told me about it." His brow furrowed. "I met some of the people who run it today at lunch, and they were very sincere."

"So basically you're worried that your dad is doing a number on you."

"Exactly. I know he wants me to take on the role of his successor, so maybe he's showing me the parts of the company he knows I'll approve of."

"That's certainly possible." Yvonne agreed, transfixed by the gold fleck in his brown eyes. "Or maybe he really has changed after all. Which scares you most? Him having changed, or you having to let up on him a little?"

"Both, I think. And then I started calculating how many people might lose their jobs if my father sells his company to a competitor or in a hostile takeover."

"So maybe you should be thinking about his offer more seriously," Yvonne suggested.

"I walked out on him once, Yvonne. It took all my courage to do that." He held her gaze. "I'm not sure if I'm strong enough to walk right back in."

"I can't tell you what the right answer is, Rio, but it sounds like you might have a lot of thinking to do."

He was still holding her hand, and their fingers were slipping and sliding and interlocking in some kind of unscripted, totally inappropriate sexual dance.

"Speaking of having a lot to think about, I've been thinking about you," Rio murmured. "I can't get you out of my head."

"I am pretty spectacular." Yvonne smiled at him.

"Yeah, and I owe you an explanation as to why I bolted from your bed."

"You do?" She blinked at him.

"You know I do. The thing is—I can't explain it." He grimaced. "I know this isn't a great time for either of us, and I know you don't want a relationship right now, but—"

"You still want me." Yvonne sighed. "Just say it. We both know it's the truth."

A second later, she found herself on her back with Rio straddling her. He had both her wrists captured in his hand and was smiling down at her.

"You don't feel like that about me, then?"

"Nope. Not at all."

"Really?" He slowly bent down, giving her all the time in the world to avoid him, and kissed her hard. "You sure about that? Because you sound pretty damn needy to me right now."

She licked her lips. "Let me up."

He immediately released her and sank back down on his knees on the couch in front of her like he was praying.

"How about we do this," Yvonne said. "We're not in a relationship, we're both free to leave, and we can have as much sex as we like for as long as we like, as long as the other person is agreeable."

"As much sex as we like?" Rio said hoarsely.

"Yes, with no strings attached." She attempted a shrug. "It's a very pragmatic, French way of solving our issues. We like each other, and neither of us wants to hurt the other person, so we promise to do our best to keep this *affaire* fun and free."

"I think they call that 'friends with benefits' these days," Rio pointed out.

"If you prefer." Yvonne held her breath. She had no idea why she'd suddenly decided to speak up, but she didn't regret it. The chemistry swirling between them was unbelievable. "What do you think?"

"It sounds okay in principle, but . . ."

"Basically, I'm giving us both a get-out clause so that we can continue to avoid facing our fear of commitment for a little while longer."

He winced. "You've been talking to Josie, haven't you?"

"No, but I'm not surprised to hear she's been giving you an earful."

Yvonne tried to sound like she didn't care what he chose to do when inside she was holding her breath. If she was ever to start trusting someone again and eventually have a proper relationship, Rio was a good place to start. Whatever happened, she knew they would still be friends.

"I don't want to hurt you," Rio said.

"I know." Yvonne nodded.

"And I still have to go back to being a bull rider for at least one more year."

"And I've got a business to run, and maybe a TV empire in the making."

They faced each other in silence until Yvonne reached out her hand and cupped his chin. The hint of stubble under her palm made her stomach do a slow roll of desire.

"We're friends, right?"

He nodded.

"And neither of us is stupid."

"Well, you certainly aren't," Rio agreed. "Me? I'm not so sure."

"We don't have to do anything."

"I think we do." His smile was pained as he took her hand and placed it over the bulge in his jeans. "I want you so badly."

"Okay." She leaned a little weight into her grip, and he groaned her name. "But this time I get to go first."

Rio almost forgot how to breathe as Yvonne undid the silver buckle of his belt and then the top button. She inhaled and then slowly lowered the zipper of his jeans, which he appreciated immensely.

"Nice," she murmured.

There was nothing he needed to say to that. He was too busy waiting to see what she'd do next to form a coherent sentence. She traced the top edge of his boxers with her fingertips, easing his jeans down over his ass. Before she could do anything else, he shoved them down completely, kicked them off and onto the floor. Nothing worse than being caught with your pants around your knees.

She spread her hands out over the jut of his hips, her thumbs lying along the sharp edge of the bone, and kissed his stomach.

"Nice abs."

"Thank you."

"I've never been a fan of them before, but yours are pretty spectacular."

"Having a strong core is essential if you ride bulls." He tried to sound nonchalant when his heart was beating like an out-of-control drum.

She kissed her way down each hip and then ran her teeth along the edge of his boxers, making him shudder with need. He almost lost it when her tongue disappeared beneath the cotton and swirled around the head of his hard, needy shaft.

He made a grab for her head, his fingers plunging into her coils of hair, and held on as she continued to explore him. His hips bucked as she drew him into her mouth, and held him there while he prayed to every god in heaven that he wouldn't disgrace himself, that the need spiraling through him could be controlled.

She pushed his boxers down, and surged forward, taking more, until he forgot about caution and simply reveled in the intensity of the feelings she aroused in him. Her fingers wrapped around his base, and she started to move on him. Everything in his world narrowed to the tightness of her mouth, the constriction of her hand, and the rhythm of his rocking hips.

His fingers curled in her hair, and he groaned. "You did say as much sex as we wanted, right?"

Her reply resonated around his arousal as she nodded.

"Good, then I won't worry if I—" Even as he spoke, the need to climax became too much, and he let go. His knees buckled, and he collapsed onto the couch like he'd been shot. Yvonne looked down at him quizzically.

"Are you okay?"

He managed a nod.

"Good, I'm going to bed now. Do you want to join me?"

She sashayed away from the couch, her hips swinging, and a victorious smile on her lips. As soon as he got his breath back, he was after her, sweeping her up into his arms while she squeaked his name. He laid her down on the bed and stripped off the rest of his clothes in record time.

Her appreciative gaze swept over him and she reached up to stroke his tattooed bicep. "You really are nice to look at."

"Thank you, so are you." He snatched a quick kiss.

"And now, it's my turn," Rio said. "And I'm not leaving this bed until I've reduced you to complete and utter exhaustion."

"You think you can do that?" Her smile was as hot as hell, and definitely a challenge. "Then go for it, cowboy."

Chapter Fourteen

Okay, so this was nice. Waking up next to Rio, his arm around her waist, and the sheets pulled down to display his spectacularly fit body. Sure, she needed to pee, but it was a simple pleasure to just lie still and breathe him in. They could make this work. They were friends, and adults, and all those good sensible things.

Eventually, she eased out of his arms and headed toward the bathroom, taking one last lingering look at his sleeping form. Today they were due to fly back to Morgantown in Chase's private jet. She'd be glad to go home. A few days in the city were quite enough to keep her happy.

Her cell was charged, and she disconnected it and plugged Rio's in. Glancing at her messages, she noticed one from Paul and carried her phone with her into the bathroom.

Delayed in New York. Can I meet with you in Morgantown sometime?

It was typical of Paul to be disorganized and to expect everyone else to accommodate him, but in this instance, she was keen to see him and get the formal separation behind her. Four years was too long to be left hanging.

Sure. Just make sure you give me enough notice. Book a room at the Hayes Historic Hotel if you plan on staying overnight.

Will do. Thanks.

Yvonne turned on the shower to heat up while she peed and then brushed her teeth. She felt slightly sore, but wasn't about to complain. Rio was a wonderful lover. . . .

Five minutes after she'd stepped into the shower, a pair of arms curled around her waist.

"Let's be good citizens and share the water?"

"Glurp." She blinked soap out of her eyes and batted at his hands as she spat. "Now I have a mouthful of shampoo suds."

"Sorry, beautiful." He kissed her throat, and her knees wobbled. "Just trying to help."

She let him caress her and gave him back every kiss and touch until they were entwined together, his hardness pressed against her stomach, and her hands digging into the flexing muscles of his shoulders.

"Damn . . ." he murmured as he slid his hand between her thighs. "I just can't get enough of you."

His strong fingers worked their magic and she was soon coming, her teeth buried in the curve of his neck, her hand between them bringing him to a climax at the same time. For a long moment, they just clung together as the water roared over their heads until Rio gently stepped back.

Yvonne smiled up at him. He wasn't that much taller than her, but his innate elegance and strength meant that, as she'd discovered last night, he could lift her like a feather. She'd never been the kind of woman who enjoyed being bossed, but something about Rio made it seem perfectly acceptable.

"I have a suggestion," Rio said as he washed himself down, and stepped out of the shower. "How about we pack your things and check you out, then you come with me to my mother's suite?"

"Sounds like a good plan to me." Yvonne bent over to gather her hair in one hand and squeezed the water out of it.

Rio groaned. "Don't do that."

"What?" Yvonne straightened up, grabbed a towel, and gathered up her long hair.

He was staring at her ass. "Don't bend over." He gestured down at the towel around his waist. "I won't be able to get my jeans on."

"Sorry." She took the second towel he handed her, and wrapped it around her torso. She pushed him gently toward the door. "Why don't you go and get dressed out there while I finish up?"

Rio barely got inside the door of the suite before his mother started on him.

"Aurelio Fatima Maria Martinez! Where have you *been* all night?"

A snort from behind him made it clear that Yvonne had heard the full list of his birth names and found it as amusing as almost every other American. He'd had to fight for his life when he'd started school. . . .

"Fatima Maria?" She nudged him in the side. "Nice."

"I'm sorry, *Mamae.* I thought Josie would've told

you where I was going." Rio came forward, took his mother's hand, and kissed it.

"I did tell her," Josie piped up. "She's just doing this for dramatic effect."

Isabelle swatted at her daughter. "I *knew* you had accompanied Yvonne back to her hotel, but I didn't realize you were intending to spend the night there."

"Neither did I." Rio shrugged. "It was one of those things that just happened."

Isabelle looked expectantly from him to Yvonne, and clasped her hands to her bosom. "You are in love? You will marry quickly, and give me lots of grandbabies?"

"Er . . . not quite. Let's not scare Yvonne away, Mom," Rio hastened to answer Isabelle. "I'll let you know how it goes, okay?"

"Well, it is certainly a step in the right direction!" Isabelle beamed at Yvonne and drew her into a hug. "You are just perfect for my son, just *perfect*."

Rio tried not to make eye contact with Yvonne. It was easy for them to agree that their relationship had no strings attached, but it wasn't so easy to explain that to his mother. . . .

"I'll go and pack," Rio said. "Are you ready, Josie? Chase is expecting you."

"Yup! I'm all ready to go." Josie nodded. "And Mom's got Graham's chauffeur coming to pick her up, and cosset her through the airport."

"Will you be okay, *Mamae*?"

"Don't you worry about me, son." Isabelle blew him a kiss. "I am perfectly used to traveling by myself."

Isabelle drew Yvonne down to sit beside her on the couch and started chatting. Rio really did appreciate how well Yvonne got on with his mother and sister. If they were able to remain friends, he hoped that would continue.

He pictured Yvonne smiling up at him as he slowly entered her body . . . and walked right into the closed door of his bedroom. No strings attached. All the freedom a man was supposed to require with the woman he desired. He was one lucky guy. . . .

His smile died as he found his suitcase and opened the closet doors. He'd never had a relationship like this before. All he could hope was that when it ended—probably went he went back on tour—that he and Yvonne could still remain friends. Even after only knowing her for a few weeks, he'd miss her terribly.

His cell buzzed with an incoming call from his father, and he reluctantly answered it.

"Aurelio?"

"What can I do for you, Graham?"

"Do you have time to come into my office before you leave this morning?"

"Not really."

"Is that the truth, or are you just avoiding me?"

"What's up?"

"It's not the kind of information I want to share with you on the phone."

"Right . . ." Maybe Graham planned to trap him in his office and never let him out again. "Then maybe I'll catch up with you when you're ready to negotiate on Mom's ranch."

"I'm leaving for the East Coast on Saturday."

"Then I won't see you for a while," Rio said evenly. "So either spit it out or suck it up."

There was a long silence.

"Your language is appalling," Graham stuttered.

"You know what I mean. I don't have time to hang on the phone right now, and I'm sure you're busy."

Graham sighed. "I'll try and amend my schedule so that I can meet you in the next week or so."

"Okay."

"Wish your mother and sister a safe trip home from me."

"Will do."

Rio waited for his father to repeat his plea for him to join the business again, but Graham signed off, leaving Rio listening to silence. That was weird. It wasn't like his father not to take an opportunity to hammer his point of view home. Graham had sounded . . . tired.

Resolutely pushing thoughts of his father to the back of his mind, Rio packed his suitcase and stowed his laptop, and other valuables, in his backpack. The nice thing about traveling with Chase was the ability to walk through shorter security lines and, hopefully, from Yvonne's point of view, no restrictions on carry-on baggage.

"Josie could've stayed with me," Yvonne pointed out as Rio followed her up the stairs to her apartment. "I've got a sofa bed."

"No, she couldn't."

"Why not?"

Yvonne opened the door and walked into her sunny kitchen. Someone had put some flowers and a sticky note saying *Welcome Home!* on the countertop, in January's familiar handwriting.

"Because I don't want to have to worry about my baby sister hearing us making passionate love every night."

"Oh, there is that." Yvonne put her keys away. "Every night?"

Rio dropped the bags by her dining room table, and straightened his back. "Well, whenever you choose to let me in your door."

"I could just give you a key." She paused. "But that would make things seem more permanent, wouldn't it?"

"Yeah. Let's not go there." He walked over to her side. "I have to go back to the ranch, and get Josie settled in."

She leaned in to kiss him. "Okay. Then I'll see you soon. Bring Josie in for coffee."

"I will." He kissed her back. "Thanks for everything."

She frowned. "That sounds very final."

"It's not meant to." He hesitated. "I mean it. Thanks for the best few days of my life."

"Better than winning that world championship?"

"Right up there."

She smiled, and just allowed herself to enjoy the moment. "Thanks."

He tipped his hat. "You're welcome." He set off down the stairs, leaving Yvonne staring after him. A minute later, his truck started up, and he was gone.

A minute after that, someone clomped up her stairs. "Hey!"

Yvonne turned around to see Nancy grinning at her.

"That was fast." Yvonne put on some coffee.

"I saw lover boy leave in his truck, so I thought I'd come over before I start my shift at the bar." Nancy sat on the couch with a bounce. "Did you get me anything in the big city?"

"How old are you?" Yvonne asked and pointed to a rainbow-striped bag. "Your gift is in there."

"Ooh!" Nancy abandoned the couch and reached for her gift. "Wow, hair colors, earrings, makeup, and a ton of samples from all the fancy store brands. Thanks! You rock."

"You're welcome."

"How did your trip go?"

"It was interesting." Yvonne checked the refrigerator and was delighted to see that January had restocked it with fresh milk and cream. "I met with the executive board of Tasty Treats, who want to do the cooking show with me, and I spent some time with Rio's family."

"You did? Are they as nice as he is?"

"Lovely. His mom is petite and dramatic, and you'll get to meet his sister Josie, as she came back with us."

Nancy placed her gift bag on the countertop, and hopped up onto one of the stools. Today, her hair was silver and black and tied up in two high pigtails like a Japanese anime character. Yvonne gave her a mug of coffee, and Nancy added way too much sugar and cream.

"How have things been around here?"

"Pretty good. Marley Hayes has been keeping everyone in line at the café, so there haven't been any real issues."

"Great. Maybe I should go away more often." Yvonne sipped her black coffee.

"With the hot cowboy?" Nancy asked. "Or for this business opp?"

"Maybe both. Rio really backed me up well at the meetings we attended."

"Who'd have thought someone who looked like that, and is a world-champion bull rider, would also have a brain?"

"I know. It's kind of unfair on all the other guys, isn't it?" Yvonne smiled at her friend.

"And I assume he's good in bed, considering that satisfied look on your face."

Yvonne winked. "Not telling."

"So you're a couple now?" Nancy asked. "Matt's going to be so sad."

"We're not officially a *couple*. We both have too much going on at the moment to deal with that kind of pressure."

"So basically you're still a commitment-phobe." Nancy raised an eyebrow. "But you're having sex?"

"Quite possibly."

"So . . . ?"

Yvonne gave her best French shrug. "That's what we're doing."

"Okay." Nancy finished her coffee and pushed her mug back across for a refill. "So tell me about the deal with Tasty Treats."

"I hate to sound like some terrible cliché, but this town is so *cute!*" Josie said. "I'm like waiting for a posse to sweep around that corner, and belly up to the saloon to drink some whisky and start shooting."

"Yeah. It's definitely got character." Rio smiled down at his sister. "The town planners are trying to keep it that way, too."

"Then maybe they should get rid of some of this traffic." Josie had to shout as a big rig muscled its way through the narrow street.

"That's on the agenda." Rio pointed toward the post office. "Yvonne's place is over there."

"With the pink and black striped awnings?"

"That's the one. Come on, I'll buy you a coffee."

Josie had loved the old ranch, and the Morgan family had taken her in as easily as they'd absorbed him. She was already an excellent rider, and had offered to help out if the family needed an extra pair of hands, which had won her even more friends.

She'd spent the early morning riding with Billy and his granddaughter Maria and then helped with the chores without being asked. Maria was already hanging on her every word. . . .

"Look, there's Yvonne." Josie pointed across the street.

Rio paused to admire the sight of his friend with benefits leaning gracefully over a guy's shoulder, pointing out items on the menu. She wore her usual black dress, white apron, and lace collar, and looked composed even in the midday sun. The guy wasn't concentrating on the menu; he was staring down Yvonne's cleavage with an idiotic smile on his face.

Rio took a menacing step forward, only to have Josie grab his sleeve.

"Watch out, idiot! There's a truck coming!"

He waited impatiently for the road to clear, and then strode across, Josie beside him. By the time he reached the café, Yvonne had gone back inside, so he contented himself with giving the jerk at the outside table a pointed stare as he walked by.

"Hey, Rio!" Lizzie greeted him with her usual sunny smile. "Did you have a good trip? Yvonne said she had a great time!"

"It was great," Rio agreed. "May I introduce you to my sister, Josie? She'll be staying at Morgan Ranch for a couple of weeks."

"Nice to meet you, Josie." Lizzie beamed at his sister. "Now, what can I get you, or did you just come in to see Yvonne?"

"Coffee would be great," Rio said. "And anything Josie wants."

His sister was already salivating over by the glass counter, so he suspected she was way ahead of him. He found a table and sat down while Josie discussed the merits of each confection with Lizzie, who obviously took her job seriously and had tried them all.

"Hi!"

He looked up to see a vaguely familiar blond woman smiling at him. She wore a bright blue skirt and a white frilly blouse, and carried a clipboard.

"I'm Margery. I was wondering if you'd like to sign my petition."

She thrust the clipboard right under his nose. He just about made out some words about housing before he pushed it gently away from his face.

"What exactly is it for?" he asked.

"Oh, I'm sorry—don't you read English? My bad." She took the seat opposite him.

"I read English just fine, but not that close up," Rio said evenly. After that comment, whatever she was selling she definitely wasn't getting his vote.

"I'm trying to stop the Morgan family dictating everything that goes on in this town."

"From what I recall, the town only exists because of the Morgans, so maybe they feel they have a duty to support it?"

"Not by bringing in cheap housing with all *that* implies," Margery snapped.

"What exactly does it imply?"

She leaned closer. "You know, undesirables . . . people who can't afford to buy their own places."

"Like most millennials, you mean?" Rio asked. "From my perspective, the best way to get good workers and families to stay put in a town is to provide them with affordable housing."

She sighed. "So you're just like the Morgans then."

"I'll take that as a compliment."

She stood and clasped the clipboard against her chest. "Luckily, not everyone in this town agrees with you. If Chase Morgan thinks he can buy himself some votes on the county board, I have enough names on this petition to say differently."

"Then good luck with it." Rio stood as well and tipped his hat to her. "It is, after all, a free country."

She turned away, and almost bumped into Yvonne, who didn't back off.

"Margery, I think you've already been asked not to come in here six times a day to badger my customers."

"I have a right to come into this space anytime I want," Margery huffed.

"Actually, that's not true." Yvonne paused. "I can go and fetch Nate Turner if you'd like him to explain the law to you?"

"Typical!" Margery snorted. "Threaten the innocent!"

"I understand that you are passionate about this, Margery, and I commend your civil spirit, but I can't have you disturbing my customers." Yvonne sounded way more sympathetic than Rio would've been. "Marley told me she's had several complaints over the past few days."

"Marley Hayes is an extremely bossy young woman."

"She was just doing her job," Yvonne said firmly. "Now, I'm asking you nicely, as a neighbor and fellow business owner, to leave my café unless you intend to purchase something."

Margery turned and went out, her head held high, and attempted to slam the door behind her.

"*Merde,* that woman." Yvonne sighed and sank down into the vacated chair opposite Rio. She looked tired. "I don't know what's up with her. Her husband died last year, and her son's gone off to university, so maybe she's lonely or needs a hobby or something."

"She's a Realtor, right?"

"Yup, she rents the property next door." Yvonne pointed to her right.

"So I guess she doesn't want to mess with the high house prices around here."

"Got it in one." Yvonne pushed an errant curl behind her ear. "I'd respect her more if she just came out and said that rather than suggesting it's an environmental issue."

"That wasn't how she put it to me," Rio said. "She suggested low-cost housing would bring in *undesirables.*"

"Well, Chase does have the money to finance new construction, so I hope he goes for it, and is ready for a fight."

"I'd bet on Chase over Margery any day." Rio smiled into her eyes and immediately forgot what he was going to say next. All he wanted was to throw her over his shoulder, take her up the stairs to her apartment, and make love to her all day. He reached for her hand. . . .

"You look tired."

"Are you suggesting I take a nap?" She briefly closed her eyes. "That sounds really appealing right now."

Rio leaned in close. "Well, not exactly a *nap*—"

"Hey, Yvonne," Josie squealed, making him jump as she pulled out the chair beside him. He hastily retracted his hand. "What's up? Did you really bake all those goodies yourself?"

Rio reluctantly sat back and let his sister chatter away. This just-friends thing was proving a lot more difficult than he'd anticipated.

"So Ruth asked me to tell you that she's expecting you for Sunday lunch tomorrow," Josie said.

"That would be lovely." Yvonne smiled at his sister. "I'm planning an early night tonight, so I'll be fresh and ready to go in the morning."

An early night . . . Rio looked up hopefully, but she gave a minute shake of her head.

"I've got a lot of baking and prep to catch up on after San Francisco, so I'm planning on working through until nine, and then going straight to bed."

"I'll come and pick you up if you like," Rio offered nonchalantly.

"Sure! That would be great." Yvonne smiled at him. "January usually brings me, but it will save her a trip."

"Or I could come," Josie suggested. "You'd lend me your truck, Rio, wouldn't you?"

"Hell, no." He smiled sweetly at his sister. "You can help Ruth cook. I'll do the chauffeuring around here."

She rolled her eyes at him. "Right, manly man, whatever you say. I'll just stay in the kitchen."

Yvonne was smiling at them both and shaking her head. "You two crack me up."

"Why?" Rio asked.

"Just because . . ." She rose to her feet and smoothed down her apron. "I've got to get on. It was nice to see you both. Enjoy the cakes, Josie. They're on me."

"She'll bankrupt you," Rio called out as she turned away, and received an elbow in the ribs from his sister.

Yvonne waved and disappeared back into the kitchen, leaving Rio feeling somewhat deprived. He hadn't even tried to kiss her hello. They hadn't discussed how public they were going to go with their casual relationship. He'd have to make sure to sort that out when he came to pick her up the next day.

Chapter Fifteen

"Are you ready to go?" Rio gave a quick knock on the open door as he walked into the pristine industrial kitchen. It was weird seeing it so empty of people and so quiet.

"Not quite." Yvonne wore fleece pants with cupcakes on them and a pink camisole top. Her hair was piled on top of her head in a messy bun. "Just got to set these trays in the cooling room."

"Let me help you." Rio set his hat to one side, washed his hands, and picked up one of the large trays.

"Thanks." Yvonne held the door open so that he could squeeze past her. The cold blast of air helped him realize she had no bra on under her top. "These are the last ones. I have some profiteroles in the refrigerator to take with me for dessert."

"Nice." Rio snatched a quick kiss as he went past her, and tasted chocolate. "How about you stay there, and I'll get the rest of these."

She didn't argue with him, which was a first, and stood patiently holding up the door while he transferred the trays into the stack of metal racks in the cooling room.

"You okay?" He glanced down at her as they headed for the stairs.

"Just tired."

"Maybe you should stay and sleep in rather than coming out to the ranch."

"No, I'm good. A quick shower, and a change of clothes, and I'll be raring to go." She gave him a bright smile as she let him into her sun-filled apartment and disappeared toward her bedroom.

"Do you need a hand?" he asked.

"No thanks, or we'll never get anywhere."

He sat on the couch. "Not a problem for me," he grumbled.

"Josie wouldn't be very happy if you didn't come back."

"Josie has practically been adopted by the Morgan family, and wouldn't notice if I disappeared for good."

"I doubt that."

Yvonne came out of her bedroom with a pile of clothes, a lacy pink bra and matching panties looped in her fingers.

Rio sat up and pointed at the lingerie. "Not fair."

Yvonne fluttered her eyelashes at him. "When you can think about me wearing it all through lunch?"

"I'd rather be taking it off you with my teeth."

"Maybe one day you will get your wish, but probably not at the Morgan family dinner table." She headed into the bathroom. "Sit tight. I'll only be a few minutes, I promise."

She was as good as her word, and within a quarter of an hour, they were on their way back to the ranch. His truck smelled like flowers and vanilla, which made a welcome change from leather and horse. It was a scent he was beginning to get used to and associate with all the best things in life. The profiterole rings were safely stowed on the back seat mats, where they couldn't shift around too much.

"Have much are we telling people about our relationship?" Rio asked.

She glanced at him over the top of her sunglasses. "What do you mean?"

"Do we say we're together? Do we pretend we're just good friends?"

"We *are* good friends."

"Yeah, I know, but does that mean I can kiss you, or put my arm around you in public?" Rio persisted.

"Would you like to do that?" She sounded slightly doubtful.

"Of *course* I would. I might even do it spontaneously, and I'm just making sure you're okay with that."

She didn't speak for quite a while, and simply stared out over the fields of cows and horses passing by as they wound their way up toward the ranch house.

Before he made the turn into the ranch proper, he drew the truck over to the side of the road, and put it in park.

"Why did you stop?" Yvonne turned to look at him.

"Because we're just about to arrive, and I still don't know what you want me to do."

"You don't know what I want you to do?" She slowly took her sunglasses off and studied him, her green eyes alight with laughter. "That's a first."

He grinned back at her. "Yeah, that's what you do to me. Turn me inside out and upside down."

She bit her lip. "The thing is—I don't want the Morgans to think we have anything really serious going on because they'll all be pleased, and will become invested in our relationship."

"So?"

"So when we go our separate ways, they might think badly of you."

"You're worried that they might think badly of *me*?" Rio asked.

"Yes."

"What about you?"

"I'll still be here. You're the one who is leaving." She paused. "So really it's up to you. How bad do you want to look?"

"I want to be able to put my arm around you and kiss you in public," Rio repeated firmly.

"Okay, then. Be it on your own head." Yvonne put her sunglasses back on. "Let's go."

Rio parked next to Chase's monster truck and went to get the dessert out of the back while Yvonne started up the steps to the porch of the ranch house. By the time he came along, she was holding the screen door open for him. A hum of chatter and laughter streamed out from inside the house meaning the Morgans were home en masse.

Rio went into the kitchen and smiled at the assembled crowd before taking the boxes over to Ruth. "You're going to need a bigger table soon."

"I know, but don't mention it to Chase or he'll start remodeling my house, and I'll have to have words with him again." Ruth placed the dessert on the countertop and went up on tiptoe to kiss Rio's cheek. "Thanks for going and getting Yvonne for me."

"You're welcome."

After hugging seemingly everyone, Yvonne came over and kissed Ruth. "You know Rio only comes over to make sure he gets dessert, Ruth."

"And other things," Rio murmured in Yvonne's ear

as he turned away from Ruth to greet the rowdier Morgans. "Don't forget those."

They managed to find a place to sit together, and for an hour or so, nothing much was discussed except the excellence of Ruth's beef stew and dumplings and the quality of the organic vegetables now being grown on the ranch.

With Yvonne pressed up against his side, Rio was happy just to sit and listen as the conversation flowed around him. Josie sat beside Maria, and the two of them were chatting like old friends. His sister had fitted into the ranch really easily and didn't seem to need him at all.

By the time they reached the coffee and dessert stage, conversation turned to other matters, and it wasn't long before Yvonne's meeting in San Francisco was mentioned by January.

"So did they offer you bazillions of dollars to star in your own show?" January asked.

"Not quite." Yvonne smiled. "We're not at that stage yet. They are still talking about how they intend to present the show, and exactly what its purpose, or what its 'selling points' to the public, will be."

"Oh, you mean their angle." January nodded like she knew all about the vagaries of television productions. "I'm more worried about how they are going to film anything when your shop is so small."

"I did mention that." Yvonne sighed. "If they put a full camera crew in my place, there won't be any room for paying customers."

"You need to rent the shop next door," Chase commented. "We own that building in town. We could certainly look at helping you out."

"And take Margery's realty office away from her?" Yvonne shook her head. "I don't think she'll be very keen on giving up that space to a friend of the Morgans right now, do you?"

"Possibly not," Chase conceded.

"She'll be screaming conspiracy theories at my customers all day long." Yvonne shuddered.

"Margery Hoffa?" Ruth frowned. "Is she being a nuisance? That doesn't sound like her at all."

"She's circulating a petition to stop the Morgan family from introducing cheap housing to the town," Yvonne said. "Unfortunately, she insists on coming into the café every time she's on a break and asks all the tourists and locals to sign the darn thing. Marley asked her to stop, but she wouldn't."

"Then I'll have to go and see what's going on with the woman." Ruth put down her napkin. "Her husband, Harry, died last year, and Spencer, her youngest, went off to San Diego to college. I wonder if she's feeling okay?"

"She hasn't paid her rent for three months," Chase said. "I was going to mention it to her when I was in town next week."

"Problem solved," Blue said as he put down his mug of coffee. "Kick Margery out for nonpayment of rent, and lease the extra space to Yvonne."

Chase groaned. "Yeah, right, BB. Let's really make her hate our guts."

"I'm just saying—"

"Then just stop, BB. I'll talk to Margery about that as well, Chase," Ruth said firmly. "No need for us all to get involved when she isn't feeling very kindly toward you boys."

Yvonne yawned discreetly behind her hand, and Ruth looked over at her. "You look worn out, my dear. Why don't you go on home and enjoy the rest of your day off in peace?"

"I'm sorry, Ruth. I don't mean to be rude," Yvonne apologized. "I haven't quite got back on schedule since my trip to the city."

"Then why don't you take her home?" Ruth looked expectantly at Rio. "I'm shut to teach Josie how to make a traditional patchwork quilt this afternoon, so there is no need for you to hurry back."

Rio sat up straight. Now all the Morgan brothers were staring at him. . . .

He turned to Yvonne. "Would you like me to take you home?"

"That would be great." She yawned again. "I am terribly tired."

"Then, if you don't mind, Ruth, we'll go right now." Rio wiped his mouth with his napkin, finished his coffee, and stood up.

Behind Ruth's back, HW winked at Rio and murmured, "Nice work, *mano.*"

Rio gave him his best *shut up right now* smile, and headed toward the door. He'd known HW for a long time, but he had no intention of giving his friend fresh ammunition to tease him with.

"I'll be back for dinner," Rio said to Ruth.

"On which day?" HW asked, and received an elbow in his side from his feisty girlfriend, Sam.

"Drop it, HW," Sam said.

"Drop what?" HW tried, and failed to look innocent. "I'm just making sure my friend is going to be okay."

Yvonne looked down at HW. "What do you think I'm going to do? Put him in a pie and cook him for dinner?"

"Maybe." HW grinned. "Definitely something hot."

Yvonne rolled her eyes at HW, and went around the table to kiss Ruth good-bye. "Thanks for having me over. I love coming here."

"Thanks for the profiteroles." Ruth patted her hand. "And don't worry about sending Rio back *too* soon."

Yvonne was just glad that neither she nor Rio were blushers because the intense but friendly scrutiny from the Morgans was getting hard to ignore. So much for not getting them involved in her and Rio's non-relationship. Everyone seemed to know what they were up to, and they were positively egging them on.

She collected her purse, promised January and Avery that they would have a girls' night out very soon, and got into Rio's truck. The moment he started the engine, she sat back in her seat, and stared up at the ceiling.

"They all know, don't they?"

"Know what?"

"That we're doing it. *How* do they know? Did you tell anyone?"

"Nope, you?"

"I didn't have to," Yvonne admitted. "Nancy was onto me the moment she saw me." She groaned. "*That's* how they know. Nancy probably shared with Avery, and then January and Sam got to hear about it, and so on and so forth."

"Which is why the Morgan brothers know," Rio added. "Basically, we're screwed."

"Because they all want us to work out and are helping us get time alone together," Yvonne concluded.

"Which is fine by me." Rio glanced over at her, his brown gaze hidden behind his sunglasses. "I'm going to be the bad guy here, remember?"

Another yawn shuddered through her, and she thought her jaw might break. "The thing is, I wasn't pretending that I was tired. . . ."

He sighed. "You're going to fall asleep the second your head hits that pillow, aren't you?"

"You know me so well."

"Then I'd better get creative." He pulled over onto the side of the road into the shade of some trees. "Come here."

"What—"

The rest of her sentence was devoured by his kiss as he leaned over, one hand wrapped around her neck, holding her close. His edge of desperation acted on her like a stimulant, making her kiss him back, and shove her hand up the back of his shirt just to rake her nails over his skin.

"Jeez . . ." Rio tore his mouth away from hers. "Right now. Let's do it right now, and then I promise I'll take you home, and you can sleep for a thousand years."

"Okay," she gasped, as he unceremoniously dragged her out of her seat and set her on his lap facing him. She moaned as her breasts were crushed against his chest, and his palm spanned her ass, pressing her against the rising tide of his need.

She fought him to undo buttons and expose the essential parts necessary to have him right where she wanted him. He found protection from somewhere, and then she was sliding down over him, taking everything as his strong fingers played with her most sensitive flesh. It only took a second for her to climax and freeze over him with her eyes tightly shut, her mouth locked on his as she lived in the moment of pure, uncomplicated pleasure.

It had only been a couple of days since she'd been with him, but it felt like a million years. She slowly opened her eyes, and framed his face with her hands.

"Thank you."

"You're welcome."

He was smiling back at her as his fingers started a

slow dance that immediately had her rocking her hips into the rhythm he demanded and created from her needy flesh.

"I can't. . . ." she gasped.

"Yeah, you can, *bonita*. Do it for me, let me watch you," he murmured against her mouth. "I want it all."

Eventually, he couldn't stay still either, and joined her thrusting upward to increase her pleasure, his booted feet planted wide, his hips rolling as he spent himself deep inside her.

She fell against his chest, wrapping her arms around his neck, and just stayed there for as long as she dared. The smell of him, the scent of *them*, infused the air, and she never wanted to move again.

"Yvonne . . ."

"What?" She opened her eyes as he gently set her away from him, back on her own side of the car.

"I'm so glad you wore a dress today."

"Me too." She smiled at him. "Now take me home, cowboy."

By the time they pulled up in the lot behind the café, Yvonne had managed to clean herself up a little, but knew that if Nancy spotted her, she'd have a lot of explaining to do. . . .

Of course, Rio had rebuttoned his shirt and jeans, and looked totally respectable. . . .

Rio got out of the truck and came around to help her descend, his keen gaze assessing her as he opened the door.

She held out her hand. "Haven't you forgotten something?"

He tried to look innocent. "Like what?"

She leaned in and whispered, "My panties?"

"Ah. What about them?"

"Do you have them?"

"Yeah."

"Then . . ." She made a hurry-up gesture. "Give them to me."

"Don't worry. I have them safe." He patted his pocket.

"What if I see someone I know?" she asked.

"How will they know whether you have a pair of pink lace panties on or not?" Rio asked in a deliberately innocent tone. "Unless they have x-ray vision or something."

She held his heated gaze. "You are incorrigible."

"Guilty." His dimple peeped out.

"One day, I'll steal your jeans and underwear, and leave you to walk home bare assed-naked."

"Okay by me."

He reached in, grabbed her around the waist, and swung her down to the ground. Yvonne was distinctly aware of a cool breeze blowing under her skirts.

"Behave yourself." She swatted him gently on the shoulder. "Put me down."

He obliged with a grin. "No point putting them on again when you're just going to take them off to shower is there?"

"Your logic is remarkable."

He kissed her nose. "And so are you."

Behind them, someone cleared his throat, and Yvonne spun around.

"*Yvonne?* Is that you?"

She backed up so fast she hit the solid wall of Rio's chest. His hand came to rest on her shoulder.

"Who is this guy?" Rio asked.

Yvonne swallowed hard. "Rio, I'd like you to meet my ex, Paul Giresse. I have *no* idea what he's doing here, but hey, that's him in a nutshell." She took a deep, steadying breath. "I hope you've booked yourself a room at the Hayes Hotel, because you're not staying with me."

Rio kept his hand on her shoulder. "Would you like me to show your ex where the hotel is?"

There was an edge to his voice that was unmistakable.

Paul's gaze flew to Yvonne and he switched to French. *"Ecoute, j'ai besoin de te parler seule, sans avoir le cowboy a cote. Tu peux envoyer balader ce plouc et me retrouve a l'hotel plus tard pour un verre?"*

He wanted her to get rid of the cowboy and have drinks with him at the hotel later?

"Are you being deliberately obtuse?" Yvonne answered him in English. "I said go and book yourself into the hotel, and I will speak to you tomorrow in the café. That's all I have to say to you right now."

Paul sighed. *"D'accord, j'y vais, mais tu n'es vraiment pas raisonnable."*

She wasn't being fair and reasonable? "Says the man who just turned up on my doorstep unannounced."

He shrugged. *"Je t'ai dit que j'allais passer."*

"This is not the kind of place you just pass by." She met his gaze head on. "That's not an adequate excuse, Paul."

"Je vois que tu as tojours la meme attitude." Paul shook his head and reverted to English. "Seeing as I don't want an argument, I'll do as you ask."

"Merci." He didn't like her *attitude?* He hadn't seen anything yet.

Yvonne turned to Rio and found a smile from somewhere.

"Would you mind showing Paul where the hotel is located, Rio?"

He inclined his head an icy inch, no hint of a smile on his normally pleasant face. "It will be my pleasure.

If he comes back, just call me, and I'll be right over with Nate Turner."

Rio didn't bother to make polite conversation as he led the way down Morgan Street toward the Hayes Historic Hotel. So this was Yvonne's ex. Paul was good looking in that smooth European way, and had the intense blue eyes of a husky dog.

"This is it? I thought they would have renovated it by now or put in something new." Paul stopped in front of the hotel. "It's . . . kind of dowdy."

"The pride of Morgantown. It's been here since the town was founded in some form or other." Rio held open the door. "After you."

Paul heaved another very French sigh and went into the lobby, which had retained its original Victorian charm and warmth.

"Hey, Tucker!" Rio called out to Avery and Marley's brother, who was manning the reception desk. "Guest for you."

"Hey, Rio." Tucker turned his professional smile toward Paul. "And who do we have here?"

"This is Paul Giresse. He's supposed to have booked."

Tucker checked his screen and nodded. "Yup, we have you in the biggest guest suite. I'll just get your key while you sign in." He handed Paul a flat-screen tablet.

Paul checked the details and scribbled his signature with his finger before turning to Rio.

"I think I can manage it from here. Thanks for the escort."

Rio frowned. "Your English is very hard to understand. Can you say that again in French?"

"What?"

Rio repeated his question. "*Ce plouc de cowboy aimerait*

que tu repetes ca en francais, connard. Et aussi, il aimerat que tu saches qu'Yvonne a beaucoup d'amis a Morgantown, alors ne fais pas le con."

Paul grabbed his key and practically ran toward the elevators. Rio suspected he'd stay put for the night.

"Wow, Rio!" Tucker's cheery voice came from behind him. "I didn't know you spoke French!"

He turned to smile at Tucker. "Obviously neither did that guy."

"What exactly did you say?"

Rio hesitated. "I'm not sure if you'll be happy to hear that I insulted one of your guests."

Tucker lowered his voice. "If he is who I think he is, I'd *love* to know what you said."

It was Rio's turn to shrug. "I said that this 'cowboy bumpkin' would like him to repeat what he said in French. And that I'd also like him to know that Yvonne has many friends in Morgantown, so he shouldn't be a dick."

Chapter Sixteen

"Nancy, stop laughing. It was embarrassing!" Yvonne spoke into her cell. "I was caught completely off guard in what could've been a terribly compromising position by the only man around who knew exactly what I'd been getting up to in that truck just by looking at my face!"

"Classic!"

Nancy cackled for quite a while longer before finally calming down enough to speak complete sentences.

"So Paul's turned up again. He must want something bad to come all this way unannounced."

"Well, he *did* say he might come here, but I wasn't convinced he would actually go through with it. You know how he is," Yvonne said. "Maybe he wants to get married to some other woman, and he needs that divorce finalized and the paperwork delivered right into my hands."

"Which would be great, right?"

"Yes, but I still resent the way he waits until he needs something to happen rather than paying attention to *my* needs."

"When did he ever do that?" Nancy countered. "I

met him quite a few times when you were setting up the café, and he was always a selfish jerk."

Yvonne sat down at the kitchen table. "I didn't see it back then. I was too excited to be home starting a business with the man I loved. His decision to walk out just before the opening took me completely by surprise."

"I remember."

"I was an idiot." Yvonne winced at the memory of her former self. "Looking back, I could see all the signs that he wasn't happy, but I ignored them because I was finally getting what I wanted, and I thought he wanted it too." She paused. "That's what he said to me afterward—that I'd made everything about me."

"Bull crap," Nancy said succinctly. "He just didn't like being in unfamiliar surroundings and not being the center of attention. Everyone liked you more than him, and he couldn't stand it."

"Well, anyway, that's in the past. I just have to work out how to deal with him right now."

"Be your usual pleasant self. That should do it."

"I'll try. I wasn't very nice to him yesterday," Yvonne confessed. "But he was so rude about Rio, and so dismissive of my concerns."

"So I heard." Nancy started to chuckle again.

"What exactly did you hear?" Yvonne said suspiciously.

"From Avery, who heard it from Tucker, who heard it at the hotel."

"What?" Yvonne almost yelled.

"Well, apparently, your cowboy speaks French, and he gave your ex a lecture *in* French about leaving you alone."

"*Rio* did?" Yvonne briefly closed her eyes. "Paul called him a hick."

"So I understand, and Rio told Paul not to behave like someone who rhymes with hick."

"Oh, God . . ." Yvonne breathed hard through her nose. "Paul's not going to be happy about that."

"So what if he isn't?" Nancy said. "Screw him!"

"You are so not helping here."

"Do you want me to come and meet Paul with you?" Nancy asked. "I'd be happy to be your wing woman."

Yvonne paused to imagine how that would go before she replied. "That's very sweet of you, but I have to speak to him alone."

"Okay, but I want a full report afterward."

"You'll get it." Yvonne checked the time. "I've got to get on. I'm glad I caught you so early."

"Actually, I was just going to bed."

"Then sleep well, and I'll talk to you later."

Nancy blew her a kiss, and Yvonne ended the call. *So, Aurelio speaks French, does he?* A slow smile spread over her face as she walked back into the main kitchen. He really was a very interesting man.

She wished she'd had a chance to get back to Chase Morgan and see whether he'd found anything out for her, but she'd been too preoccupied with Rio. Now all she had to do was find out exactly what Paul wanted so that she could use it to get what she deserved—a complete and final parting of ways.

Rio leaned against the wall of the post office while he waited for Josie to post her letter to their mother, who was back at her ranch in Sao Paulo. It was a beautiful morning with the sky a sheer, cloudless blue, and just a hint of a breeze coming down off the Sierras. He was due back at the ranch after lunch to help Ry and Roy take a group of newbies out on their first trail ride. The three R's, as they were now nicknamed, were deemed to have the patience and quiet temperaments to deal with the most skittish of the guests.

Sometimes an enthusiastic new rider thought he was in a western, and kicked his horse into a gallop. . . . That never went well. The Morgan horses had been trained to stop at a whistle, but the occasional one did get away. So far, they'd had a broken collarbone from an overenthusiastic teen who'd ignored every attempt to restrain him and taken off into the pine forest.

BB had been more furious about the damage to the horse, but Ry had taken care of the kid, who had hopefully learned his lesson. . . .

"Hey, *mano*, shall we go and say hi to Yvonne?" Josie rejoined him at the front of the building.

"Sure! I'll buy you a coffee."

Rio straightened up, checked his truck was locked, and walked past the shop that separated the post office from Yvonne's. The smell of good coffee and melting chocolate reached him and immediately made him yearn for the chance to kiss a certain naked café owner all over her luscious, willing body. . . .

"What's up, Josie?" Lizzie called out as they entered the shop. "Hey, Rio!"

Rio joined the short line while Josie checked out the pastries and cakes on offer.

"*Bonjour.*"

Rio turned to see that Paul Giresse had come into the café and wasn't looking very pleased to see him— which was just fine with Rio. Paul wore some kind of expensive brand polo shirt and pressed jeans. His short blond hair was gelled into spikes.

"Hey." Rio nodded. "Did you sleep well?"

"The hotel was comfortable, I'll give them that," Paul said grudgingly. "Do you live around here?"

Rio wanted to say he lived with Yvonne, but he knew that wouldn't go down well with her, or her ex.

"I'm working at the Morgan Ranch this summer."

"Oh, you're a seasonal worker. Do you go back home for the winter?"

"Home as in?" Rio pretended to look confused.

"You know, to wherever you come from."

"Nah, Boston's too damn cold for me. I prefer to stay on the West Coast, or visit my mom in Brazil."

"So you were one of those . . ." Paul paused. "Let me think of the American phrase—anchor babies? Do I have that right?"

"Wow." Rio shook his head. "I can see why Yvonne let you go back to France."

Paul laughed. "I'm just kidding, my friend."

"Right." Rio moved forward in the line. "When are *you* going back to France?"

"When I've finished my business meetings here, and settled things with Yvonne."

"So pretty soon, then." Rio didn't add the *good*, but suspected Paul would pick up on it.

Paul lowered his voice. "Are you and Yvonne a couple? She hasn't mentioned you at all."

"We're just good friends," Rio replied evenly.

"Looked like more than that to me. Perhaps you have a thing for her and she isn't interested, yes?"

"I can't comment." Rio shrugged. "You'll have to talk to Yvonne."

"Oh, don't worry. I will." Paul nodded toward the counter. "I believe it is your turn."

"Thanks." Rio caught Josie's attention as she came up to him. "Hey, have you chosen what you want?"

She smiled at him. "Yup, Lizzie's got my order. I'm going to find us a table, okay?"

Rio ordered his usual coffee and, after a brisk nod to Paul, went over to where Josie had already sat down. The table gave him a good view of the café, and the entrance to the kitchen.

Paul smiled at Lizzie. "Yvonne's expecting me. Will you tell her Paul's here?"

Josie nudged Rio. "Who's that with the fancy French accent?"

"Yvonne's ex-husband."

"He's definitely prettier than you."

"And I could definitely take him in a fight," Rio muttered.

"For a man who won't even confirm that he's going out with Yvonne, you sure are a dog in the manger," Josie murmured back. "Look! Yvonne's coming out to see him. She doesn't look happy, and she hasn't even noticed us."

Rio had already noticed that.

Paul was speaking, and after a long hesitation, Yvonne turned to Lizzie.

"Can you cope for a few minutes while I talk to Paul?"

"Sure!" Lizzie said brightly. "Just don't leave me alone to face the lunch rush."

"I won't be that long." Yvonne took off her apron, and held the door into the kitchen open. "Come on then, Paul."

Rio was only aware that he'd risen from his seat when Josie tugged on his sleeve.

"Sit down, tiger."

"I don't trust him."

"Yvonne won't let him do anything she doesn't like." She tugged harder. "Sit *down*. People are staring at you."

He sank back into his seat and picked up his coffee. It wasn't like him to feel so strongly about anyone. When women he'd dated in the past had moved on, he'd kissed them good-bye and sent them on their way with a smile. Now he wanted to chase Paul down and keep him as far away from Yvonne as possible.

There was no longer a way to deny it. His feelings for Yvonne went far deeper than the casual. And what the heck was he supposed to do about that when they'd both decided to steer clear of anything complicated?

Yvonne led the way up the stairs to her apartment, and waited by the countertop, her arms folded for Paul to join her.

"It looks great up here!" Paul took a long look around her home. "I was convinced it would be too small and cramped, but you really opened the space up."

She resisted the urge to say, *I told you so.* They'd lived in a rented apartment down the street while the café was remodeled. She'd shown him her design for their upstairs space, and he'd claimed not to understand what she was trying to achieve and constantly criticized her choices.

"I'm happy here." She moved to the refrigerator. "Would you like some water?"

"That would be great." He walked over to the big window that looked out over the street and then sat in her favorite chair. "Ice and lemon if you have it please."

She took the drinks over with her and placed them on the coffee table between the small couch and his chair.

"So what can I do for you, Paul? Did you come to deliver my divorce papers by hand?"

"Well, as to that." He took a sip of water before placing the glass back down. "It's still in progress. I've been thinking about you a lot."

"In progress?" The hairs on the back of her neck rose. "Meaning?"

He raised his gaze to hers, his expression solemn. "I keep wondering whether I bailed on you too easily."

Yvonne just stared at him, her thoughts in turmoil.

"We were both young, and I was so homesick that I suspect I didn't give our relationship enough attention." He sighed. "I didn't give *you* enough attention. All I cared about was getting back to France, and when you didn't want to come with me, I blamed you, and ran away."

It was so not what Yvonne had expected to hear that she had to check her mouth wasn't hanging open in shock.

"The last four years have been great for me financially and professionally, I can't deny it, but personally?" Paul stared right into her eyes. "Life has never felt the same since I left you."

"Hold on a minute." Yvonne finally found her voice. "Is this you finally apologizing to me after four long years of nothing?"

Paul leaned forward and reached for her hands. "Not only apologizing, but hoping that you'll give me another chance?"

"Hell, *no.*" Yvonne yanked her hands free. "You didn't just leave because you were homesick, Paul. You left because I wasn't the malleable teenager you married, and I no longer did every single thing you told me to do. You *left* when I began to challenge you, and you told me *I* was the problem, that I'd grown angry and aggressive and *opinionated,* and that wasn't my place in your world."

Paul shifted in his seat. "I think you're being rather harsh, Yvonne, I hardly—"

"Whether you agree with my assessment of what went wrong or not, and whether that's what you *meant*, is irrelevant now, isn't it? We've both moved on. We're both different people, and maybe that's what was meant to happen."

"But I'd like the chance to get to know you *again*," Paul said earnestly. "As you said, we're both different people now. I think we could appreciate each other's strengths and successes. I can certainly appreciate what you've achieved here."

"I'm very proud of my café," Yvonne said. "And I'm sure you're proud of your chain of restaurants."

He shrugged. "I had more financial help than you did. If we were together again, I could—"

She held up her hand. "Thanks for the offer, but I don't need your money."

"But if you want to expand the business, I have the resources to help you in the USA. That's one of the reasons why I'm over here—to discuss finances for a new restaurant chain."

"I'm really not interested in that kind of enterprise," Yvonne said. "It was never my dream, but I know it was always one of yours."

"Something of a family tradition." Paul smiled. "How could I resist the temptation to make my own fortune?"

"And you've succeeded very well." Yvonne finished her water. "I really need to get back to work. One of my staff is sick, and we're shorthanded."

"Will you at least think about what I've said?" Paul asked.

"About my business opportunities? I'm quite happy

right here in Morgantown." Yvonne stood up and took her glass over to the dishwasher. She wasn't about to mention the Tasty Treats TV thing.

Paul followed her over, trapping her in the small galley kitchen. "Not just the business deals, but about us."

"There is no 'us,' Paul." She looked him right in the eyes and felt nothing, no rage, no jealousy, just a hint of sadness. "I wish you all the best with everything in the future, but I've moved on. I couldn't go back and be the girl you married again."

"I wouldn't want you to." His voice softened. "I want you to think about me as a new man who wants to get to know you, the *new* you. Please, Yvonne, think it over and give me your answer before I leave. Surely you owe me that?"

His pleading blue gaze met hers, and she slowly let out her breath. "My answer will still be the same."

"But I'd still like to hear it." He stepped in and kissed her on each cheek. "Thank you for at least listening to me."

"I could hardly throw you out now, could I? You're bigger than me."

"You could've called in that cowboy. I suspect he's dying for an excuse to run me out of town."

"He's a good friend," Yvonne said.

Paul raised an eyebrow. "I suspect he's a lot more than that. Did he mention he threatened me last night?"

"Rio did?" Yvonne tried hard not to smile. "In which language?"

"Oh, you heard about that, did you?" A reluctant smile crossed Paul's even features. "I suppose when you work all over the place, as itinerants tend to do, you pick up languages fairly easily."

"*Itinerants*?" Yvonne couldn't hold her amusement back any longer. "You have no idea who he is, do you?" She walked toward the apartment door. "Let me help you out with that. Google 'Rio Martinez, bull rider,' and let me know how that goes for you."

She was still smiling as she came down the stairs, let Paul out into the back parking lot, and went on into the main kitchen. It was getting close to lunchtime, and Antonio was already prepping his selection of meals. Lizzie would need help at the counter. She was going to have to split her time between that and making up for Tom's absence.

She wasn't even going to think about Paul's ridiculous plea for them to get back together. It just felt wrong, but she'd have to deal with it at some point. Her answer wouldn't change. Had Paul really suggested that the divorce wasn't even final? What the heck was she supposed to do about that? She really was very proud of what she'd achieved in Morgantown, and nothing could take that away from her.

Her steps slowed. Could she go back to being an adoring wife who thought her husband was the sun, moon, and stars? Did losing that amazing capacity to blindly love and trust someone make her a harder and less sympathetic person? She guessed Paul would say it did, but she wasn't so sure. She liked herself so much better now, and she was so happy to have a man like Rio in her life who liked and respected her just the way she was.

Rio . . .

Yvonne pushed the swing door and entered the café, but the table where she'd glimpsed Josie and her brother sitting at earlier was empty. She was aware of disappointment settling in her stomach. Had Rio watched her talk to Paul, and take him up to her apartment? Had he cared?

She knew she had no right to ask him those questions. She'd been the one to define their relationship as just good friends, but just this once, she'd dearly like to know what he was feeling right now. . . .

The door of the café opened, and right on schedule, a stream of people from the various businesses in Morgantown came in for lunch. Yvonne found her apron, tied it around her waist, and went to work.

Rio checked out the boots at Maureen's General Store while Josie chose herself a new hat, and a couple of shirts to complement the Morgan Ranch T-shirts January had given her. The back of the shop was packed with everything a local rancher could ever need, and supplemented with food for the tourists who constantly drove through the town on the old gold trail.

When Josie was finally done, they made their way through to the front of the store and found Nancy at the cash register.

Josie put down the considerable pile of clothes she'd accumulated and pointed to the white straw hat on her head. "And this please."

Rio smiled at Nancy as she checked the price tag still attached to the hat.

"Hey, I didn't know you worked here as well."

"Maureen's my mom." Nancy snipped off the ticket. "I help her out when she needs it."

"You don't look much alike," Josie chimed in.

"Apparently I favored my father." Nancy carried on

checking out the clothes. "Not that I've actually met him, so I can't confirm that."

"My father died when I was quite young," Josie said. "I don't remember much about him either."

"That sucks." Nancy found a large paper bag, set it on the counter, expertly folded the shirts, and put them inside.

"How much is it going to be?" Rio inquired as he hunted for his wallet in the back pocket of his jeans.

Josie gave him her best glare. "I can afford to buy my own clothes, Aurelio, so put your card away right now."

Rio shrugged. "Just offering. I know how expensive college can be."

"Like either of us had to pay a dime for it. Your father paid for you, and mine paid for me out of my trust fund." Josie handed over her own credit card.

"And I'm sure Nancy doesn't need to hear all about that," Rio said.

"I dunno, I'm really nosey. That's why I like to work at the only bar in town. You wouldn't *believe* the stuff I hear there." Nancy ran the card through the machine. "But I promise I won't tell anyone that you're both filthy rich."

"I'd appreciate that," Rio said gravely. "My sister is sometimes a little bit too honest for her own good."

"Yeah, we wouldn't want her being kidnapped or anything," Nancy agreed.

"Unlikely in Morgantown, but you never know." Rio winked at his sister.

"So are you and Yvonne dating now?" Nancy asked as she handed over the receipt to Josie.

"You'd better ask Yvonne." Rio gave her his sweetest smile. "I'd hate to speak out of turn."

"Because her ex-husband is back, and I've never trusted him an inch." Nancy paused. "He's a bit of a charmer, and I'm worried that she's going to let him sweet-talk her into something."

"Like what?" Rio asked, despite himself.

"I dunno. I just know what he's like." Nancy shrugged. "I think he's leaving soon, so hopefully he won't have much of a chance to get to her."

"I think you underestimate your friend." Rio picked up the heavy bag. "She is more than capable of taking care of herself."

"Usually I'd agree with you, but she has a soft spot for that loser a mile wide." Nancy wrinkled her nose. "First love and all that crap."

Rio had a sense Nancy was trying to convey something to him, but he wasn't sure exactly what she wanted.

"Do you think I should talk to her about it?"

"God, no." Nancy shuddered. "You know what Yvonne's like."

"Then what do you suggest I do?" Rio asked patiently.

"Do?" She blinked at him. "Nothing. I'm just bringing you up to speed."

"Okay." Rio nodded to her. "Thanks."

"You're welcome!" Nancy called out to them as they exited the store.

Rio stole a glance at his sister as she walked along beside him. "Did I miss something important back there?"

"With Nancy?"

"Yeah."

"No, she was just letting you know what was going on with the woman you are secretly dating."

"I know that's what she *said*, but am I meant to be doing something more proactive?"

"Typical man," Josie sighed. "You can't go rushing

in there and fight for your fair lady's honor, you know. Nancy really was just giving you a heads-up."

"Okay."

Rio kept walking toward the parking lot behind Yvonne's café, where he'd left his truck. The problem was, even though he trusted Yvonne to sort out her ex, he hated not doing something directly to get rid of Paul himself. It made him feel . . . useless. He imagined Yvonne laughing her ass off at that stupid macho statement—and then demanding to know why he cared so much when they were supposed to be just friends. . . .

Liking and respecting someone was good. Getting passionate and hotheaded was a recipe for disaster. He'd watched that movie in real-time action with his volatile parents, and didn't want a rerun. Yvonne brought out a side of him he'd never realized he possessed, and he didn't like that feeling at all.

"Oh!" Josie stopped right by the truck. "I'm supposed to pick up some live yeast from Lizzie for Ruth. I'll just go and get it."

She went running off to the shop before Rio could offer to go in her stead. He opened up the truck and placed the big bag full of Josie's new purchases on the back seat.

"May I speak to you for a moment?"

At the unexpected voice, Rio almost banged his head as he exited the back of the vehicle. He turned to find Paul standing by the truck.

"What can I help you with?" Rio asked.

"It's about Yvonne."

Rio raised his eyebrow and waited to hear what the man had to say.

"I just wanted to ask you, as a gentleman, whether

you'd consider doing me a favor and backing off from Yvonne for the next day or two."

"Backing off?"

"I'm . . . trying to make things right between us again. I'd like her to have the opportunity to think things through without any outside influences."

"Like me, you mean."

"Exactly." Paul hesitated. "We were married very young, and we made some stupid mistakes, but I've never stopped loving her."

"If Yvonne wants to talk about it, I'm not going to stop her," Rio said even as Paul's softly spoken words burned a hole in his gut. "We're friends."

"But you won't try and dissuade her from thinking things through?"

"That wouldn't be my place." Rio looked past Paul to where Josie was rapidly approaching. "I have to go."

"Do I have your word on this?" Paul insisted.

"Sure." Rio tipped his hat to Paul. "I won't interfere."

He got into the truck, started the engine, and stared grimly out over the half-empty parking lot. Josie got in, and he released the break and put the truck into drive.

"What did Yvonne's ex want?" Josie asked.

"He was just making conversation."

"Didn't look like that from where I was standing," Josie scoffed. "Was he warning you off, or did he challenge you to a duel?"

"This isn't a movie, Josie," Rio said as he turned out of the parking lot.

"Well, I think you *should* challenge him to a duel, and then kick his skinny butt all the way back to France. Yvonne shouldn't have to deal with that idiot."

Rio gripped the steering wheel hard as he straightened up the truck. "You know what? I'm sick and tired

of other people telling me what I should and should
not be doing with Yvonne Payet!"

"There's no need to shout, Rio. I'm just saying—"

"Then maybe, just for once, you could keep it to
yourself?"

She didn't say anything until they turned off the
county road onto Morgan Ranch land and waited for
the automatic gate to open.

"You know *why* you're mad at me, don't you?"

Rio let out a breath. "I'm not mad at you. I'm sorry
I shouted." What was wrong with him? He *never* raised
his voice to his sister or his mother.

"You're mad because, for the first time in your life,
you actually care about someone, and you don't know
how to handle it."

He whipped off his sunglasses to glare at her. "I said
I was sorry!"

"I know you did, but that still doesn't change my
point, does it?" Josie gave him a sympathetic smile.
"Maybe it's time for you to stop hiding, and reach out
for what you really want."

Chapter Seventeen

"What are you doing in my kitchen?"

Yvonne rubbed the sleep from her eyes, and stared at Paul, who was washing his hands in the sink. It was four-thirty in the morning, and she was usually the only person in Morgantown apart from the deputy sheriff who was up and about.

"You said you were shorthanded. I thought I could help out today."

"How did you get in here?"

He shrugged. "I met your cleaners coming out, and they kindly let me in. Otherwise I would still be standing on the step waiting for you to come down."

"You don't need to do this," Yvonne said.

"I'd like to. There's nothing else to do around here." His smile was both charming and self-deprecating. "It's a whole month since I've been in a kitchen. I'm getting worried I'm forgetting my basics."

"I'm not sure—"

"I've already put the ovens on, so you might want to check the temperatures and show me your work order list for the day."

Yvonne considered all she had to do without Tom

around, and conceded defeat. If Paul thought working alongside him would make her go all romantic again, he was way off base. With a sigh, she got out her notebook and accessed the calendar on her tablet.

"Here's the list of extras." She pointed at the written orders. "The regular daily batches are on my tablet."

"You are quite productive." He came over to look at the list. "Where do all these large-batch orders go out to?"

"The Morgan Ranch and the Hayes Hotel." Yvonne put on her apron. "What would you like to help out with?"

"Not the bread. That was always your specialty. I'll work on the patisserie, and if I have time, I'll start on the cakes."

"Great."

The rest of her staff came in around seven for the café to open at eight. Aside from Antonio and trainee Tom, she had two additional staff in the kitchen who finished up the batch jobs and sorted them into the correct boxes for collection. After checking the temperature of the ovens, she started assembling the basic ingredients for her first batch of bread.

Hauling huge bags of flour, fresh yeast, and other essentials kept her in shape and gave her something to work her rage off on if she was having a bad day. With Paul in her space, she might need all her strength just to get through the day.

An hour later, she glanced up to see him working competently, rolling out pastry, buttering it, and refolding it before placing it in the refrigerator. Unlike Tom, he worked at the speed of an expert in a professional kitchen. He noticed her looking at him and winked.

"This is fun."

"Hmm . . ." Yvonne wasn't going to let him charm her. "There's still a long way to go."

She lugged a mass of dough into the kneading machine and turned it on. When she made smaller quantities, she liked to do the kneading herself, but for the batch orders there was never enough time. She walked over to the window where she kept her cell phone and surreptitiously checked her messages. There was nothing from Rio, which wasn't really a surprise. He'd probably be in to see her in person later.

And then she'd have to decide whether to tell him about Paul's offer to make a go of their marriage again and the current complicated unknown status of her divorce. . . . Would Rio want to know? Would he expect her to tell him? Things had gotten thorny so quickly that she wasn't sure anymore. Seeing as she had no intention of *agreeing* to Paul's proposal, maybe it would be better not to mention it at all?

She checked the dough and moved on to the next thing on her list. There was plenty to do, and worrying about Rio would have to wait.

Ruth smiled up at Rio and patted his arm. "You've been so helpful today, I'll buy you a cup of coffee at Yvonne's."

"You don't have to do that—"

Rio's protest died away as Ruth grabbed his hand and headed into the café. She'd asked him to bring her to town, saying no one else was available to help her, so how could he refuse? She'd spoken to her lawyer, visited every other shop in town, including the Realtors, and they'd ended up outside Yvonne's, where he wasn't supposed to be.

Did Ruth know that? Had she sensed his reluctance

to proceed and made the decision for him? He wouldn't put anything past Ruth Morgan.

"Sit here and save the table," Ruth said. "I'll go and get the coffee. You drink yours black, don't you?"

"Yes, but please let me—"

She patted him on the shoulder like he was five years old. "My treat."

He sat down. They'd missed most of the lunchtime rush, and Lizzie was by herself at the counter. But not for long . . .

The kitchen door swung open, and Yvonne emerged with a fresh tray of pastries. Her face broke into a smile when she saw Ruth, and Rio couldn't look away. He didn't want her thinking about Paul. He wanted her thoughts firmly centered on him.

A moment later, her gaze turned his way and he instinctively rose to his feet. She took the smallest of steps backward before she made the decision to come over.

"Hey, stranger."

"Hey yourself." He gestured at the seat. "How are things going?"

She made a face as she sat down. "They are a bit . . . complicated."

"Anything you need to share with a friend? I'm available most evenings until nine."

"That's very sweet of you, but I think this is something I'm going to have to work out for myself."

"Well, you know where I am if you need me," Rio said.

It was the right thing to say, even though the thought that she'd chosen *not* to confide in him hurt more than it should have.

"Rio . . ." She reached across the table and took his

hand. "I'm not trying to shut you out. I really don't think any of my friends can help me with this decision."

He wondered if she knew her ex was already trying to ensure that her friends didn't have any input on her state of mind. Just as he was about to reply, the kitchen door opened again, and Paul came out dusting his floury hands on his apron.

"Yvonne, do you have—?" Paul stopped talking and stared down at Rio. "Hey."

"Hey, are you working here now?" Rio asked as he eased his fingers away from Yvonne's.

"Just for a day or so. Yvonne needed some help."

"Oh, that's right. Tom's sick, isn't he?" Rio directed his question at Yvonne, who nodded. She didn't seem worried about Paul seeing her with him so he wasn't going to worry about it either. "When's he due back?"

"The weekend, I think. I might just tell him to stay home until Monday." Yvonne smiled.

"Seeing as *I'm* here until Sunday," Paul chimed in. "You're in the clear."

Yvonne rolled her eyes at Rio. "Yeah, lucky old me."

She didn't look like a woman trying to get remarried. . . . She looked like she wanted Paul to leave. Rio sat up straighter.

"Any news from Tasty Treats?"

"Nope." Yvonne frowned. "Did you hear from your father?"

"Yeah, he sent me a package detailing the offer. It's a damn good one, but I'm still not tempted."

"Good for you." Yvonne stood up and kissed him on each cheek. She smelled so delicious he wanted to inhale her whole. "I'd better get back. I'll speak to you soon, okay?"

She and Paul disappeared into the kitchen, and Rio

let out his breath. Ruth came back with the coffee and a selection of pastries, and settled in opposite Rio.

"She likes you."

"Who does?"

"Yvonne."

"So why does she have her ex working in the kitchen right now?" Rio inquired.

"Probably because she needed the help? You know how hard it is to find good staff around here." Ruth sipped her coffee. "And speaking of which, I spoke to Margery next door. She's definitely not right. The moment she saw me, she started crying. I couldn't get much sense out of her at all, except that she's lonely, and that she doesn't want her town changing as well as everything else in her life."

"I can kind of see her point," Rio said cautiously. "But—"

"The town needs new blood and new housing opportunities," Ruth said. "I'll drop a word in Dr. Ortiz's ear about checking in with her. I also suggested she might consider moving her business somewhere closer to her son."

"What did she say about that?"

"She promised me she would consider it." Ruth sighed. "It's hard when your family leave you. For a long while, I thought I was going to die on the ranch all alone."

"Until you persuaded Chase to come home."

She winked at him. "And all the rest of them."

"Even HW." He shook his head. "You must be some kind of magician."

"Family is the magic word, Rio." She held his gaze, her blue eyes bright with unshed tears. "Forgive the past, and make new plans for the future. That's what my grandsons have done."

"Sometimes families aren't worth saving, Ruth," Rio reminded her gently.

"Like yours? You love your mother and sister, don't you?"

"Yes, of course."

"But you struggle with your father."

"He was not good to me or my mother."

"And yet Josie says Isabelle has forgiven him. Why can't you do that?"

"Because he hasn't changed one bit," Rio said.

"Is that really the truth, or is that just how you prefer to see it?" Ruth asked. "Everyone changes. Look at my son, Billy. He became a drunk and walked out on his home and his family. He even went to prison. But now his sons are all trying in their different ways to connect with him."

"Because he's accepted responsibility for what he did? My father—" Rio paused and considered the last conversation he'd had with Graham, where certain things had come to light and he'd surprised his parent into apologizing.

"You've got to start seeing your father through your adult eyes, not through the eyes of a frightened child."

"And what good will that do?"

Ruth's smile was full of warmth and wisdom. "Free you from all that hurt you keep inside you. Now drink your coffee, eat one of these delicious pastries, and let's take the rest of them back to the ranch."

"So what is Tasty Treats?" Paul asked as they stood side by side at the sink, washing up various utensils.

"Nothing important." Yvonne carefully wiped down her favorite knife and placed it back in its block.

"It sounds like something related to your business."

He paused. "If you don't tell me, I'm just going to Google it anyway."

Yvonne mentally pictured herself duct-taping up Rio's mouth. But then she wouldn't be able to kiss him, and she enjoyed that far too much.

"It's a TV production company. One of the producers came by recently and really enjoyed my baking and the atmosphere of the café." She shrugged. "She might feature us at some point."

"That's good, right?"

"I suppose so." Yvonne finished washing up and wiped her hands. "I doubt it will come to anything— you know how these things go."

"What does your cowboy friend have to do with this potential business opportunity?"

"He happened to be in the café when the producer was saying how great my cakes were." Jeez, Yvonne hated lying, but she had a sense that if Paul discovered the extent of the production company's interest in her, he'd never leave. He'd always wanted to be a TV chef.

"Oh." Paul wiped down the countertop and took the cloth through to the laundry bag. "The restaurant chain I'm hoping to start on the East Coast would be perfect for a production company to feature. Do you happen to have the producer's number?"

Yvonne relaxed. Of course Paul was primarily thinking about himself. "I don't have it on me right now."

"No rush. If you find it, I'd love to have it." Paul took off his apron and stretched. "Wow, that was some workload we got through today."

"Yes, sometimes I feel like I never stop."

"Not sure how you manage all by yourself."

"After you walked out, I didn't really have much choice, did I?" Yvonne said sweetly.

"I Googled your cowboy. He's quite something, isn't he?"

"I guess he is." Yvonne took another look around the kitchen, making sure everything was in its correct place.

"How did you meet him?"

"He came in for coffee just like everyone else around here. Why are you asking so many questions?"

Paul shrugged. "I was just wondering. It seemed like a bit of a coincidence."

"In what way?"

"Just odd that a man like him would find himself in an out-of-the-way place like this."

"He's friends with the Morgan brothers up at the ranch. They asked him to come and do a master class on bull riding this summer. What's so odd about that?"

"So you were just in the right place at the right time for him to hook up with you." Paul washed his hands and dried them.

"So what?" Yvonne raised her chin and looked him right in the eye. "What's it got to do with you?"

"I'm just looking out for you. Men like him aren't exactly known for sustaining long-term relationships."

"Apparently most men aren't." She pointed at the back door. "Good-bye, Paul. Thanks for all your help."

"I was going to take you out to dinner."

"No thanks." She stomped over to the door and opened it wide. "Have a great evening. The food at the hotel is good. If you prefer something with livelier company go to the Red Dragon Bar on the corner of Morgan Street."

He slowly came to the door and paused right in front of her. "He's not going to stick around for you, Yvonne."

"And you are? What about your business interests

in France, and your family over there—the people you couldn't live without when we were married?"

"I intend to spend the majority of my time in the USA. I told you I want to do better."

Even though he was staring right into her eyes, she still didn't quite believe him. Call her paranoid, but there was something missing here . . . something that explained why he'd contacted her, and why he suddenly wanted to be part of her life again.

"Bye, Paul. Thanks for your help today."

She stepped back, closed the door with him safely on the other side of it and locked it. With Paul helping out in the kitchen, she actually wasn't as tired as she normally was, and she craved company. Her first thought was Rio, but she couldn't go there. . . .

Yvonne stared out of the window. When had Rio Martinez become her go-to person? What was going on? She grabbed her phone and sent a text to Nancy.

R U around?

Till 6, why?

Can U come over?

Sure.

Rio wasn't sure how he ended up at the Red Dragon when the only place he wanted to be was in Yvonne Payet's bed. But at least this was better than sitting at the ranch reading through all the information his father had sent him about the position on the board, and imagining how he'd change and improve things. . . .

He could do it.

If he wanted to give up his soul to his father.

He finished his beer and Jay Williams, the bar

owner, who had reactions like a cat, immediately held up another one, a question on his face.

Rio nodded. "*Obrigado*."

"You're welcome." Jay sent it down the bar.

It was early in the evening. Most of the tourists had left, and the locals hadn't yet taken back their favorite space to meet and drink. Some sports game was playing on the giant screens, but the volume was off, and it wasn't annoying him. He rarely drank alone or indeed came out without at least one companion. He'd needed to think, and the Morgans, much as he loved them, were way too ready to give him their thoughts and opinions on everything under the sun.

Ruth's comments about him not letting go of the past and giving his father a chance had hit home. He'd watched Billy at dinner, seen the way his sons interacted with him, and the love that was willingly being offered and shared despite their fractured pasts. If Billy Morgan was forgivable, how about Graham Howatch?

Nah . . .

"We meet again."

Rio looked up from his beer to see Paul sliding onto the bar stool beside him.

"It's a small town."

"Yvonne said I could eat at the hotel or here. It is a shame that she does not open her place in the evenings. The town could do with a good restaurant."

"And she'd be working eighteen-hour days."

"Not if she used my franchise opportunity."

"You have one?"

Paul shrugged. "I'm currently working on an opportunity to do so in the USA."

Which explained why Paul thought he had a chance

to get back together with Yvonne. He was going to be hanging around all the time.

Great.

Rio finished off his second beer in one long swallow.

"The attrition rate for restaurant franchises is quite high, but I wish you all the best with yours."

"Well, you would know, wouldn't you?" Paul's smile wasn't friendly.

"Meaning?"

"With your family connections."

"I don't have anything to do with that anymore," Rio said firmly.

"Really? That's not what I heard." Paul sipped the wine he'd ordered and grimaced. "I hear you're now on the board, and ready to take over when your father retires."

Rio eased his wallet out of his back pocket and beckoned to Jay. "I've got to get back to the ranch. Nice talking to you, Paul."

"Yes, I wouldn't advise you to go over to Yvonne's. She said she's having an early night."

Rio got off the stool and faced Paul. "You don't get to advise me about anything, okay? Yvonne is her own person, and she gets to decide whether she wants to hang out with me or not."

"I beg to disagree. I think I still *do* have some say in things." Paul's sympathetic smile made the hairs on the back of Rio's neck stand up.

"Why's that?"

"She didn't tell you, did she?" Paul paused. "I'm sorry, but that was really unfair of her. We're actually still married."

Rio took out a twenty-dollar bill, wedged it under the empty bottle, and left the bar, his feet automatically taking him into the parking lot before he stopped to let what Paul had said sink into his head.

Yvonne was married.

For the first time ever, he actually agreed with something that lying snake in the grass had said. It would sure have been nice if Yvonne had mentioned it. He tried to laugh it off and found it impossible. His last coherent thought was that he needed to speak to Yvonne right now.

"Paul's up to something, but what?" Yvonne said to Nancy as they sat on her couch, drinking coffee and eating left over ham-and-swiss-cheese croissants from the café.

"I'm not arguing with you about that," Nancy mused. "So what do we know? He's got a new business venture in the US. What does he think you can bring to that?"

"Not money. He has enough to last him several lifetimes from his family," Yvonne said. "Or creative input. He always hated my ideas, and I suspect nothing has changed there."

"Influence?"

"From my one tiny café in the gold country? I doubt it."

"Then what?" Nancy sat up straight. "Ooh! Did he know about the TV thing? He'd love to be involved in that."

"He only knew about it because Rio mentioned it to me in his hearing. I played it down, but you're correct. He was definitely interested." Yvonne bit her lip. "Maybe he knew about it already, and was just pretending to find out?"

"I wouldn't put it past him," Nancy agreed. "He's all

about the glorification of himself, and being on TV would probably be a dream come true."

"It would." Yvonne nodded. "So that's one thing. Maybe I should ask him straight out what he's up to. He can't seriously believe I'd get back together with him again, can he?"

"With his ego? Sure, but I think you're on the right track. This isn't about rekindling lost love. This is all about him, and his business interests."

Yvonne flopped back on the couch. "I'm just going to have to ask him, flat out, aren't I?"

"Yeah," Nancy sighed. "Any chance we could get him blind drunk, tie him up, and make him confess everything?"

"He's French. He never gets drunk," Yvonne said gloomily.

Nancy uncurled from her position on the couch. "Gotta go, girlfriend. I'm due at the bar."

Yvonne rose as well. "Thanks for coming over. I really appreciate it."

Nancy drew her into a quick hug. "That's what friends are for, right? And seeing as we're the only two sensible women left in town since the Morgan brothers returned, we need to stick together."

"I'm not feeling very sensible right now," Yvonne confessed. "Every moment I spend with Paul reminds me how much I like Rio."

Nancy drew back and searched her face. "You *really* like him, don't you?"

"Yeah."

"And?"

"It's terrifying. What if I make another huge mistake and get lust and love mixed up? What if he's really cool with us just staying friends, and will blow me a kiss and ride off into the sunset never to be seen again?"

"Okay, relax," Nancy said firmly. "That man is not going anywhere. He is *totally* into you."

"You think?"

"I know. Get rid of Paul, sort out the divorce, and make sure you tell Rio how you feel before he gets the *chance* to ride away."

"Okay." Yvonne nodded. "It's not like me to be so indecisive."

"Which only confirms that this dude has done a number on you." Nancy smiled. "It's quite fun to watch, actually."

Yvonne laughed and walked her friend to the door. "Go away. You're way too happy at my expense."

She gathered up the empty plates to bring down to the shop as Nancy clomped down the stairs in her wedged heels. It appeared to be raining, but as Nancy was quite close to the bar, Yvonne didn't think she'd need an umbrella.

Unlocking the back door, she kissed Nancy's cheek. "Bye, girlfriend, love you."

"Same here." Nancy headed out, drawing the hood of her jacket over her white and black hair to protect her from the rain.

"Hey."

Yvonne almost jumped as a deep familiar voice called out to her.

"Rio?"

His cowboy hat was lowered over his face against the drift of the rain, and he wore his favorite all-black ensemble.

"May I speak to you for a minute?"

"Sure, come on in." Yvonne held the door open to allow him to come through into the hall that separated the kitchen from the stairs up to her apartment.

She started up the stairs and then realized he wasn't following her.

"Are you coming?"

"I'd rather talk to you down here."

She retraced her steps and took in his body language. Her usually easygoing, elegant lover had disappeared, and been replaced by someone she barely recognized.

"What's up?"

He finally looked at her. "We're supposed to be friends, right?"

"Yes."

"So was there some minor detail you should have shared with me recently? Something important?"

"Such as?"

"The fact that you're still married to that godawful French jerk?"

Shock fisted in her gut. "Who told you that?"

"Guess?"

She crossed her arms over her chest. "It's not that simple."

"It damn well sounds like it to me!"

"Well, it isn't. The thing is, I thought—"

"You know whether you're married or not, Yvonne, so which is it?"

She drew herself up to her full height. "Are you *shouting* at me?"

"What's that got to do with answering the question?"

Hurt blasted through her. "Why do you care so much anyway? I don't tell my friends everything."

"So no one knew except you and the asshole?"

Yvonne hesitated long enough for him to shake his head.

"I bet all your friends knew, so what does that say about us?"

"You *agreed* that we could only be friends," Yvonne pointed out. "You said you didn't want a long-term relationship."

"So this is my fault? I accidentally put myself in the wrong friends category? I have no right to ask you what the hell is going on?"

"That's not what I said!"

"I don't have affairs, Yvonne. I don't get mixed up with married women, period. I saw my father doing that to my mother. It's screwed up."

"So you're angry because in your eyes I'm apparently an *adulteress*?"

"No! I'm *angry* because you didn't mention it before we went to bed together."

Silence fell for a moment, punctuated only by their harsh breathing.

She took a couple of steps backward until her heel hit the bottom step. Her fingers shook as she gripped the bannister. She could explain to him exactly what had happened with Paul, but there didn't seem much point. His anger, and her response to it, told her they were way beyond just being friends now. And, hey, she had made the decision not to tell him what was going on with her ex, so maybe she deserved at least some of his ire.

"Okay. Maybe you have a point." With a tremendous effort, Yvonne pulled herself together. "Maybe I haven't been a very good friend to you after all. I apologize for that."

"That's not what I . . ." He stopped talking, and shook his head.

She couldn't find a smile. His accusation hurt far more than it should've. Which meant that, despite her best efforts, her heart had become involved, too. What a terrible moment to realize how much she'd come to value him. . . .

"Can you let yourself out? I'm expecting a phone call. I have to go."

He swept his hat off his head, and came toward her, his brown eyes intent.

"Please, Yvonne . . . I was out of line, I apologize—"

"I really do have to go."

Just on cue, her cell phone on her kitchen counter-top started ringing, and she ran up the stairs, slamming her apartment door behind her. Grabbing her phone, she forced her shaking voice to cooperate.

"Hi, this is Yvonne. How are you doing, Priscilla?"

Chapter Eighteen

"Hey, Rio, we're all really grateful you've been out here doing our chores for hours, but Ruth wants you to come in and eat something."

Rio straightened up from dumping a load of soiled straw on the manure heap and faced HW, who was leaning casually against the corner of the barn, hands in his pockets, watching him.

Rio wiped his hands on his jeans and let out his breath. "Seeing as I've run out of things to do, I suppose I have no choice but to come in." He walked toward the tack room. "Just give me a minute to wash up, and I'll be there."

HW followed him over and propped up another doorframe. "What's up?"

"Nothing much."

"I don't believe you." HW paused. "Woman trouble?"

Rio snorted. "Like I'm going to tell you."

"Why not? I'm your friend, and I've had a whole crap load of advice dumped on me about my relationship with Sam. The least I can do is help another guy avoid some of the pitfalls."

"It's too late for that."

"You screwed up?"

"Nope." Rio reluctantly faced HW.

"*Yvonne* screwed up?"

"You could say that." Rio dried his hands and turned off the faucet. "She forgot to give me some important information before we hooked up."

"Like what?"

"She's still married to that French asshole."

HW frowned. "You sure about that?"

"The asshole told me himself."

"And Yvonne admitted it?"

"She . . ." Rio paused to run his conversation with Yvonne back through his head. "She didn't deny it."

"That's not the same thing, bro. In my experience, women get super pissed when you get on their case and start accusing them of stuff. Now, a guy would just give you an explanation right off or punch your lights out, but a woman? She'll clam up, get all upset, and storm off."

"Really?" Rio raised an eyebrow. "Because I heard that you were the one who kept storming out on Sam."

"I'm the exception that proves the rule." HW waved that inconvenient fact aside. "And this isn't about me, so stay focused."

"Yvonne did get pissed with me, which is unfair because I'm not the one at fault this time. I don't mess around with married women, HW. You know that."

"The thing is—I'm sure Chase said he was looking into something for Yvonne in France a while back." HW frowned. "I usually try and tune him out when he gets technical, so I can't remember the details. Maybe you should ask him about it."

"Maybe she was looking for air tickets home," Rio muttered.

HW punched his arm. "Don't be such an ass."

"So what do you think I should do, oh wise man?" Rio said.

"Go and talk to her instead of staying on the ranch fuming and fretting."

"Like I should take advice from you?"

"Well, I am the one who's in a fantastic relationship with a woman I love." HW smirked. "And you're the one running scared, so maybe just for once, yeah, maybe you should."

Rio showered and went back down to the kitchen to eat the dinner Ruth had set aside for him. He braced himself for another Morgan intervention, but Ruth was in the parlor with Roy watching some reality show they both loved, and he had the place to himself. Unfortunately, it gave him too much time to think, which was what he'd been avoiding by doing the chores.

His cell buzzed, and he took it out of his pocket. Maybe it was Yvonne wanting to talk to him after all. . . .

Landing at Morgan ranch in ten minutes. Please be there to meet me.

Rio stared at his father's message and reread it several times before replying.

What the hell are you talking about?

I'm arriving by helicopter. Need to speak to you.

"*Deus todo poderoso* . . ." Rio murmured. "What now?"

He hastily downed his coffee and went to knock on the door of the parlor.

"Ruth, I'm sorry to interrupt, but do you know how to operate the landing strip controls on the ranch?"

Ruth turned to look at him. "Is the emergency heli-copter coming in?"

"No, apparently it's my father," Rio confessed. "I'm really sorry about this. I had no idea he was even in the area until I got his text a few minutes ago."

Roy stood and put on his cowboy hat. "Don't worry, son. I can take you out there."

"Thank you."

Ruth smiled at Rio. "And bring your father back to the ranch. I'd love to meet him. I'll find him a bed if he needs it."

Ten minutes later, he and Roy were bumping up a side road that snaked between the abandoned silver mine and the ghost town of Morgansville.

"I called Chase, and he said the landing lights are preset to come on when radar makes contact with a plane," Roy said as he peered into the gathering gloom.

"Good to know." Rio hung on to the strap as the truck almost went sideways. Luckily, it didn't take that long to reach the flat strip of land, which was already blazing with light. "Looks like he's already here."

"Yup." Roy brought the truck to a stop. "I'll wait. Let me know what you need."

"Thanks, Roy."

Rio exited the truck and made his way toward the helicopter parked on the landing pad. The blades were still turning, but were obviously winding down.

"Mr. Martinez?" Someone stepped out of the gloom. "Mr. Howatch asks that you please join him on board."

Rio nodded and went up the lowered steps to the back end of the helicopter, where his father was seated in comfort in a relatively large space.

"Hey. What can I do for you?" Rio asked.

"Come and sit down."

Graham pointed at the seat opposite him, Graham wasn't wearing his usual suit and tie combination, and had a blanket over his knees. Either the interior lighting sucked, or his father's skin had a yellowish tinge to it.

"Are you okay?" The words left Rio's lips before he could stop himself.

"I hate helicopters."

"Then why take one just to come out here and see me?" Rio asked.

"Because I wanted to share some information with you in person."

"We've been through this once before. Why can't you tell me over the phone?"

"Phones aren't secure." Graham picked up a folder on his desk. "I have some information about Yvonne Payet I think you should know."

"Let me guess." Rio sat back in his chair. "She's married to a French guy. I already know all about that, so shall I go before I get into what a gross intrusion that is into Yvonne's privacy?"

"I always investigate anyone who comes close to my family." Graham shrugged. "There are many people out there who are attracted to wealth. You know that."

"Seeing as I've never considered myself that wealthy, not really."

"Don't be flippant, Aurelio. You are a world champion. You aren't exactly a pauper, and I've seen the women you chose to surround yourself with. You are also my son."

"So you've been spying on me as well? Great."

"The report on Yvonne brought up another interesting anomaly. Her connection with Paul Giresse."

"What about him?"

"He is currently in the country discussing acquiring

a chain of restaurants and rebranding them to reflect his personality and cooking expertise."

"So I hear." Rio snorted. "It doesn't surprise me. Have you met the guy?"

"He's seeking funding from Howatch International."

"From *you*?" For the first time, Rio smiled. "Then you know what to do. Turn him down and send his sorry ass back to France."

Graham studied him for a long moment. "Do you see him as a rival for Yvonne's affections?"

"No, I just don't like the guy."

"The Giresse family is very wealthy," Graham said. "Don't you think it's strange that Yvonne managed to attract the attention of Paul Giresse, and then you?"

Rio tensed. "What exactly are you trying to suggest?"

"Don't bite my head off, but is it possible that she is the kind of woman who seeks out men with money?"

After a stunned second, Rio laughed out loud. "No, not at all. You've met her. How can you even entertain that thought? She's the real deal—hardworking, honest, and as determined as hell."

"You really do like her, don't you?" Graham said slowly.

"How I feel about her has nothing to do with how I view her character."

"I beg to disagree." To Rio's surprise, Graham was smiling. "Seeing as you've made your position clear, perhaps you would care to read through the proposal Paul put forward?"

"Why would I do that?"

"Because I value your advice, and you might find out something interesting as to his motivation and need to ensure the deal goes through as soon as possible."

"What the hell is that supposed to mean?" Rio said slowly.

Graham held out a folder. "Why don't you find out?"

"Today at eleven? That sounds great!" Yvonne lied, and inwardly screamed as Priscilla apologized for the short notice and waffled on about contracts, camera crews, and all kinds of stuff that she couldn't yet envision filling up her café. "I look forward to it. Bye for now."

It was six in the morning, and she was in her usual spot in her kitchen. After briefly talking to Priscilla the night before she'd been waiting for an update, but hadn't expected Priscilla to want to come and see her that very same day. The bread was trying. The ovens were heating up, and she'd made a start on the brioche dough for the next morning.

There was no sign of Paul, which made her happy. She hoped he'd left town but had a sinking sensation that he'd make sure she knew about it, which probably meant he was still at the hotel. After her falling-out with Rio, she hadn't slept well. Her decision not to argue with him about the sham of her marriage still seemed the lesser of two evils.

If she'd tried to convince him that she'd believed she was single when they'd gotten together, she'd have to admit to herself that he deserved an explanation because they really cared about each other. Maybe he'd just been angry about being deceived and not hurt at all. Maybe she was the only one who needed to step back and protect her vulnerable heart.

But she couldn't forget the look in his eyes when he'd confronted her—like she'd destroyed his world as well as her own. She needed to talk to him. She owed him that. If only the day hadn't already gotten so overcrowded . . .

"Are you coming?" Josie called out to Rio as he came down the stairs of the ranch house.

"Coming where?" Rio answered.

"Into town. Mom said she's written me a letter, and I want to pick it up from the post office."

Rio paused on the bottom step to consider his options. On his return from seeing his father, he'd thrown the file onto the desk in his bedroom and left it there unopened. He wasn't sure he wanted to know what was in it. It felt disloyal to Yvonne to even consider reading it.

He wanted to see her—just to check that she was okay, and to really listen to what she had to say to him—rather than reacting like an idiot. She deserved that. She'd never struck him as the kind of person who would deliberately deceive him, and his bullshit meter was quite high. So there must be more to it.

"Shame you didn't think on your feet when you actually saw her," Rio murmured to himself. "Serves you right if she doesn't want to speak to you ever again."

"Are you talking to me?" Josie demanded as she came out of the kitchen.

"No, just reminding myself not to be an idiot."

"Too late for that." She gave him a sunny smile. "So, are you coming, or can I borrow your truck and go myself?"

"Like I'd lend you my truck." Rio showed her the keys, and then put them right back in his pocket. Going into town with his sister was a perfectly legitimate excuse to drop in at the café. "Let me just get my boots on, and I'll be right there."

* * *

For once, Yvonne was glad that the weather was lousy, and that the tourists who usually dropped in at the café were largely absent. Tom was back in the kitchen, and she'd added another person to the wait-staff roster, meaning she had more time to deal with weird stuff like TV production companies.

Priscilla arrived at the café promptly at eleven, and brought a guy Yvonne hadn't met before.

"Hey, Yvonne. This is John Jordan. He's—"

Before Priscilla could finish her sentence, John reached over, grabbed Yvonne's hand, and shook it vigorously.

"Hi, I represent Howatch International. We own the majority share in Tasty Treats." His appreciative gaze scanned her from head to toe. "I'm sorry I was out of town when you visited our offices in San Francisco. It's a pleasure to finally meet you."

"You, too."

Yvonne eased her hand out of his overly enthusiastic grasp. *Howatch International?* Wasn't that the company contemplating financing Paul's restaurant business? Maybe he *had* known about her potential TV deal before he'd descended on Morgantown. . . .

"Oh, look! There's Rio!" Priscilla pointed at the door, where Rio and his sister, Josie, had just arrived. She waved at Rio. "Come on over and meet John! You're just in time!"

Rio looked helplessly at Yvonne, who shrugged even as her heart rate tripled, and it suddenly became hard to breathe.

"I'm not sure if Rio has time for this meeting or not. He's on vacation with his sister," Yvonne said.

"Don't worry about me." Josie gave her brother a

shove in Yvonne's direction. "I'll just sit and have my coffee over there. I'm not in any rush."

Rio slowly closed the gap between them, and lowered his voice. "I'm happy to sit in on this if you want me to, but I understand if—"

She cut him off. "Look, let's talk about that later. I'd love you to stay."

He held her gaze. "Are you sure? I know I've behaved like a complete ass."

"Let's just see this through, shall we? If you disappear on me now, Priscilla's probably going to cry."

A reluctant smile flickered across his face. "Okay. Whatever you want."

He turned to John. "Hi, I'm Rio Martinez."

"Wow!" John's eyes widened. "You're—"

Yvonne suppressed a smile. Who would've thought that the polished businessman was a PBR fan?

"Let's not worry about what I am or not at this point," Rio said firmly. "I'd prefer to keep the focus on Yvonne and her café."

"Okay, then." John sat down and looked around the café. "One of the first issues I see here is lack of space. Is there any potential to expand?"

"I'm certainly considering it," Yvonne said. "The kitchen at the rear of the property is extensive. I assumed you'd be doing most of your filming out there."

"Possibly," John agreed. "If we do go ahead, there are ways to use smaller static cameras to cover some areas like the entrances and exits, so we could get around it if we have to."

"I'll take you through to the kitchen after we've talked, and you can see what you think," Yvonne said. "I assumed you'd be more interested in featuring my cooking skills than my daily interactions with my customers."

"There's a balance to be found between those two elements," John agreed. "But having met you, I'm inclined to suggest that the spotlight remains firmly on you."

"What do you mean?" Yvonne asked.

"Well, look at you." John waved a hand at her face. "You're a multi-talented immigrant probably with a fascinating backstory that would go over really well with our audiences."

"*Immigrant*?" Yvonne sat up straight.

"You're African and French, right? Where *exactly* were you born? You've got a beautiful *exotic* look our viewers will love."

Yvonne slowly opened and closed her mouth before gathering her resources. "Not that it is any of your business, but I was born in the United States to an American citizen. That makes me *American*, right?"

"Sure, if you want to push that angle." John shrugged. "I'm just saying that having an exotic mysterious heritage would play better."

Yvonne abruptly stood up. "Would you like to see the kitchen?"

She was shaking so hard with the desire to smack John in his stupid smiling face. He wasn't the first person to make the same assumptions, and he probably wouldn't be the last. She'd learned to smile and ignore such people, but sometimes it was hard. It was a good thing they hadn't been in her kitchen within reach of her favorite cast-iron pans and knives. . . .

She and Priscilla led the way into the kitchen, where she hoped her team was working away. She held open the door to let Priscilla go past her and turned just in time to see Rio nose to nose with John, his finger jabbing the other guy in the chest as he shoved him up against the wall.

"You want to talk about someone's heritage? Why don't you show what a complete asshole you are, and ask about mine?"

"Rio . . ." Yvonne took a step toward him.

Rio gave John one last icy glare. "Keep your outdated opinions to yourself in future, okay?"

John put his hands up as if he was surrendering. "Sure . . . I didn't mean to offend anyone. I was just making a suggestion."

"Then don't." Rio looked over at Yvonne, his expression like granite. "Do you want to call this whole thing off? I'll back you one hundred percent if you do."

"It's okay." She offered him a smile. "It's not exactly the first time I've heard it."

"Me neither, but that isn't an excuse." Rio motioned for John to follow Priscilla into the kitchen, and lingered beside Yvonne. "You okay?"

"Yes, thanks for standing up for me."

He brushed his thumb over her lips. "You're welcome."

John would probably return to his employer and immediately pull the plug on any reality show ever involving her. In fact, she was surprised he hadn't walked out already. Yvonne was at peace with it. Being asked to falsify her heritage just to increase ratings wasn't her thing. Her only surprise was that John hadn't gotten back in Rio's face. He'd capitulated really easily, but then he would have the pleasure of nixing the show.

He must really love the PBR. . . .

"Yeah, so the kitchen is great, lots of light and space in here," John was saying heartily. "I just wish you could expand the front-end."

"You and me both," Yvonne said.

John turned to Rio. "Have you considered investing in this?"

Yvonne hastened to intervene. "Why would he? He's just my business adviser. He doesn't take a share of my profit or anything."

"Er . . . okay." John looked confused, his gaze sliding from her to Rio. Yvonne wondered exactly what Priscilla had told him about their relationship.

"Shall we go back to the café?" Yvonne suggested. "We still haven't had our coffee."

John was typing notes into his phone. "I think I'm good, actually. If Rio is okay with this venture, then I'm hardly going to argue with him, am I?"

"Why not?" Yvonne paused by the kitchen door to look back at him.

"Disagree with the boss's son?" John laughed rather unconvincingly. "Not happening. I like my job too much."

"I don't understand." Yvonne noticed that Rio had gone very still. "Who owns Howatch International?"

"Graham Howatch." John looked from her to Priscilla as he continued to walk through to the front of the café. "You said she'd met him in San Francisco?"

Priscilla frowned. "It was certainly mentioned in the latest notes."

John smiled. "Thought I was right. I'm going to liaise with Mr. Howatch at the hotel after this meeting, so I'll give him your best." He nodded warily at Rio, and then shook Yvonne's hand. "Pleasure to meet you."

She didn't say anything as he shook her hand, and departed with Priscilla, who gave one longing look back at the pastries in the glass cabinet.

Yvonne let them leave and then pointed at Rio. "May I speak to you for a moment, please?"

She walked back into the hallway that separated the kitchen from the outer door, and made sure both doors were closed.

"Your *father* owns Howatch International?"

"Yes."

"*That's* the company he wants you to take over?"

Rio nodded.

"He must be a fricking *billionaire!* Why didn't you *tell* me?"

A crease appeared on his brow. "Which part?"

"That your father not only owns Tasty Treats, but is contemplating financing Paul's restaurants!"

"One, that's the first I've heard about him owning a controlling share of Tasty Treats. He oversees over five hundred business interests worldwide. I doubt he knows all of them by name. Two, I only just found out myself that he's behind Paul's potential empire."

"I thought John was overawed by you because he was into the PBR!"

Rio's mouth quirked up at the corner and he quickly suppressed it. "Really?"

Yvonne pushed a hand through her now-disheveled hair and briefly considered screaming like a banshee.

"I know this is all messed up, but I genuinely didn't know that my father had any involvement in Tasty Treats until now," Rio said softly.

"Okay."

"There's something else I need to talk to you about," Rio continued.

She forced herself to focus on his face.

"Before I lost my temper with you the other night, I should have let you explain."

"Explain what?"

"Your current relationship with Paul. Whatever it is, it's your own business and has nothing to do with me.

Infidelity is a bit of an issue for me." He took his hat off and twirled the brim through his fingers. "And I was . . . hurt that you hadn't confided in me."

"Even though we'd both agreed we'd just have sex with none of the unnecessary entanglements?"

"Yes, even though." He met her gaze, his brown eyes steady.

"I don't *owe* you an explanation for anything," Yvonne said.

"You're right, you don't, and I'm not asking you for one."

A curious sense of disappointment flooded through her. Here she was, offering him all kinds of opportunities to disagree with her, and tell her how he *really* felt, and he kept failing them.

"Okay, then."

"Is that all you have to say?" Rio asked cautiously.

"What would you like me to say?"

"That you at least forgive me for getting mad?"

"Of course, I forgive you." She finally found a smile. "We're friends, aren't we? And thanks for helping me out in there."

She half turned away so that he wouldn't see how close she was to crying. Nothing had changed. He was still leaving, and it would be better for both of them if he went away not knowing how close she'd come to trying to make him stay. It hadn't worked with Paul, and she wasn't going to break her heart again trying to make a man stay when he'd just resent her for it.

"You'd better go find Josie," she said brightly. "She'll be wondering where you've gotten to by now."

He caught her elbow. "Yvonne . . ."

"Did John say your father is at the Hayes Hotel? How on earth did he end up there?"

Was she babbling now? Was she too much of a

coward to risk looking at him for too long in case she blurted out something pathetic like *don't leave me*?

"He arrived last night by helicopter at Morgan Ranch. I didn't know he'd hung around until now either. Look—"

"Paul's there as well."

"So?"

"If Paul works out whom your father is—and knowing how chatty the Hayes family are, he probably will—then Paul will be sucking up to him like crazy."

"You've met my father. He's not going to fall for Paul's brand of suck-upage."

"Suck-upage? Did you just make that up?"

"It seemed appropriate." Rio shrugged. He was still holding on to her. "Are you going to keep this up?"

"I'm not sure what you're talking about." Yvonne stared hard at the kitchen door.

"Not looking at me, not—letting me in."

"I'm just being practical."

"Then why are you still so upset?"

"Because everything in my world is upside-down crazy at the moment, okay?"

His face softened. "I'm sorry. I'm not helping much, am I?" He dropped a kiss on her nose. "How about we wait until my father and Paul have gone back to wherever hellholes they came from, and then sort out our stuff, okay?"

"What stuff?" she whispered.

"This."

He bent his head and kissed her until she kissed him back. She balled her hands into fists at her sides to stop her grabbing hold of him and never letting go.

When he finally lifted his head, all she could do was stare helplessly into his eyes.

"See?" He smiled down at her. "We can both say

anything we want to deny it, but there's something between us. Something neither of us can ignore." He kissed her again. "I know things are a mess, and that we both have issues to sort out, *querida*, but I'm not giving up on this, or on you, just yet."

"Okay."

He stepped back and put his hat back on. "Stay strong." He blew her a kiss and went back through to the café.

Yvonne rolled her eyes at his departing form. She *was* strong. She'd let him walk away from her. She'd keep doing it until he went back to defend his stupid championship and forgot all about her.

Which would be much easier if he would just stop kissing her, and telling her everything was going to be all right. . . .

She risked a glance into both the kitchen and the café to check everything was going well and then went upstairs. She had a shrewd idea what *querida* meant, but that didn't mean she wouldn't Google it anyway.

Chapter Nineteen

Yvonne rolled over onto her back, and stared up at the ceiling. She had a sense that she wasn't going to be able to sleep tonight—what with worrying about Paul, and the TV show, and Rio . . .

Rio hadn't walked away from her yet. In fact, he'd indicated that he still had things to say that would wait until she'd sorted out her other problems. Did she want to hear what he had to say? She has a sneaking suspicion that, despite everything, she did.

What if he saw a future for them together?

She tried to imagine that, and ended up smiling foolishly in the darkness before sitting bolt upright in bed. She was way too into him. Not just because he was a hot and sexy man who made her see stars in bed, but also because he was a good person. A man who tried to stay true to what he believed in. A man who loved his mother and sister and was loyal to a fault.

And the son of a billionaire.

Yvonne groaned. She was never going to get back to sleep now. She picked up her cell phone and noticed a text message from Chase Morgan.

Attached: confirmation that your divorce petition has cleared the French courts. Asked my international lawyers to hasten it along for you. Best. Chase.

Her *divorce* settlement?

Yvonne clicked on the attachment. In all the recent excitement, she'd forgotten to check back with Chase to see what he could find out from the French authorities about the status of the divorce petition. She read through the document and then sent it to print, jumping out of bed for a quick wash while it whirred through her old printer. Paul had to have known about this . . .

Fueled by rage, she pulled on a pair of leggings, and a long sweater, and slid her bare feet into the first pair of sandals she came across in her closet. It was only nine-thirty in the evening. She reckoned her prey would still be awake, and hopefully not expecting her.

Rio closed his bedroom door and crossed over to the open window. The old barn was a grey silhouette in the gathering darkness, and the sweet scents of lavender, and the other herbs January grew in the yard, danced and perfumed the slight breeze. It was too early to sleep, and he'd done all the chores he could find—including putting the chickens away for the night—which Chase hated doing.

He let out his breath. Had he made any headway with Yvonne, or had all the revelations about his father's business interests driven her even further away from him? At least she was still talking to him. . . .

And she'd kissed him back and hadn't told him to take a hike when he'd suggested they weren't done. . . .

There still remained the small matter of Paul and her potential TV show. He knew in his soul that the chance of her staying with the Frenchman was non-existent. She'd gotten over the idiot, which was good because he didn't think anyone else could love her the way he would.

He banged his head against the old glass-paned window. Yeah. There was no point denying it any longer. Any woman who could tie him up in knots, make him lose his temper, and still make him want to fall at her feet and worship her was definitely the one.

Now all he had to do was find a way to tell her that. He had a sense that all the other issues—her work, his current profession, and all the other everyday stuff—were doable and fixable if they were both in it together. He was going to have to be brave, step up, and tell her how he felt.

He checked the time and realized it was almost nine, about when Yvonne went to bed. He didn't want to rush down there and disturb her sleep. Getting it right, saying what he meant needed time and space. He could wait another day. His father and Paul were supposedly leaving tomorrow as well.

After that, he and Yvonne would talk. He closed the window and drew the drapes. Now all he had to do was find a way to sleep through the night. His gaze fell on the folder his father had given him about Paul's business venture. If anything would put him to sleep, that would probably be it.

He kicked off his boots and lay down on his bed, the folder by his side, and started to read. Five minutes in, he stopped and carefully reread the last few paragraphs of the private investigator's report.

"*Filho da puta*," Rio cursed softly. He swung his legs over the side of the bed and hurried to put on his boots again. His night was about to get a lot more exciting than he had envisioned.

Yvonne arrived at the reception desk of the Hayes Hotel brandishing her printout and possibly, judging from Marley's startled expression, breathing actual fire.

"I need to speak to Paul Giresse."

Marley tapped away at her keyboard. "Is he expecting you?"

"I damn well hope not."

"Then I should probably call, and let him know you're in the lobby, okay?" Marley said brightly and looked hopefully at Yvonne.

"Sure, whatever you need to do. I'll wait."

Yvonne turned away and paced the polished wooden floor of the lobby from the bar and back to the entrance of the dining room, which was also open to the public for lunch and dinner. The smell of roast beef and stewed apples flavored the air, making her stomach gurgle.

As she made her third circle past the bar, an all-too-familiar laugh rang out, and she tensed.

"Yvonne?" Marley called out. "Mr. Giresse isn't answering his phone. He might be in the dining room, or he's gone out somewhere for the evening."

"Don't worry." Yvonne smiled through her teeth. Paul wouldn't be laughing for much longer. "I think I've found him."

She marched into the bar, nodded at Mr. Hayes, who always worked the evening shift, and kept moving until she discovered Paul sitting in a booth opposite another familiar face.

"Paul." She fixed him with her best intimidating stare. "Just the man I was hoping to see."

He half rose to his feet, his fair skin flushing. "*Bonsoir*, Yvonne. Have you met Mr. Graham Howatch?"

"Yes, we've met." Yvonne offered Rio's father a polite smile. "What brings you to Morgantown, Graham? Protecting your investments?"

"I actually stopped off to deliver some information to my son." Graham didn't look at all fazed by her sudden appearance. "Have you seen him today?"

"I saw him." Yvonne nodded. "I didn't realize he'd taken his mother's last name instead of yours."

"Come on, Yvonne," Paul interjected with a laugh. "You must have known who 'Rio' was. It took me a couple of seconds on the web to work it out."

"Only because I gave you a honking great clue where to start." She took a quick breath. "There's something I'd like to talk to you about, Paul. I'm sure Graham won't mind if I borrow you for a few minutes."

"And *I'd* like to talk to both of them." Rio's voice sounded behind her and she jumped. How come he got to turn up like the cavalry just at the right moment? Not that she wasn't extremely glad to see him. . . . "Maybe we can find somewhere more private?"

"Good evening, Aurelio." Graham rose slowly to his feet. "I'm so glad you decided to join us."

"You might change your mind about that shortly," Rio said as he squeezed Yvonne's shoulder. "Let's check in with Marley, and find a usable space."

Yvonne hesitated as Paul slid out of his seat, and docilely followed Rio out the door. He wasn't going to make a fuss as long as the billionaire who could further his career was in his orbit. Graham paused as he came out of the booth, stumbled, and hung on to the back of the seat. On impulse Yvonne offered him her arm, and to her surprise, he took it.

"Thank you, my dear."

He actually had to lean on her to make any progress. She slowed her pace and followed Rio and Paul down to one of the offices through the back hallway. The only sound was her companion's labored breathing. Rio hadn't mentioned that his father was ill. It was possible he hadn't even noticed.

Inside the room, she guided Graham into the nearest chair and closed the door behind them.

She and Rio both started talking at the same time, and Graham held up his hand.

"Aurelio, where are your manners? Perhaps you might allow Yvonne to speak first?"

Yvonne glanced over at Rio, who was grim faced and practically vibrating.

"What I have to say *concerns* Yvonne," Rio snapped. "She might wish to hear it."

"Then go for it." Fascinated, Yvonne stepped back and sat beside Graham.

Rio approached Paul. "I just read the proposal you and your team put together for the restaurant franchise."

"I thought you weren't involved in your father's business empire anymore?" Paul said, glancing nervously over at Graham.

"He asked me to take a look at it." Rio nodded at his father. "Thanks for that."

"You're welcome." Graham cleared his throat. "Which particular part of the proposal made you turn up here in a rage, I wonder?"

"Well, in the first place, the assumptions about the growth and volume of the business don't add up considering he is basically an unknown in the USA."

"Agreed," Graham said.

"And secondly, his remaining in the USA for any length of time relies on him retaining his green card through his American wife."

"Ha! *That's* why he came here!" Yvonne jumped up and waved her paper in the air. "Then he's screwed!"

Rio looked over at her. "What?"

"Chase hurried the petition along for me!" She gave it to Rio. "Look."

A slow smile emerged on his face as he scanned the paper, and then handed it over to Paul. "Looks like you might have a problem here, buddy."

Yvonne faced Paul. "I knew you weren't really interested in getting back together with me, but I couldn't quite figure out why you were even *trying*. I should've known it was all about your wants and needs."

"Says the woman who made me leave my family and friends in France just so she could have her own little business in California," Paul snapped.

"Paul, that's not *true*. I *loved* you. You *wanted* to come to this country, you voluntarily went through that whole green card process with me." She hesitated. "Unless you're saying that even then you did it just to gain residency here?"

"My father thought it would be a good idea for me to come to the USA," Paul said sulkily. "He was keen to expand our family business interests here."

"That's why you didn't want me to stay in Morgantown, isn't it?" Yvonne shook her head. "Your family wanted you to be in New York or San Francisco or somewhere you could help *them*, not me."

She took the paper out of his unresisting hand. "Was

your decision to delay getting our marriage dissolved also based on your father's recommendation? Was he the one who told you to lie and string me along for four years?" Her voice broke. "I thought we were already divorced, and you just hadn't sent me the details out of spite." She pointed at Rio. "I dragged a good man into a situation where he believed he'd been lied to, when the only liar around was you."

"My father controls the money, Yvonne. You know that." Paul avoided her gaze. "If I don't do what he says I'll be cut out of his will."

Yvonne's gaze flew to Rio, who shrugged.

"Never stopped me doing anything I wanted to."

Graham sighed. "You are celebrating your own stubbornness now?"

Rio pointed at Paul. "You'd really want me to be like *this* guy?"

Graham considered Paul. "No, not really."

"Good," Rio said. "Because being spineless isn't really my thing."

"That's hardly fair," Paul protested. "I'm the youngest in my family. It's been hard for me to make my own way in France. They didn't want me to marry a nonentity like you. I almost lost everything once by defying them, and I wasn't willing to do it again."

"With all that money and name recognition behind you?" Yvonne asked sweetly. "You expect me to feel *sorry* for you?"

Paul took a hasty step toward her. "Why not? You'll obviously be fine, regardless, won't you? Dump me, and latch on to a man who just *happens* to be richer than dirt!"

"I'm not rich." Rio stepped right in front of her, blocking Paul's path. "My father is. Unlike my father,

I grew up in a world where, if you don't shut the hell up right now, I'm going to take you down."

"No, you're not." Yvonne put her hand on Rio's rigid arm. "If you hit him, Paul will call the cops, and I don't want my name plastered all over the Internet, thank you very much." She smiled up at Rio. "Not that I don't appreciate you standing up for me."

"Any time. So if I can't deck him, I'll go for a more civilized route." He turned to his father. "My recommendation to your board is not to go ahead with the Giresse project."

"That's totally unfair!" Paul protested. "You're making your decision on a purely personal basis."

"I sure as hell am," Rio said. "Would you prefer me to return to option one?"

"Rio . . ." Yvonne gave him her best glare. "Will you *please* drop it?"

"I'll certainly consider your opinion, Aurelio," Graham intervened. "Of course, it would make things a lot easier if you took your seat on the board, and could tell everyone yourself."

"We can talk about that later," Rio said firmly. "I'm not discussing family business in front of Paul Giresse."

"Because you've already said quite enough," Yvonne murmured.

"And just to make things clear, Paul, I promised you an answer as to whether I'd consider ever getting back together with you before you left." She paused until he had the guts to look her in the eye. "My first response was hell no, and my second remains the same."

"Then don't expect my family to honor any financial demands you make on us since we are now officially divorced," Paul snapped.

"I haven't asked for a penny, and I don't intend to

do so," Yvonne said evenly. "You're free to go. You and your family don't owe me anything."

Paul tried to stare her down, but she was having none of it. She'd loved him once, she'd learned to live without him, and she had no regrets about either decision.

With one last glare, Paul left the room, slamming the door behind him. Yvonne sat down abruptly in the nearest chair.

"Are you all right, Yvonne?" Graham asked gently.

"Not really." She gulped in some air. "I just realized that the whole of my marriage was one big scam."

"No, remember Paul just admitted he loved you enough to marry you against his family's wishes." Rio crouched down in front of her, and took her hand. "The fact that they eventually overwhelmed him with their needs and demands, and he let them, is totally on him."

"I feel pretty damn stupid right now," Yvonne whispered.

"Did you *want* him back?" Rio asked.

"No." She shuddered. "When I saw him, I felt nothing."

"Then that's okay, isn't it?"

She studied his patient features. "I suppose so."

"What Aurelio is trying to say, my dear, is that your feelings for Paul are entirely appropriate, and that he appreciates that you are not hung up on the past."

Rio gave his father an exasperated look. "Who asked you?"

"I am just trying to help, son."

"Then please stop."

It was Yvonne's turn to frown. "There's no need to

be so rude to your father, Rio. It was very sweet of him to consider my feelings."

Graham smiled at her. "He's a good boy at heart."

Rio groaned and rose from his crouch in front of Yvonne. "Now, see what you've done by encouraging him? He's gone nuts."

"You are a good man," Yvonne insisted. "I said it myself earlier, I—"

Graham and Rio's cell phones buzzed at the same time, drowning her out.

"Is it a weather warning?" Graham reached inside the jacket of his suit. "Oh, obviously not." He looked up. "Do you know a lady by the name of Ruth Morgan, Aurelio? She's insisting that we all come to her ranch for a late supper."

Rio glanced at Yvonne and shrugged. "She asked me to give her my father's number in case he needed a bed at the ranch. I just got the same message. Are you up for it?"

Yvonne stood and mentally shook herself down. The night couldn't get any stranger. She wouldn't be able to sleep, and she certainly wasn't going to let Rio and his father alone to bicker all night. It wasn't good for either of them.

"Sure. Why not?"

"Great. We can all go together in my truck," Rio said. "I'll bring it round to the front of the hotel, and pick you both up."

"Sounds good to me."

The Morgans were the closest thing Yvonne had to family. If anyone could make her feel better about being played for a fool by her now officially ex-husband, it would be Ruth.

* * *

Rio pulled into the circular drive at the ranch, and glanced over at Yvonne, who had taken the back seat, allowing Graham to sit up front. She looked more composed now, but his heart hurt for her, and he still *really* wanted to kick Paul's ass.

"Okay, let's get this over with." Rio bailed out and went to open Graham and Yvonne's doors. To his surprise, by the time he got around there, Yvonne was helping his father out of his seat.

"You two okay?" he asked.

"We're good." Yvonne waved at him to go on. "Why don't you go ahead and tell Ruth we're here?"

After one last puzzled glance backward, Rio did what she'd suggested, and bounded up the steps to the side door. Ruth appeared in the hallway and beckoned to him.

"Did you bring your father?"

"Yes, he's just coming." Rio paused to study her face. "Excuse me if this sounds impolite, but are you up to something?"

"I might be." She winked at him. "Is Yvonne there as well?"

Just as he went to answer, the screen door opened behind him to reveal his father and Yvonne. Graham looked exhausted, and doubt shook through Rio. His father was out of his usual time zone and hated traveling. The last thing he probably should be doing was having a late supper.

"We're here, Ruth," Yvonne called out.

"Then come on through to the kitchen. I've made pie and chocolate cake."

"It was very kind of you to invite us to the ranch, Mrs. Morgan." Graham put down his mug. "I hope

Aurelio has been behaving himself while residing here."

Ruth smiled. "He's been a great help. In fact, I'll miss him terribly when he goes." She pushed the plate of pie toward Graham. "Do have some more. I made plenty."

"Thank you. It is absolutely delicious, but I'm completely full." Graham smiled across at Ruth.

"I hear there was a bit of a fracas at the hotel this evening." Ruth turned to Yvonne. "Was everything all right?"

Yvonne winked at Graham. "You've heard of the Oracle at Delphi? This is the Morgantown equivalent. *Nothing* gets past this woman."

"So I see." Graham used his napkin. "I was asked to dinner by a man named Paul Giresse. You might have heard of him? After we'd eaten, we retired to the bar for a brandy, which was where first Yvonne, and then my son, turned up to confront my dining companion."

Yvonne leaned in. "To put it in a nutshell, Paul lied about our divorce because he wanted to invest in the USA, and needed to keep his green card by marriage."

Ruth shook her head and tutted. "That was a horrible thing to do."

"I think we can all agree on that," Graham said. "And seeing as I'm the one who currently controls the board of Howatch International, I can assure you that his dreams will not be realized using my money. If his family really thinks it is a good idea, they can finance it themselves. I suspect they aren't completely convinced of his success either."

"Good." Ruth contemplated her mug of coffee. "What else do you use all that money for?"

Graham raised an eyebrow. "I have a charitable foundation, if that's what you are asking."

"And how does that work?"

"I invest in infrastructure projects both here and overseas that benefit local communities."

"That's right. Josie told me about it." Ruth nodded. "Do you ever invest in low-cost housing?"

Rio locked gazes with Yvonne, who shrugged.

"Occasionally. Why?"

"Because I have an investment opportunity for you right here in Morgantown." Ruth smiled at him. "After breakfast tomorrow morning, you can sit down with my oldest grandson, Chase, and talk it through."

"I wasn't aware I was staying the night," Graham murmured.

"Of course you are. I dragged you all the way out here, so it's the least I can do to make amends." Ruth reached over and patted his hand. "I've made you up a bed in my parlor."

Rio held his breath, and waited to see how his autocratic father would deal with the unstoppable force of Ruth Morgan.

"That is very kind of you. Seeing as my helicopter is currently parked up on your airstrip, it will make my return journey much easier." Graham rose to his feet. "In fact, I'd rather like to retire, if that's all right with everyone?"

"Of course." Ruth rose as well. "Let me show you the way."

Rio contemplated the closed door his father had just gone through and sipped his coffee. "That was weird."

Yvonne looked over at him. "Ruth trying to go into

business with your father? Yeah." She sighed and shoved the hair out of her face. "What an unbelievable night."

"Can't argue with that." He caught her yawning. "Are you going to stay here, too?"

She grimaced. "If Ruth's reduced to stashing your father in the parlor, I doubt there's any room left for me."

"There's my bed." He reached across the table and took her hand. "I don't have to be in it with you."

"That's very sweet of you, but—"

"I'll wake you up in time to get back to the café to bake." He tugged gently on her hand. "Come on, you're exhausted. Let me do this one thing for you."

She allowed him to pull her to her feet, her green eyes unusually solemn as she studied him. With a soft sound, he came around the table and gathered her in his arms.

"It's okay."

"It's not, and you know it."

He smoothed a hand over her hair as she rubbed her cheek against his chest. "I know it feels like everything is wrong at the moment, but just sleep on it, and things will get better, I promise you."

Her sigh ended in a shuddering yawn as he continued to hold her. "Come on, go to bed. I'll check in on you later, okay?"

"But where are you going to sleep?"

"Don't worry about that. I'll sort something out."

He drew her toward the door. When she dawdled, he simply swept her up into his arms, and carried her right up to his bedroom, kicked the door open, and deposited her gently on his bed.

She gazed up at him and he kissed her mouth. "Sleep, okay?"

She cupped his cheek. "Thank you."

"You're welcome." He took her hand in his and kissed her fingers. "*Boa noite, querida.*"

"Querida means darling, right?" she said sleepily.

"Yes, because that's what you are to me." He paused as her eyes closed and he drew the covers up over her. "*Cada dia que passa eu me apaixono mais por voce.*"

"That sounds lovely. What does it mean?"

Rio hesitated and then bent to whisper in her ear. "With every day that passes, I fall in love with you more."

"Oh . . ."

He waited hopefully for another few seconds to see if she'd react to what he'd said until he registered a tiny snore. He found himself smiling into the darkness. It was eleven-thirty, and well past Yvonne's bedtime. He didn't blame her one bit for falling asleep on him. Now that he'd said the words out loud, he wouldn't take them back even if she'd missed them.

Next time, he'd make sure she was upright, awake, and listening.

After one last kiss on her cheek, he drew the curtains, tiptoed out of the room and down the stairs. Ruth was just coming out of the parlor, and she turned to wait for him.

"Is Yvonne up there?"

"Yeah." He smiled at Ruth. "I hope you don't mind. She was exhausted."

"Not at all."

Rio gestured at the closed door. "Was my father all right?"

Ruth hesitated. "I'm not sure."

"Do you think I should go check on him?"

She met his gaze. "Yes. I think that would be an excellent idea." He went to move past her, and she put her hand on his arm. "And, Rio? Try and listen to him, okay? I know it's hard, but maybe it's time to give him a chance."

Rio knocked on the door and went in to find his father sitting up in bed, a glass of water, and a collection of pill bottles that rivaled a pharmacy, at his side.

"What's all this for?" Rio pointed at the side table.

Graham looked up from his tablet and took his glasses off. "Vitamins and other things my doctor insists I need at my age."

"I'm not buying it." Rio dragged over a chair and sat down right in front of his father. "You look like crap. What's going on?"

"Before we get into that, I meant to tell you that I've accepted your offer for your mother's ranch."

"What?"

"I've accepted your offer. My lawyers are drawing up the paperwork for you to sign. I've proposed two ways to pay. Either in full right now, or if you do decide to join my board through a series of deductions to your dividends."

"That's . . . very good of you."

Graham shrugged. "It seemed fair."

"You've never cared about fair in your dealings with me and Mom. It's always been about winning."

"Then maybe you won this round."

"No, that would mean you lost, and you don't play that game. What's going on? You're starting to worry me now." Rio pointed at the pills. "Does it have something to do with all the drugs you're taking? Are they making you behave differently?"

A slight smile edged Graham's lips. "You could say that."

Rio straightened in his seat as something tightened in his gut. "Tell me."

"I have a hepatocellular carcinoma."

"Meaning?"

"Cancer of the liver. I am lucky in that it was spotted fairly early, but—"

"How are they going to fix it?" Rio interrupted his father. "It's beatable, right?"

"They are planning a partial surgical resection in a month's time. That's apparently the best they can do to contain it."

"What's the difference between beating it and containing it?"

Graham sighed. "There's a high chance that, even if they get as much as they can out next month, it will reoccur within five years."

"What kind of chance?"

"Seventy percent."

Rio felt like the breath had been knocked out of him. "That . . . sucks."

"I am aware of that."

Silence fell, broken only by the ticking of the clock on the mantelpiece over the log fire.

"Were you going to tell me at some point, or did you intend to keep me and Mom in the dark?" Rio asked.

"I intended to mention it when I asked you both to meet me in San Francisco, but—" Graham stopped talking.

"What?"

"I know you won't believe me, but it was such a pleasure to see you both again—especially because your mother appears to have forgiven me—that I didn't wish to spoil the moment."

"You could have used it as leverage to get me back into your company," Rio pointed out.

"That's true, but it didn't seem fair. I'd rather you

came back because you believed in the company and the people within it than force you out of some kind of twisted guilt."

"If you'd tried to force me to come back using your illness as a reason, I'm not sure what I would've done," Rio confessed. "I'm not certain I wouldn't have resented the hell out of you and walked away forever."

"I understand." Graham cleared his throat. "I've reached a financial settlement with Jennifer, and we'll be divorcing fairly soon. As she pointed out, she didn't sign on to nurse an elderly sick man. I quite understand how she feels."

"I don't. What a fricking coward," Rio said. "Good riddance." He tried to clear his throat, which had suddenly gotten really tight. "Do you want me to tell Mom?"

"It might be best to wait until after I have the surgery. I don't want to alarm her."

"Okay." Rio considered that and looked his father in the eye. "And what do you want from me?"

"You know what I want."

"Me back in the saddle at Howatch International as opposed to riding bareback on a bull."

"Perhaps a compromise?"

Rio blinked at Graham. "A *what?* You really are sick, aren't you?"

"Indeed. When I am unable to handle my responsibilities, I would like you to step up and act in my interests."

"Vote on the board and make the big decisions?" Rio whistled. "That's a big ask."

"I know." Graham hesitated. "I won't hold you to any promise to succeed me, and I don't expect you to be there full-time. If you choose to walk away once

I've recovered, I won't stop you, but I would hope, if you make that decision, that you will have found someone to replace you, and eventually, me." His faint smile was laced with exhaustion. "It might take me several years to die, so at least we have that."

"I can't promise anything right now," Rio said carefully. "I need to think about this."

He stood and stared down at his father, who was wearing a Morgan Ranch T-shirt and an old dressing gown that looked like it had once belonged to Roy. He must have left his belongings at the hotel. Graham looked smaller without the armor of his bespoke suit, like he was wasting away into the darkness.

"How can you be so calm?" Rio burst out. "Why aren't you screaming and railing against the unfairness of this?"

"It's a lot to take in," Graham agreed. "I've known for a few months, so I've had time to make some plans, but it is still a shock." He chuckled. "I thought I had everything under control—my life, my work, and my health—and guess what? It was all an illusion." He put his glasses on the side table. "There's a lesson in there for all of us, Aurelio. Even you."

"Yeah." Rio nodded. "You should get some sleep. I'll see you in the morning."

"Good night, son." Graham eased himself back against the pillow. "Turn the main light out on your way, will you?"

Yvonne woke up in a panic in an unfamiliar bed that smelled of lavender, leather, and her favorite cowboy. She flung out a hand, but there was no one else there. She lay on her back and tried to remember where she was.

Morgan Ranch. Rio's bed.

He'd placed her on the sheets, kissed her, and gone away. At least, she didn't remember him leaving because she'd fallen asleep, but he'd obviously left. She peered at the clock on the bedside cabinet, and realized it was two-thirty in the morning. Where *was* he?

She eased her feet down onto the scarred oak floorboards and cotton rag rug. She was still fully dressed, and had left her sandals downstairs in the boot room. Opening the door, she went and used the bathroom, and then hesitated on the landing. At the bottom of the stairs, there was a faint glow of light that she figured came from the kitchen.

She tiptoed down the stairs and along the hallway, pausing in the half-open doorway to see Rio sitting at the kitchen table with his head in his hands. Her heart constricted at the sight of his bowed shoulders. She'd never seen him look totally defeated before. Without alerting him to her presence, she went to sit opposite him.

He didn't look up, but she knew from the way he braced himself that he knew he was no longer alone. She reached out, curved her hand around his elbow, and just stayed quiet. Keeping him company in his distress, which was so obvious he couldn't even pretend he wasn't feeling it.

Eventually he spoke.

"I'm not really up for company right now, Yvonne."

"Okay." She assumed her most neutral tone. "But remember that friends thing? If you want to share, I'm right here."

"My father is sick."

Yvonne considered her next words. "I thought he didn't look too well today. Is he going to be able to fly out tomorrow?"

"I don't know." He sighed. "He'll probably leave regardless."

"Did you fight?"

"No." He still hadn't looked at her. "We talked about what was wrong with him, and when I should tell my mother."

The stark pain in his words reached her and made her catch her breath. "Are you saying he's really sick?"

"Yeah. Cancer."

She struggled to find words. "He's receiving treatment though, good treatment?"

"The best money can buy, but it might not make any difference in the end." He eased his hands away from his head, and spread them flat on the pine table. "He's going in for surgery next month."

"Rio, I'm so sorry. . . ."

He cut her off. "Don't be sorry for me. I'm fine." He stood and headed for the door. "I just need to think things through."

Yvonne followed him out of the house, down the steps, and toward the barn. Despite the season, it was cold outside, and she fought a shiver.

He finally stopped by the tack room and watched her approach, his expression devoid of its usual good humor.

"You don't need to follow me around."

"I'm worried about you," Yvonne said. "Just *talk* to me, okay?"

She held her breath as he considered her for a long moment, and then suddenly started speaking.

"Why should I care what happens to a man I've spent the majority of my life hating, ignoring, or despising?"

"Because, despite everything, he's still your father?"

"What the hell does that even mean?" he demanded. "He gave me life, he made that life as difficult as he could when I was a kid, and now . . ." He shook his head. "*Now,* I'm upset? What the hell is *wrong* with me?"

"Maybe because, for the first time, you were beginning to see a different side to him?" Yvonne suggested gently.

"He's not a good man, Yvonne. Don't try and make this into some kind of goddam fairytale where I forgive all his sins, and everything is okay again."

"I would never do that." She shook her head. "Life isn't that simple."

"Good, so we finally agree on something." He lapsed into silence again.

"You shouldn't blame yourself."

He frowned. "I don't."

"At some level, maybe you *are* blaming yourself for everything from your parents splitting up to hating your own father, to him getting sick."

"No, I'm trying to work out how I *feel* right now."

"Nothing happens in a vacuum, Rio. The way you feel now is a reflection on what happened before."

"I couldn't stop my parents splitting up."

"Exactly."

"I can't change anything." His mouth set into a hard line.

"You can change how you feel about it," Yvonne suggested.

"Don't give me that psychological bullshit," he retorted. "He's *dying.* I shouldn't be sad. I should be fricking delighted, but I can't be, so what does that say about me?"

"That you're a good person?"

He looked away, and shook his head. "I'm an idiot. I can tell you that right now."

"Okay."

His gaze snapped back to hers. "What the hell does that mean?"

"So you're an idiot." She shrugged. "You're just like everyone else, a confused mass of good, bad, and everything in between. You can be *angry* with your father *and* feel sorry for what he's going through right now. You're not that child who had to stick up for their mother one hundred percent anymore. You're *you*."

He stared at her as if she had two heads, and she tried again.

"Can't you just accept that you can both love and hate someone at the same time?"

"*No*."

"Then I can't help you." She held out her hand. "I need to get home. Can I borrow your truck?"

"I'll take you."

"There's no need." She smiled at him. "You probably want to spend some time with your father before he leaves."

"I'd rather see you safely home. I'll be back before he even wakes up."

She didn't have the energy to argue with him at this point. "Fine. I'll just get my shoes, and leave a note for Ruth."

She walked back into the house, wrote her note, and propped it up against the coffeepot. When she came out, Rio's truck was right next to the house. Unlike the grim-faced man beside her, it was already warming up.

She didn't speak on the return journey, her thoughts far away with her parents, and the choices she'd made about Paul, and coming back to California. . . . Her anger with herself and her parents had mellowed over time, and become manageable. It wasn't their fault that they'd died so suddenly in a car crash. They hadn't deliberately abandoned her. She remembered the good times as well as the bad—that her parents had loved each other, which was why she existed.

Maybe Rio would reach that point eventually. Maybe she'd been a fool to push him to understand things that he just wasn't ready to hear. It was hardly her business anyway, was it? She pressed a hand over her aching heart, watched the darkness start to lift, and deliberately counted her blessings. Paul was leaving today. She was a one hundred percent officially divorced woman with a business to run, and a lot of good friends. Rio would be leaving town soon, too—whether to go back to bull riding, or to help out his father, she had no clue.

She couldn't make his decisions for him. She couldn't make him care enough to listen to her, just like Paul, and she wasn't going to knock herself out begging for something she could never have.

Rio drew the truck to a stop at the back of the shop, and she immediately grabbed the door handle, and jumped out.

"Thanks for bringing me home."

"Yvonne . . ."

"Can we leave it right now? I'm tired, you're tired, and you obviously don't want to listen to anything I have to say. Talk to Josie, talk to your mom. I'm sure you'll work things out." She slammed the truck door, and walked away from him.

It was the only thing left for her to do.

Chapter Twenty

Despite Ruth's pleas for him to stay, Graham left the ranch without insisting Rio give him any answers at all. That was a first. Rio watched the helicopter rise in a swirl of choking dust, got back in his truck, and sat there staring at nothing. He didn't feel angry anymore, just numb, like he'd come off a bull and had the breath knocked out of him.

The last thing he'd said to his father was to call him when he got back to Boston. He'd never done that before. For the last five years, all the overtures had come from Graham. Which led to another question. Graham hadn't just called him when he knew he was sick, and he hadn't initially used his illness to force Rio back on his board.

Hell, Graham wasn't even doing that now. Not that he needed to. Rio obviously had enough sense of family responsibility to consider helping out a man he'd despised his entire life. But why did that rile him so much?

Can't you just accept that you can both love and hate someone at the same time?

Yvonne's words floated back into his head. Dammit,

he needed to talk to her, and apologize for snarling like a savage beast. She, of all people, didn't deserve his anger. Decision made, he started the truck, turned in a circle, and made his way down toward Morgantown.

It was still relatively early, and Yvonne would be baking in her kitchen before the café officially opened at eight. He pictured her there, moving through her endless list of tasks with the grace and charm of a ballerina, and the discipline of a five-star general.

Had she finally given up on him last night? Had she realized he was another idiot like Paul who didn't appreciate her? She'd looked tired and defeated. . . . He'd done that to her. One thing he did know was that she'd survive him, her capacity to deal with betrayal and the vagaries of life was apparent in every bone of her body. That was one of the reasons why he admired her so much.

He parked in the lot behind the row of shops, and went to the back door of the café. Just as he was about to knock, his attention fixed on the business next door. The door was wedged open by a body and an out-flung arm.

"*Deus,*" he whispered. "Margery!" and rushed over to kneel beside the woman, who was stretched out on the floor, papers scattered all around her. He immediately felt for a pulse, and found a weak one. A quick check revealed no obvious injuries, so he took off his jacket, made a pillow for her head, and stood up.

"Yvonne!" He ran and hammered on her door.

Her face appeared at the window, and she slowly unlocked the door.

"If you're here to start shouting at me again, Aurelio Martinez get lost."

"Margery's collapsed," Rio said. "Can you call an ambulance while I find Nate Turner?"

"Oh! Of course!" She wiped her hands on her apron. "I'll be right there."

He went back to Margery, who still hadn't stirred. Her skin was quite cold, and her fingertips were blue. He wondered how long she'd been lying there as he sent a text to Nate.

To his relief, the deputy sheriff appeared around the corner of the row of shops, talking into his mic as he ran toward Rio.

"Ambulance is on its way," Nate confirmed.

"Great."

"Has she been robbed?" Nate asked, one hand on the weapon at his hip.

"I didn't look in the shop," Rio confessed. "I was more concerned about her."

"Then hang there while I go take a look."

Rio focused his attention on Margery as Nate drew his weapon and stepped over the body, disappearing into the gloom of the interior.

"Is she all right?" Rio looked up as Yvonne crouched down beside him, a blanket in her hands.

"She's still alive," Rio said. "Nate's inside checking the place out."

As he spoke, Nate returned, a frown on his face. "Everything looks great in there. No sign of a break-in or a struggle at all." His mic clicked, and he listened to some communication that sounded more like frying bacon than actual words.

"Got it." Nate nodded. "Ambulance is almost here."

"Look." Yvonne, who had been spreading the blanket, pointed at something in Margery's clenched hand.

Nate crouched down, pulled on a pair of gloves,

and gently eased her fingers away from the two brown plastic prescription bottles. "*Shit.* Oxycodone and anti-depressants."

The ambulance turned into the parking lot, and two paramedics emerged. Nate handed them the pills.

"Possible overdose."

The woman knelt and shone a light into Margery's eyes. "Yeah, her pupils are like pinpricks. We'll take her to the ER."

Within a few minutes, the ambulance was loaded up and heading out of town, lights flashing and sirens blaring. Rio bent to pick up his jacket just as Yvonne gathered up her blanket.

"You okay?" Rio asked her.

"I'm fine." Yvonne looked down at the blanket as she folded it into a precise set of squares. "I'm glad you found her. She wasn't here when I arrived last night, and I haven't been out since. Ruth said Margery wasn't herself. I wish I'd paid more attention to her and not just got mad about that stupid petition."

"To quote a wise person I know, you can't blame yourself for everything."

Yvonne almost smiled. "Who was that incredibly wise person?" She turned toward her door. "Were you coming to get coffee or something? The café isn't open yet, but you're welcome to help yourself."

"Actually, I wanted to talk to you."

"I don't have a lot of time to talk right now." She went to move past him. "I was already behind because I slept in, and now it's going to be even worse."

"Yvonne." He caught her elbow. "Just give me a minute, okay?"

She still wouldn't look properly at him, but she at

least allowed him through the door into the entrance lobby.

"I want to apologize for taking out my frustrations on you last night rather than keeping them to myself."

She shrugged. "As I keep telling you, that's what friends are for."

"I was still out of line."

"Okay. Apology accepted." She nodded and flashed him a brief smile. "I've got to get on."

She already had her back to him before he could get out another coherent sentence. He had to break through the wall he'd created, and he knew just how to do it. The first time he'd asked her out, he'd made an ass of himself, and he was more than willing to do it again.

"Is this what you meant about loving someone, and wanting to smack them over the head at the same time?" Rio asked.

"*What*?" She swung back around to confront him.

He shrugged. "You know, how you're feeling about me right now."

"Smacking you over the head with my best cast-iron pan? Hugely appealing. You *telling* me how I'm feeling? Not cool at all."

"You didn't address something I said."

She narrowed her eyes. "Wow, you are feeling brave, aren't you? Can you hang around while I go get that pan?"

"I hate getting angry," Rio said quietly. "It reminds me of when I was a kid, so when I do lose my temper I don't know what to do with it—stuff it back inside me, ride it out on a bull, shout at the wrong person . . ." Rio gathered his courage. "You're the first person

I've ever truly felt comfortable showing that side of myself to."

"So what?"

"So I realized something important this morning." He took a deep breath. "I love you. I love that I can finally be myself with you, because you make me feel safe."

"So you're saying I have to put up with all your crap just because you love me?"

He met her gaze. "You do, if you love me back, and apparently I'm a good guy most of the time. Someone special told me that recently."

She still wasn't buying it. He held out his hand to her.

"What can I do to show you that I'm sincere?" Rio asked. "That I love you, and want to spend the rest of my life with you?"

She regarded him for so long that he almost forgot how to breathe before she replied.

"We can't be friends anymore."

Rio stared at her in stunned silence before clearing his throat. "Why *not*? I *love* you. I want to make things right. What can I do? There must be *something*."

"Go away."

The bottom dropped out of his world, and he struggled not to fall to his knees and start begging.

"You want me to leave?" He nodded, his throat tight. "Okay, I guess I deserve that—"

Her green eyes sparkled. "I *want* you to leave, and do your stupid bull-riding thing, and then I want you to keep coming back whenever you have the opportunity."

"To see you?" he asked cautiously.

She dipped her head. "*Duh.*"

"And what will that accomplish?" he said, still feeling his way.

She shrugged. "It will prove to me that you really mean it."

"That I love you?"

"Yes."

He considered that for a long moment. "You'll be here?"

"I'm not planning on going anywhere else."

"Waiting for me?" Rio said hopefully.

She snorted. "I'm hardly going to be sitting around waiting, because I'm a busy woman, but—"

"You'd like to see me." Rio smiled for the first time in ages as a chorus of heavenly angels sang through his heart. "So you *do* love me back, and that's why you think we can't be friends."

"Wow, you're *quick* today," she said approvingly. "I thought you weren't going to work it out there for a moment."

"You'll have to forgive me, English not being my first language and everything." He moved toward her and pinned her against the door before cupping her cheek. "*Te amo, querida.*"

She sighed and leaned into him, her body relaxing into his arms.

"Okay."

"*Okay?* That's all I'm getting?" Rio kissed her.

"Yes, because you need to prove yourself to me."

"Just like your bread dough, because you really 'need' me?"

With a groan, she went on tiptoe and nipped his lip. "Stop it."

With her mouth firmly over his, he was quite happy to stop talking and focus on far more exciting ways to convince her that he was the only man for her. He'd come back to her, and they'd work everything out. She drew him like a lodestar, and she deserved every ounce of devotion he would offer to convince her he'd never walk away like that idiot Paul Giresse.

Knowing Yvonne, it would probably take him a lifetime to persuade her he was good enough. But that was okay. They'd share that journey together, and he'd enjoy every single moment of it.

Epilogue

"He did it!"

Yvonne grabbed hold of Isabelle, Josie, and HW, and they all screamed and jumped up and down as Rio finished his last ride at the T-Mobile Arena with the highest score yet and clinched his second world championship. Pandemonium broke out in the arena as the jumbotron focused in on Rio's grinning face while he gathered his rope, and waved to the crowd.

"Come on." Josie took Yvonne's hand again, and started towing her down toward the barrier. "Let's go see him."

By the time they reached the front of the crowd, Rio was fending off fellow competitors and backslapping fans, his gaze scanning the bucking chutes.

"Yvonne!"

He saw her and beckoned for them to come forward, before finally striding over himself and getting the security guy to let them through. He was dressed in his usual black, his safety vest buckled over his chest with his number on his back. He hugged Isabelle and

Josie, and then picked Yvonne up and spun her around in a circle.

"*Querida.*"

He smelled like hot, sexy man with just a hint of leather and cattle to send her wild. After a month away from him while he focused on his preparations for the finals, she buried her face in the heat of his throat and drank him in.

He finally put her down, and she grinned at him.

"You were awesome."

"Thanks." He kissed her fingers and kept hold of her hand. "Don't go anywhere."

Turning to one side, he grabbed one of the TV commentators waiting to interview him, and nodded.

"Okay, shoot."

The guy launched into a series of questions about the last ride and the finals and all kinds of bull-riding stuff that Yvonne had made herself learn for Rio's sake, but couldn't really say turned her on. She tried to ease away, but Rio kept her locked to his side.

"Anything else you'd like to say to the fans, Rio?" the interviewer asked.

"Just a couple of things." Rio cleared his throat. "Firstly, thanks to all my sponsors, my fellow competitors, and every single one of you who has supported me through the last few years. I couldn't have done it without you."

He waited until the crowd finished applauding and then continued. "Secondly, this seems a great moment to announce that I am retiring from the PBR. It's best to go out at the very top, right?"

The crowd groaned, and he pressed his fist to his heart and thumped his chest.

Yvonne blinked at him. Sure, he'd *talked* about retiring, but her old insecurities had made her wonder whether winning again would change his mind. He'd been working with his father on and off during the last year, but hadn't made any firm commitment to rejoin Howatch International as Graham had recovered sufficiently to regain most of his control.

They both knew Graham's long-term prospects weren't good, but to his credit, Graham hadn't forced the issue. He'd been enjoying spending time with Isabelle, of all people, and willingly taken Josie into the company to work as Rio's assistant.

Thanks to Rio's new influence with Howatch International, Tasty Treats had agreed to slow down the proposal to shoot a reality show in her café until she'd finished doubling the size of her store. She'd arranged with Chase to rent Margery's former space after the shaken Realtor had left to live near her son in San Diego.

Yvonne glanced longingly at the exit as the guy with the microphone asked one last question. Right now, she'd much rather be celebrating with her world champion in a far more up close and personal manner. . . .

"If you're going to retire, what comes next for you, Rio?"

"This." She jumped as he went down on one knee and looked up into her eyes. "Yvonne Payet, will you marry me?"

His hand was shaking as much as hers and the crowd went wild. Did he really think she was going to turn him down flat in front of all these people, and the thousands of people watching on TV at home?

She smiled and his eyes narrowed. "Don't you dare," he breathed.

"Yes."

"Really?" Rio croaked.

She nodded again, and he came back to his feet and wrapped her in his arms.

"I love you, Aurelio Fatima Maria Martinez Howatch," she murmured.

"It's about time, too," he said, and kissed the living daylights out of her.

Flourless Sin Cake for Ruth

(Recipe courtesy of Angela Ollivett Smith
from Sweet Eatz LLC)

12 oz. semisweet chocolate
4 oz. unsweetened chocolate
2 cups butter
1 cup espresso
1 cup brown sugar
8 eggs, beaten

- Set oven to 350 degrees F.
- Grease and line a 9-inch springform tin—wrap outside in foil.
- Boil butter, espresso, and sugar.
- Pour over chocolate and whisk until smooth.
- Whisk in eggs.
- Pour into pan.
- Bake until just set in the center, about 30 minutes.
- Cool and then chill overnight.
- Unmold.
- Glaze with chocolate glaze. (1 cup chocolate chips, 1½ cups of heavy cream—simmer and whisk smooth; pour over cake.)

Connect with Us

Visit us online at
KensingtonBooks.com
to read more from your favorite authors, see books
by series, view reading group guides, and more.

Join us on social media
for sneak peeks, chances to win books and prize packs,
and to share your thoughts with other readers.

facebook.com/kensingtonpublishing
twitter.com/kensingtonbooks

Tell us what you think!

To share your thoughts, submit a review,
or sign up for our eNewsletters, please visit:
KensingtonBooks.com/TellUs.